WE DON'T MEET PEOPLE
BY ACCIDENT.
THEY ARE MEANT TO CROSS
OUR PATH FOR A REASON.

Dedication

To the FBI, MI6, and whatever other government agencies may have been watching my search history while I researched for this book! I promise all those things were research purposes only, I have no intention of doing any of it!

To my Literati - thank you for indulging my need to explore new ideas and for keeping me amused while I write.

Be Aware

Rook contains scenes of kidnapping, and mild torture.

1

Magdalena

"F—five hundred dollars... upfront, like you asked." I cursed myself when I stumbled over the words I'd practiced over and over in front of the mirror before coming to the diner. How did I *still* manage to sound like an idiot?

The man at table twelve paused, a forkful of food halfway to his lips, and looked up at me. I wasn't typically a nervous person, but I shivered, my mind convincing me I could feel his eyes skimming over my skin. He scanned me from head to toe, his brows dipping into a frown, but he didn't speak. I held out the white envelope, my hand shaking. His frown deepened, dark eyes dropping to look at it, but he made no move to take it from me. After an awkward couple of seconds, I placed it on the table beside his plate.

"Five hundred," I repeated, firmer this time. "That's how much you said the platinum package would cost." I tried to inject more confidence in my voice—a far cry from the way my stomach was doing backflips, my mind screaming at me to turn around and walk away, and my dry mouth.

This was such a bad idea. Why had I let Jasmine talk me into it?

He leaned back in his seat; the fork dropping onto his plate with a loud clatter. I jumped, and those eyes lifted to look at me again. My entire body locked up at the contact. His eyes were dark, almost black in the dim light of the diner, and cold ... *so cold.*

I swallowed. *This* was the man Jasmine had said would be perfect? He looked more like a hitman in his dark suit and white shirt.

Wait! She hadn't hired someone to off my mother, had she?

I was giving serious thought to turning around and fleeing when he spoke.

"Honey, I have no idea what you're talking about." His voice was pitched low—deep and rich. He slid the envelope back toward me with one long finger.

My lips parted, and I forced myself to press them back together to stop the shaky intake of breath at his words. "We ... *you* told me to meet you here. Well, not *me.* Jasmine ... my friend, I mean. *She* contacted you. You arranged all the details with her, but insisted I was the one to come and pay you. I guess that's because you need to meet me before Saturday. Of course you'd need to know what I look like ... otherwise you wouldn't know who you were supposed to be spending the evening with ..."

One dark eyebrow rose above those cold eyes, and I

stammered to a stop.

Oh no! I mentally slapped myself. Obviously, he didn't want everyone around to know what he was doing, what *I* was hiring him to do.

"I'm sorry! I'm such an idiot. Before talking about money and the job, I should have introduced myself. I didn't think about how it would look. This isn't something I do ... I mean ... I've *never* done something like this before!" I dropped onto the bench seat opposite him. "I don't think anyone noticed, though."

"Noticed what?" He glanced around the diner, and I did the same.

There were three people other than me and this man inside the small building—two women chatting over coffee, and another man sitting alone, drumming his fingers on the table. I assumed that's why he picked it—because it was quiet. The perfect location for a meeting. None of the other diners paid attention to what we were doing.

I pushed the envelope toward him again. "I put the name and address of a tailor in the envelope. I've already paid for your suit, and booked the appointment for tomorrow at two-thirty."

He didn't respond. Desperately wanting to get this meeting over with, I soldiered on, "I—I would also like you to hire a car, as discussed. Not something too expensive looking, but ..." My tongue swept out to wet my lips. *Why had I let Jasmine talk me into this?* "You know ... something decent ... *clean*. One that suggests you're a safe driver."

"A car and a suit," he repeated. His frown hadn't smoothed out. In fact, I was certain he was glaring at me, although there was no hint of irritation in his voice, and his expression hadn't changed. There was no hint of *anything*. But it was the way his eyes looked *at* me, *through* me—it sent a slither of alarm up my spine. He reached up and scratched his jaw. "Remind me again what you're paying for?"

"The platinum package?" My heart hammered against my ribs. Nausea threatened to make this situation even more unbearable than it already was. If I threw up on the table, *on* his lunch …

This was such a huge mistake. I wasn't this person. I didn't hire strangers to make my life easier. I didn't lie to my family.

He studied me, and the silence lengthened. I shifted on the seat.

This was definitely a bad idea.

I reached out to take back the envelope, and that's when he spoke.

"Which platinum package did you want?"

I frowned at him.

Was this a test? Did he want to see how serious I was? Maybe he was hoping I was going to cancel. Oh god, what if he didn't want to be seen with me?

"Well … umm … when my friend spoke to you, she said you agreed from mid-afternoon into the evening …" My cheeks heated. "And that if I paid to hire a car, you would pick me up to drive there and back as well."

"Day *and* evening?"

When I nodded, he pursed full lips. "And when is this for?"

"Saturday."

He gave a slow nod. "And you want the *full* package, right?"

"That's right." I tried to swallow down my nerves.

"The *full* package?" There was a note to his voice that woke up butterflies in my stomach.

"Yes." God, why was he making this sound way weirder than it already was? *I should never have listened to Jasmine's insane ideas.*

His fingers tapped the envelope. "And this contains five hundred dollars ... in cash?"

"Cash, yes." I whispered the words, my eyes closing briefly while I hoped no one could hear us, and prayed that the floor would open up and swallow me.

Why did I feel like I was taking part in something illegal?

I shifted on the hard and uncomfortable seat. "That's how much you asked for. Unless ..." I bit my lip, then blurted, "Have you changed your mind?"

He didn't reply, those cold eyes tracking over my face.

Why was this man even hiring himself out, anyway? He could make a fortune as a male model with those brooding good looks.

"This is stupid. I never should have—"

"Write the address and time I need to pick you up on the envelope." He spoke over me, reached into his jacket and pulled out a pen, then held it out to me.

I stared at it.

This was happening then? I was really about to hire someone—a stranger—to pose as my boyfriend in front of my parents?

"Sometime today would be good, honey." The dry words snapped my attention back to the moment.

"My address is already in the envelope, along with the itinerary for the evening."

"There's an *itinerary?*" One eyebrow shot upward.

I nodded. "I'm afraid so. My parents ... well, my mother likes things done a certain way. So, we have to be at the house at three for drinks and mingling, which means we need to set off at two. Dinner will be served at seven."

"Sounds very formal. Are we eating at the house or a restaurant?"

"The house."

"And we're looking at something that's going to go through late into the evening?"

"Yes. Afternoon and evening. Is that ... will that be a problem for you?"

He shook his head. "Not at all. I assume you need a plus one, and that's where I come in?"

I bit my lip. "Kind of."

"What's the occasion?"

"It's my birthday."

That dark eyebrow hiked again. "You're hiring me to accompany you to a birthday dinner with your *parents?*"

"Didn't Jasmine explain when she called you?" What had she told him was the reason I was hiring him?

"I get hired for a lot of things, honey, and take a lot of calls.

So, humor me. Remind me what I agreed to do."

"I ... umm ... well ..." Was it possible to erupt into flames from embarrassment? If it was, I expected to be ashes on the bench seat in the next few seconds. "It was Jasmine's idea, really."

"Jasmine? She's the one ... I spoke to?"

I nodded, grateful to be on common ground at last. "That's right. She saw your ad in the newspaper, listing the services you offer." My cheeks burned hotter. *That sounded like he sold sexual favors.* "Umm ..." I took in a deep breath, then started again. "I told them ... my parents, I mean, that I am dating someone. It was a couple of months ago, so I didn't actually expect them to invite that person to my birthday dinner."

"You didn't expect them to want to meet your boyfriend?"

"Well ... no. I'd forgotten I said anything to them."

I sounded like an idiot. He must have been questioning what kind of stupid person hires a stranger to be their boyfriend. Hell, I was questioning my sanity! But then, if he advertised this kind of service, maybe more people than I thought needed a pretend boyfriend.

"You're not actually dating someone, then?"

"No. Otherwise, I wouldn't need to hire someone to pretend to be my boyfriend." Any second now, I was going to spontaneously combust. The heat in my cheeks couldn't get any hotter. Did I look as red as I felt?

"Fair point." He picked up his fork and ate a mouthful of pie. "Okay, I get a nice suit, pick up a hire car and take you for dinner with your parents. Is that it? Or ..." He paused, that eyebrow hiking up again. "Was there more? Do you want a full boyfriend experience? Dinner, dancing ... *seduction?*" His voice dropped an octave on that last word, drawing it out, *savoring* it.

I almost swallowed my tongue.

"What?" *Oh my god!* Was he asking if I was paying to have sex with him? What kind of guy had Jasmine hired? Was he a ... a gigolo? "No!"

"Then what happens afterward?" His voice returned to normal. "We go to dinner and then break up? Do you dump me or I you? Are you paying for a big heartbreak scene *during* dinner, perhaps? Or do I need to block-book my weekends for the next six months so we can play happy families, and slowly devolve into disgust? Or are we thinking of a more long-term con? Get married, have kids, and then throw in a divorce in a year or two?"

"No!" My voice was higher this time. "I'll tell them it didn't work out in a few weeks."

"Hmm." He tapped the fork against his lips. "Our relationship has become serious enough for you to introduce me to your parents, but not serious enough for it to devastate you when we break up? I think I'm already more invested in this relationship than you are."

I blinked, gaping at him. *Was he serious?* There was no hint of his thoughts on his face or in his voice that I could see. "I'll tell them *you* dumped *me*. It doesn't matter. I just need to get through this dinner without my mother—" I pressed my lips together. He didn't need to know the details of the relationship I had with my mother.

He eyed me while he ate another piece of pie.

"Which platinum package do you want? The perfect besotted boyfriend or the jerk?"

"I... umm... I didn't realize there were options." My voice was faint. He was throwing all these things I hadn't considered at me.

"There are *always* options, honey. If I'm to be besotted with you, then we'll need pet names, handholding, stolen kisses. If I'm a jerk, then that's easier. I'll get drunk and flirt with the female guests... I assume there *will* be female guests? Maybe I could just hit on your mom and ignore you."

I gaped. "The only female guests will be my mother and sister, so I would rather you didn't do any of that."

"Besotted boyfriend it is, then." He nodded. His fork clattered to the plate again, and he held out his hand. "Rook."

The hand hovering in front of me was large, tanned, and... was that a tattoo peeking out from beneath the cuff of his sleeve? I took it gingerly, and his fingers wrapped around mine in a warm, firm grip.

"I'm... umm... my name is Magdalena."

L. ANN

2

Rook

Magdalena.

I repeated her name in my head. Turned it over, examined it, and *tasted* how it felt on my tongue. It wasn't one I'd heard often.

Who named their kid Magdalena these days?

Not that the woman opposite me could *ever* be mistaken for a child—not with those curves. I wasn't ashamed to admit that her fifties pin-up figure was the sole reason I'd given her the time of day, and not sent her running with a well-placed *'fuck off'*. Well, that and the fact she began to talk, oblivious to my disinterest. Disinterest, which turned to confusion when she offered money. When I finally caught up with her babbled explanation and realized she thought I was available as a body to hire, curiosity got the better of me, and I didn't set her straight. Instead, I let her believe I was the guy she was here to meet, just to see where she was leading.

Because there was no way she was hiring me for what people usually hired me for.

I *wasn't* the guy she was supposed to be meeting, and I'm not sure how she had mistaken me for him. A quick glance around the diner told me exactly who she was supposed to meet—the guy tapping his fingers against the table and casting impatient glances toward the door—and I gave brief thought to pointing her in his direction. But then, at some point during her blush-charged explanation, I decided I was going to take the job. Solely to be there to witness the car crash of events she was describing up close and personal—because there was *no way* this girl hiring a stranger to pretend to be her boyfriend was going to go as smoothly as she seemed to think. By the time we got to her admission that it was a birthday dinner, I was invested enough in the insanity of her plan to want to see it through to the obvious disastrous end.

"Do you want to check it's all there?"

I picked up the envelope, turned it over, and smacked it against the palm of my other hand. "No, honey, I'm sure it's fine. If you're short-changing me, I simply won't turn up and you'll have lost your money."

Did I feel guilty for taking money meant for someone else? Not in the slightest. The guy sitting at table twenty-one and constantly checking the time on his cell was the person she should talk to, but he looked sketchy as fuck. At least *my* hair was clean—which was more than could be said for him. You could have fried eggs on the grease making *his* hair shine.

But that also begged the question—if *he* regularly posed as a boyfriend for hire, and got paid for it, how fucking desperate were the women who hired him?

"Okay, you need to pick me up at two, so we're not late." My new fake girlfriend's voice dragged my attention back to her.

"Got it."

"And you'll go for the suit fitting and hire a car?"

"I will." I *wouldn't* hire a car. My car was better than anything I could hire. I'd take the suit, though. I did like a well-made suit.

"Okay. Good." She rose to her feet. "If that's everything? My cell number is in the envelope. Unless you have any further questions, I'll see you on Saturday, Mr. ... Rook?"

I hid a smile at her stilted formality. "Just Rook."

She gave a small nod, turned, and walked toward the exit without another word. I was admiring the sway of her hips when she was blocked from my view.

"Sorry I'm late." My brother took the seat the lovely Magdalena had vacated. He twisted around, following the direction of my gaze. "What are you staring at?"

I ate the last piece of pie on my plate, rubbed a hand over my jaw, and leaned back in the seat. "Apparently, I have a date on Saturday."

"A ... *date?*"

"Yeah."

"Is *date* code for fucking? Since when do you date?" He lifted a hand to get the attention of one of the roaming servers.

"Not in this case, no, and since she paid me five hundred dollars *in cash* and booked me in for a suit fitting."

Bishop stared at me. "Five hundred dollars?"

I lifted my mug to the server, who stopped at the side of the table. "Thanks, honey," I said when she refilled it. Bishop ordered coffee, and she headed back to the counter to get him a clean mug. "Yeah. Five hundred dollars to take her to dinner with her parents on Saturday night." I picked up the conversation again.

"You can't be *that* desperate for money or female company, surely?"

I shrugged. It wasn't a question requiring a reply. He *knew* I didn't need the money or female attention. Picking up the envelope she left on the table, I tore it open. Inside was a wad of twenty-dollar bills and a folded piece of paper. "There's an extra two fifty for the suit and another hundred to hire a car. Can you even hire a car for less than a hundred dollars these days?"

"Eight hundred and fifty dollars for a single date ... and you said yes? Are you *sure* you don't need the money, or was she simply that desperate to spend the night with you?"

"Not doing it for the money. And it was the strangest thing. She wasn't hitting on me. She was hiring a boyfriend for the evening. She just assumed she was talking to the right person."

My brother's jaw dropped. I could count the number of times I'd rendered him speechless on one hand—guess I was adding this occasion to that short list. "Let me get this straight. You're going on a date with a girl who *thought* she was hiring you to be her boyfriend ... but *wasn't?*"

"Pretty much."

"Why?"

I nodded my head toward table twenty-one. "I'm fairly sure *that's* the guy she was supposed to talk to."

Bishop twisted around on his seat and we both regarded the scruffy guy across the way.

"He doesn't look like your typical gigolo," Bishop said finally.

"Right? He looks skeevy as fuck." I wasn't exaggerating—there were sweat stains on his t-shirt and patchy stubble on his chin. "It became a matter of principle to take the job from him."

"Is she hot at least?"

I laughed. "Didn't really pay that much attention." That was a lie. She had a figure that made my mouth water, and her voice had set off tiny explosions in my blood. "She's cute enough, I guess."

I arrived in Glenville six months ago and bought the old rundown manor house on the furthest edge—on the opposite side of town to the home my oldest brother had purchased. It had been his idea to move here.

I hadn't come here to make friends, hold hands, go on dates or form a relationship, but that didn't stop the constant stream of women knocking at my door. They didn't seem to grasp, or care, that I wanted to be left alone, and I was absolutely against shitting where I slept. Whenever I had an itch that needed scratching, I drove out of town and found a willing woman.

A single fuck—that was my rule. Once and done. No repeats, no sleepovers, no cuddles. One tussle between the sheets in a random hotel. I didn't want to get to know them. I barely even *spoke* to them. And yet, *every single one* thought it would be different. What they didn't understand was that I wasn't *capable* of giving them what they wanted, and if they knew why, they'd run screaming, anyway.

That thought made me stop and ask myself for the hundredth time why I'd let a girl believe she'd hired me to be her boyfriend for the evening, and more to the point, why I was going through with it.

I rolled over, reaching down to check the time on my cell.

"Do you want to stay over?" The woman's lips skated over my left shoulder, probably thinking her mouth could convince me to agree.

"Fuck, no." I grunted and shrugged, dislodging her from where she sprawled against my back.

"But I thought we had a good time." The whine in her voice was like nails on a chalkboard.

I climbed off the bed and grabbed my shirt from the floor. Dragging it over my arms, I moved toward the door, pulling on my pants as I went. "It passed the time." I threw open the bedroom door. "I'm going to take a shower and then call a cab. The hotel room is paid up for the day, so if you want to stick around, you can. I have a busy day ahead, and don't have time to stay."

"But Rook…"

I stopped short of rolling my eyes. This was why I never took women back to my place. Don't get me wrong, I *liked* women. I liked fucking. What I *didn't* like was the clinging afterward. Why the fuck did these women want to cuddle and stay in bed once we were done? I couldn't figure it out. It wasn't like I didn't lay down the terms of how it would go before we even reached a bedroom. But it didn't stop them from trying to convince me to take a second go on the merry-go-round.

"Come back to bed."

I glanced back. "Sorry, honey. I've got a meeting in a couple of hours and need to get ready and get gone. Leave your number, and maybe I'll call you." I shut the bedroom door behind me and walked into the bathroom.

By the time I'd showered and returned to the main room, the woman who'd shared my bed for the last few hours was gone. She'd left a piece of paper on the nightstand with her name and cell number. I tossed it into the trash can without even looking at it, left the hotel room, and headed back home.

By the time I got there, I had just enough time for coffee before I went to the appointment with the tailor my new pretend girlfriend had booked for later that day. I frowned.

That reminded me ...

Pulling out my cell, I scrolled through my contacts until I found the number I'd added for her.

```
ME—It's Rook. The info you provided doesn't
really tell me anything a long-term boyfriend
needs to know. I have questions. Got a couple
of minutes to answer them?
```

Her answer came through a couple of minutes later.

DALLY—What sort of questions?

Yeah, I'd already shortened that fucking long-ass name of hers so it fit easier in my cell

ME—I was thinking if we've been dating for a while, then I need to know some things. Do you prefer the right or left side of the bed? Do you sleep clothed or unclothed?

They were stupid questions, but I wanted to get a feel for her personality.

DALLY—I doubt anyone is going to ask you questions about that.

ME—How do you know? They might. Okay, let's start with something simple. Favorite color?

DALLY—Purple.

ME—Movie? Book? Are you a reader or a watcher?

DALLY—I listen to audiobooks. My favorite is Kill Switch by Penelope Douglas. Favorite movie is Love, Actually.

I looked up the book and movie she'd mentioned and discovered they were opposite ends of a spectrum. What that spectrum was, I wasn't entirely sure. "Love, Actually" was a cutesy romance movie and "Kill Switch"... Well, from flicking through it, *that* wasn't as cute but, surprisingly, I caught myself reading a few pages on Amazon's Look Inside feature.

Damon seemed cool in a psycho-killer kind of way. I thought

we could be friends. But it made me wonder about the girl I was about to go and hang out with. Did she lean more toward the pretty 'happy ever after' of "Love, Actually", or was she more about the down and dirty of "Kill Switch"? I knew which one I'd prefer, and it *wasn't* the movie option.

```
ME - Interesting. That'll do for now. See
you on Saturday.
```

When Saturday finally rolled around, I took the suit she'd had tailored for me out of the closet.

Yes, I was actually going to go through with the date.

Why?

Fuck knows.

It wasn't like I needed the money. Five hundred dollars was pocket change.

Then why?

The answer was simple. I just didn't want to acknowledge it.

Because I was bored.

Maybe I needed a change of pace.

Maybe it also had something to do with the note that had been in the envelope with the eight hundred and fifty dollars from my fake girlfriend's friend.

'Mags needs to live a little. Show her a REALLY good time!'

It struck a nerve. I was thirty-eight years old, and I had nothing to show for it, other than a lot of money and a bad reputation. And by bad, I didn't mean a small-town reputation for getting into fights and breaking women's hearts. Nor did I mean breaking and entering or holding up 7-11's. No, when I said I had a bad reputation, I meant it literally. There was blood on my hands. *Lots* of it.

But I was *very* good at showing women a good time, yet I rarely enjoyed the time I spent with them. The words felt like a challenge, like the woman was going to be resistant to having some fun, and I wanted to prove to myself that *I* could give her a good time *and* also have one, too.

I frowned.

Fuck, she'd said it was her birthday.

I should at least get the girl a card. It's what a boyfriend—fake or not—would do, surely. With that in mind, I stopped at a florist and bought her a bouquet and a card on my way to pick her up.

3

Magdalena

I put the finishing touches to my makeup, checked that my hair was still in the chignon my mother expected to see, and slipped my feet into flat black pumps.

"I don't understand why you continue to put yourself through these things," Jasmine, my friend and roommate, said from the doorway.

"You've met my mother. It's easier to go along with her wishes than it is to argue. I'd rather just get it over with and not deal with the constant phone calls and comments about *'that one time'* I refused to keep with her traditions."

"Well, at least you have a date this time. That should ease *some* of the pressure, right?" A tap sounded on the front door as she spoke, saving me from answering. Jasmine grinned. "Guess he heard me. Perfect timing! Are you ready?"

"I don't even know why I let you talk me into this. My mother will never believe I've been dating this guy for months."

"Did you give him all the information I wrote out?"

I nodded. "He texted me a few questions as well."

"Then it'll be fine. They don't know him, so they won't be able to tell if *you're* lying about him, but they *do* know you, which means he needs to know things to show that you've been together for a while."

"I'm glad *you* feel confident about it."

Another rap at the door had us both turning toward it.

"Want me to answer it?" Jasmin offered, and I shook my head.

"No, let's get it over with." I grabbed my purse from the couch on they way past as I headed toward the door. "I'll call you when I get there."

"I should walk out with you and take a note of the license plate."

I stopped and stared at her. "What? Why?"

"Just in case."

"Jas …" My eyes sought where my friend stood. "Am I going to be murdered?"

She laughed. "Don't be ridiculous!" She glanced toward the door. "Maybe I'll follow you out, though, and get a photograph of him as well."

I shook my head. "We have his cell number. I think it'll be fine. Stay here. This is awkward enough without having an audience."

Before I could talk myself out of it, I pulled the door open … and blinked. He'd been sitting down when I saw him. Well, *sprawled* on the bench seat in the diner, all long limbs and casual elegance. On the ad he'd posted, it had stated he was five foot nine, only a couple of inches taller than my five-seven, but standing in front of me was a guy who had to be at *least* six three! My eyes were level with his throat—a throat that showed the barest hint of a colorful tattoo creeping up from beneath the collar of his shirt. I tipped my head back to look at his face, which was partially covered by dark glasses and stubble.

"Hi." His voice was low and gravelly. "Ready to go?"

I nodded. "Were you able to hire a car for the day?"

He walked along the hallway toward the elevator bay, then stopped and turned back, holding out the bouquet he held. "I have a car, yeah. And these are for you. Happy birthday."

"Oh!" I took them from him, burying my face in the petals. "Thank you! Let me go back inside and put them in water." I hurried back into the apartment before he could speak.

Jasmine's eyes dropped to the flowers. "Wow, they're pretty. Guess he's really embracing the role, huh?" She grinned and took them from me. "You need to go, or you'll be late. I'll make sure these go into a vase." She pushed me back toward the door and I hurried to catch up to the man waiting for me.

"Did you have time to read everything?"

He leaned forward and stabbed at the call button. "I did. Your mother sounds like a royal pain in the ass."

I gaped at him, a little taken aback by his bluntness. "She's just ..." I frowned, searching for the best way to describe her. "Well, she's set in her ways." *What had Jasmine written down?*

"Set in her ways? Are you sure you don't mean overbearing?

Or maybe controlling?" One eyebrow rose from behind the glasses covering his face.

The elevator doors slid open, and he waited while I stepped inside before following me. He pushed the button for the ground floor and moved to stand on the opposite side of the small compartment.

"You don't even know her. That's a judgment call based upon whatever Jasmine wrote." I scowled. "What *did* she write?"

His head tilted. "You don't know?"

"I *told* you. She arranged this whole thing."

"Very trusting of you not to read what she was telling your pretend boyfriend about you."

I frowned. "Why?" The smile which curled his lips caused my stomach to twist in sudden concern. "What did she write?"

"She was very ... thorough."

"About?"

"Isn't it a bit late to be worrying about that?" He pushed away from the wall when the elevator doors slid open.

"I'm not going anywhere until you tell me."

One broad shoulder lifted in a shrug. I folded my arms and narrowed my eyes.

He laughed, the sound low and husky. "Alright, Miss Defiant. She told me it's your twenty-fourth birthday. Happy birthday, darlin'. That makes me way too old for you and should cause an indecent amount of outrage. You're the youngest of three—one older brother and one older sister. You were the surprise child when your parents thought they were done. Unplanned and unexpected. From the things your friend wrote, I'd also guess that you were unwanted."

I held back a flinch at that. It was too close to a truth I tried not to think about.

"You were raised by various nannies and the household staff, and when you grew older and moved out, your parents demanded that you always come home for your birthday. Last year, you were blindsided by them inviting a man they viewed as potential husband material. This year you're hoping to avoid a repeat performance of *that* disaster by bringing a date of your own choosing."

"That's … umm …" Hearing him list what had happened in such a dispassionate voice made everything sound much worse.

He turned and walked away. I watched him for a second, as did the woman who was collecting her mail, and I met her eyes when I stepped out of the elevator. Her expression said everything she wasn't verbalizing. How did *you* catch *him*? I couldn't help the smile which tugged my lips up.

He gave off quite the impression, as he prowled to the entrance of the building. He stopped by the doors and turned back.

"Are you coming?" That eyebrow lifted again.

I followed him out of the building and down the steps. A black sports car was parked nearby, and he stopped beside it.

"*This* is the car you hired?" I asked when he opened the passenger door.

"Don't you like it?"

"It's beautiful, but it must have cost a lot more than I gave you." There was *no way* he could have hired a sports car for the day with one hundred dollars. I climbed in and fiddled with the seatbelt.

"I imagine it would *if* I'd hired it." He slammed the door, sealing me inside, and strode around to the driver's side. "The car's mine," he explained once he was behind the wheel.

"*Yours?*" I winced at the clear disbelief in my voice.

"I can't have a nice car?"

I was beginning to hate the eyebrow rising from behind his glasses.

"Of course you can! It's just ... well ... I didn't ..." I fell silent. How was I supposed to say I'd assumed someone who was hiring themselves out as a temporary boyfriend was doing it because they needed the money and not sound demeaning?

He pulled out into the traffic. "I'm surprised you aren't driving."

I turned my head to look at him. "Why?"

"Two reasons. First, you're in a car with a strange man. That's very trusting of you. Didn't your parents ever teach you not to go with strangers? Second, there was eight hundred and fifty dollars in that envelope. You're clearly not short of money if you can throw that away on hiring a random man to take you on a date. Surely you have your own car?"

"You're assuming I can drive."

"Can't you?"

I *couldn't,* but that wasn't the point. "Maybe I thought it'd look better if my boyfriend drove us to the house?"

His head swung around to glance at me before returning his attention to the road. "You *can't* drive, can you?"

I sighed. "No. It never interested me." That wasn't the truth. I couldn't drive because when I did Driver's Ed at school, I crashed into the cones so much the instructor refused to continue the lessons. Because I often confused my left and right. Because, until I was nineteen, I thought I was stupid.

L. ANN

4

Rook

The pink tinge on her cheeks told me everything I needed to know about what she was thinking about my car. In her defense, had I been the guy who'd been sitting at table twenty-one, she wouldn't have been wrong. There was no way the sleaze she'd meant to hire would own a less-than-year-old Mustang GT convertible.

She didn't speak again until we'd left the town behind us and were on the freeway heading to her parent's place.

"Did Jasmine put anything about me in her notes, other than it being my birthday?"

"She put a few things in, yeah." I didn't expand on that. I wasn't sure she'd appreciate knowing her friend had listed a bunch of sexual positions she thought Magdalena would enjoy, her ideal date situation, and a comment that she enjoyed bully romance—whatever *that* was. I guessed it had something to do with the 'Kill Switch' book—which, according to her friend, meant she had the potential to be a wildcat in bed. Along with those details, thankfully she'd remembered to jot down random likes and dislikes, and the fact she didn't drink alcohol. Other than that, and the few things I'd asked her directly, I was working blind.

But hey, what was life without a little challenge?

"Tell me about what we're walking into. It's your birthday and we're both dressed like we're going to a formal dinner. Why is that?"

"Family tradition." She glanced over at me and chewed on her bottom lip for a second before continuing. "As you rightfully pointed out, my parents like me to celebrate my birthday at home with them. My mother ..."

She looked away, and I frowned. "She didn't have an easy pregnancy with me. She was older and thought her childbearing days were over. It caused her a lot of stress. She likes to ..." Another hesitation. "Well, once we all grew up and left home, she insisted I continue to go home on my birthday."

"You've never blown it off and done your own thing?" I kept my eyes on the road, watching for the turnoff, which would take us to the town her parents lived in.

"Definitely not!" The shock in her voice interested me.

"Why not? What would they do?"

"Do? They wouldn't *do* anything."

"Then why are you going? Surely you have better things to do than sit through a meal on your birthday? Friends you could go out with?"

"It's not just a meal. My parents ... well, mostly my mother likes to spend the afternoon catching up on all our lives."

"That can't be done via a phone call?"

She sighed. "It'll be easier to understand when we get there."

I shrugged. "It's your money you're wasting." I followed the signs for Gerard's Bay—the small town where her parents lived—and, after a few more minutes, drove down a long curved drive and pulled up outside a sprawling ranch house.

"Can you park over by the trees?" She pointed to where a cluster of three or four trees stood, and two other cars were parked.

"Sure."

Once we parked, I turned in my seat to look at her. She sat, knees together, hands tucked between her thighs, back ramrod straight. She was so stiff and formal. There was no way anyone was going to believe we were in an intimate relationship. "They're expecting you to bring your long-term, committed boyfriend, right? Will they be watching for you? You *did* tell them you were bringing someone?"

"Yes, and yes." She fumbled with her seatbelt, not looking at me.

"Alright. Stay there." I climbed out and strode around to the passenger side. Throwing open the door, I bent and held out a hand. "We should start as we mean to go on," I said in response to her confused frown. "Take my hand."

Frown firmly in place, she rested her hand on mine. I curled my fingers around hers and drew her out of the car. When she straightened from smoothing her knee-length skirt back into place, I dropped her hand and stepped closer.

"What are you doing?"

"Making it clear that we're dating to anyone who's watching. You wanted the besotted boyfriend package, right? The platinum version?" I waited for her nod. "That means being cooped up in the car for the past hour has been too long, and now I need to kiss you, so put your arms around my neck."

"What?" She stiffened, eyes going wide. "No, you absolutely do *not* need to kiss me. That's ridiculous."

"Oh honey, I really do. Now do as you're told." I caught her hand, lifted it to my shoulder, and took another step forward, backing her against the side of my car. I lowered my head. "Now remember, if you punch me, it'll ruin all the lies you've been telling," I cautioned, and kissed her.

The hand on my shoulder moved, her fingers curling into the material of my shirt. Her eyes were huge, and would have been locked on mine if she could see them through the dark lenses of my sunglasses. I fisted a hand into her hair, disrupting the neat style she had it pinned in, and tugged her head back. The silky strands spilled over my fingers, and the faint scent of honey reached me. She held herself still and stiff, making no attempt to take part in the kiss.

Separating my mouth from hers, I left just enough space for me to whisper against her lips. "If you don't kiss me back, they're going to question what kind of relationship we have."

"We don't *have* a relationship!"

"That's my point. And if we walk in without making it

look like we *do*, then they'll know you're lying and you'll have wasted all that money. So... *kiss me*." I didn't wait for her to reply, lowering my head and capturing her lips with mine.

For a split second, I thought she would push me away. Her mouth stayed closed, refusing to part under mine. I brushed my lips across her cheek until I reached her ear. "What was the point in hiring a boyfriend to convince your parents you're off the market, if you're not going to live the pretense? Or are you out of practice? Scared I'm going to think you can't kiss?"

That got through to her. She braced herself against my shoulder, lifted on her toes, turned her head, and found my lips with hers.

She tasted like peppermint—probably the toothpaste she'd used—but she smelled like *summer*. That intangible, indescribable scent that you simply recognized and linked to hot, lazy days under the sun. I curved a hand around her waist, tightened the fingers of my other hand in her hair and pulled her closer, until I could feel the warmth of her body against mine. She didn't protest, her free hand sliding up to hook around my neck, and her lips parted beneath the pressure of my tongue.

"Mags!" A sharp, high-pitched voice broke us apart, and Magdalena stepped back, hands immediately dropping away from me. "What on earth are you doing? Mother is watching from the window!"

Magdalena didn't reply, her focus locked on me. I hadn't really noticed her eyes before now. We hadn't been close enough. They were a light brown, hazel with little flecks of green—unnoticeable from any kind of distance, but this close... this close they were clear. Her tongue came out to sweep over her lips and slowly, as though it was difficult to do, she turned to face the newcomer.

"Charlie, I thought you weren't coming until this evening." Her voice was a little breathless.

"You know I don't like that name. It's *Charlotte*. Charlie makes me sound like a boy."

Curiosity got the better of me, and I turned to see the woman talking to Magdalena. It was obvious they were related—they had the same brunette hair, similar features, but Charlie... *Charlotte*... was shorter than Dally, and her build was not as... generous with the curves that had caught my attention on the woman with me. I paused in my perusal of the two women. *Dally?* When did the name I'd put in my cell become the name I called her in my head?

"This is Rook." Dally's hand on my arm snapped my attention back to the two women. "My..." She licked her lips. "My... umm... my boyfriend." The words came out in a rush.

I placed my hand on top of hers and squeezed her fingers. Her gaze jumped to me. I smiled.

"Pleasure to meet you. Magdalena has told me so much about you." That was a lie. I knew barely anything. Based on the similarities between them, I had to assume that this woman was her sister. It was a good job I was excellent at winging my way through a situation.

"Has she?" Charlotte's voice was cool. "That's interesting,

because she's said *nothing* about you."

"And that's why I'm here. To rectify that," I said before my fake-date could. From the way her cheeks were turning pink, lying was *not* in her skill set and I was pretty sure she was on the verge of blurting out the truth of the situation, which seemed counterproductive to why I was here.

I draped an arm across her shoulders. "Come on, darlin'. Why don't we go and say hi to your parents?"

She slanted an unreadable look in my direction, but nodded her head. "If Mother was watching, that means she must be in the Summer Room." She raised her voice. "Is that where she is, *Charlotte*?"

"Yes. So is Father."

"What about Randall and the kids?"

Charlotte's lips thinned. "Randall decided he should stay at home with the boys. I'm leaving straight after dinner. I agreed that there was no point in dragging them all this way as well. It's not a big deal or anything, just your birthday."

Just her birthday?

"That's true." There was nothing in Magdalena's voice to show her sister's words had upset her.

"If it's not a *big deal*, then why the insistence on coming here at all?" I received an angry look from Charlotte in return for my question.

The woman shook her head, then turned to Dally. "Go and greet our mother before she comes looking for you." She ignored my question while Dally slid out from beneath my arm and moved ahead of me.

5

Magdalena

I led Rook toward the front door and inside the house I grew up in. I could still feel his lips against mine, the hand he'd wrapped in my hair.

Oh shoot, my hair!

My hand flew up and felt the strands loose around my face. My mother was going to lose her mind when she saw it wasn't in the expected chignon. I stopped and cast a glance toward the stairs.

"Problem?" Rook asked from beside me.

"Not yet," I muttered. I was about to say I needed to use the bathroom when my mother's voice spoke.

"Magdalena, stop haunting the hallway like you're an unhappy spirit. Come in here and introduce me to the man you've been talking about for the past two months." Her voice was crisp, and my spine snapped straight.

"Been talking all about me for two months, huh?" I swear I could hear laughter in his voice.

I sliced a look at him. "This was a bad idea."

He chuckled. "It really was, darlin', but you're in too deep to back out now. Come on." He slung an arm back across my shoulders, and the action was so casual, as though he'd done it a thousand times before, it froze me to the spot. "Dally, Dally, Dally," he murmured. "This isn't going to work, if you can't play pretend."

I frowned. Wait. Had he just called me ... *Dally*?

"Did you ever play with dolls when you were a kid?"

I blinked at him. "Of course I did."

"And did you ever steal your brother's action figures and marry them off?"

"No. Fraser didn't play with action figures."

Rook rolled his eyes at me, and I realized he'd taken his sunglasses off somewhere between kissing me and coming indoors. "Work with me here. Did you ever play pretend weddings with your friends?"

"Sure."

"Then use that. Remember what you used to do ... or you can follow my lead, if you like. I was often the test subject for my neighbor's daughter to practice her kissing technique on."

"I just bet you were." I couldn't help the tart response. I licked my lips. They felt sensitive, tender. Did they *look* like I'd been thoroughly kissed?

He grinned and squeezed my shoulder. "Trust me. You're paying me good money not to fuck this up. Follow my lead, and we'll be out of here with your parents firmly believing you're happy and not in the market for any more blind dates."

I took a breath, then nodded. "Okay, but please ... don't do anything ... outrageous."

He chuckled again. "*Trust* me." And with those words, he urged me forward.

My mother was in the Summer Room, right where I'd expected to find her—perched on the edge of her chair, with a perfect view out of the window where she would have seen Rook kiss me. Her lips pressed together into a thin line, and her eyes narrowed as they swept over me. Contrary to what my sister had said, there was no sign of my father.

"Magdalena, please fix your hair. You look a mess."

"Yes, mother." The response was automatic, and I'd half-turned back toward the door before remembering I hadn't introduced Rook to her. I stopped and faced her. "Mother, this is Rook."

Rook held out one hand. "Glad to make your acquaintance. Dally has told me so much about you."

"Dally?" My mother's voice was sharp.

I vented a silent groan. I should have warned him my mother didn't like shortened versions of our names, but in my defense, I didn't *know* he'd shortened it until thirty seconds ago.

"It suits her, don't you think?" Rook seemed oblivious to the chill in my mother's tone.

She ignored him. "*Magdalena*, your hair. Before dinner is served."

I sent Rook an apologetic look, dipped my head and dashed

out of the room. Charlotte was coming toward me as I hurried across the floor to the staircase.

"Where are you going?"

"Mother demanded I fix my hair."

My sister's eyes flicked over my face. "He did make quite a mess of it when he kissed you." She glanced around. "Where is he?"

I pulled a face. "In the Summer Room."

Charlotte laughed. "You've left him alone with her? Are you *insane?*"

"I didn't really have much of a choice, Charl—Charlotte." I caught myself before I called her Charlie—the name I'd always used growing up, before we'd grown apart, distant, before she'd married the man our mother chose for her.

"Where did you find him? Isn't he a little old for you? I didn't think you were into older men."

My mind blanked. We hadn't worked out a meet-cute story to tell everyone. "I'll tell you all about him later. I need to clean up before Mother sends someone to look for me." I touched my hair.

"Then hurry up and sort it out, before you find he's been driven away. I'll try to keep the peace."

I almost speed-walked to the bedroom my mother insisted I kept at the house, and into the attached bathroom. The first glimpse of my hair in the mirror widened my eyes. I looked like I'd just climbed out of bed after spending a night with a lover. My hair was a tangled mess around my shoulders instead of the tightly pinned-in-place chignon I'd worked on before leaving my apartment. The lipstick I'd worn was gone, kissed away by the man downstairs. My tongue swept over my lips again at the memory.

It hadn't seemed like a first kiss, not any I'd ever had from a new boyfriend—they'd always been hesitant, stumbling, *awkward* as we both tried to work out pace, angle and firmness. But Rook's kiss had been assured, as though he already knew how I liked to be kissed... or how I *should* be kissed. I pressed my lips together. It had been an act, a pretense, a way to dissuade any questions when we arrived.

I reached up to unpin the rest of my hair, found a brush, untangled it, and ten minutes later, my chignon was back in place. I found a lipstick on the dresser in my bedroom, a pale pink which I slicked across my lips, then headed back downstairs. I hoped... *prayed*... Rook would still be there when I returned, that my mother hadn't sent him running. Without him, I wouldn't be able to get home without calling a cab, or asking my mother to lend me a car and her driver—neither of which I wanted. But as I descended the stairs, I could hear voices, and one of them was Rook's. The tension in my spine eased a little, knowing he was still here, that my escape route was still intact. Taking a deep breath, I stepped inside the Summer Room.

My mother was still seated in her chair near the window. Rook stood near the fireplace, one hand in his pants pocket, the other holding a glass of ... I frowned. *Was he drinking alcohol?* I hoped not. I wanted to go home tonight, not have to stay, and if he was drinking, he certainly couldn't drive back to town. He caught my eyes, and one corner of his lips tilted upward.

"Welcome back, darlin'." He stepped forward, placing the glass down onto a coaster on the table as he passed, and walked across the floor to me. All eyes were on us as his hand slid around my waist and tugged me into his side. "I was just telling your mom how we met."

"You ... were?" My stomach knotted. *What had he told her?* I'd been very vague about having a boyfriend any time I spoke to my mother, and I hadn't thought to discuss it with him before we arrived. My mother had never shown much interest in my love life, beyond whether or not I was going to get married, so it was easy to change the subject any time she raised it. But now I'd have to work with whatever story he'd shared and, from the gleam in his eye, I was certain it wasn't going to be easy.

His head dipped, and his lips brushed over my forehead. "Don't look so worried. I kept the more ... x-rated parts to myself."

"X-rated?" I repeated faintly. *Dear god, what had he said?*

His smile widened. "There are some things you don't share with your family."

My eyes sought my mother, where she sat staring at us, her lips still set in a thin line. "There is no x-rated story to tell. He's just teasing. It's what he does. I bet he hasn't even told you the real story of how we met." The hand on my waist squeezed, and I glanced up at the man beside me. "What did you tell them?"

"Relax, darlin'. I told them we met at Rory's Diner. You thought I was someone else and struck up a conversation. I was confused but too polite to tell you that you'd got the wrong person. Sparks flew, we hit it off, and agreed to see each other again." His eyes laughed at me. "What part of it was wrong?"

Rory's Diner—that was where we'd agreed to meet and pay for him to be here today. He had mixed in enough truth for it to sound believable. But there was something in his tone, to the curl of his lip, that made me wonder ... for a second ... whether there was more truth to his words than I realized.

Was he telling me he wasn't the person I'd gone there to meet? Oh god. Was he?

"How is it possible to even do that?" Charlotte asked, and I looked at Rook. He'd started this, so he could damn well continue it.

He gave my sister an easy smile. "She was supposed to go to table twenty-one, but rolled up to table twelve, where I was finishing my lunch. She was half-way through her speech about arranging to meet me before I could even get a word out. By that point ..." He shrugged. "I was too fascinated to tell her she was talking to the wrong guy."

L. ANN

6

Rook

I could almost see her mind working as she listened to the story I'd told her family. None of it was a lie. I just hadn't added the *reason* why she had spoken to me. I wondered if she'd realize the mistake she had made with the table numbers and whether she'd mention it. But she stood there, a small frown furrowing her brow as she stared at me.

Most of my attention was on her mother, though. That woman had a face that could spoil milk. Thin lipped, fine lines around her eyes and mouth that weren't from laughter, but she was beautiful in a cold, *don't touch me* kind of way, and I could see where Dally and her sister had inherited at least some of their looks from.

I glanced at Dally—I'd told my brother she was cute, but the fact was she was fucking stunning. I hadn't paid much attention to her looks when she'd approached me in the diner. But the weird hairstyle she was currently sporting, pulled tightly into place, showed off her high cheekbones and huge brown eyes. She had coated her lips in a pale pink lipstick, lighter than the one I'd kissed off her mouth earlier, and it suited her skin tone more.

Why the fuck was I analyzing her skin?

Maybe because when I'd touched it outside on the drive, her skin had been warm, smooth, and soft.

"Where did you go on your first date?" The question had me searching out the speaker—Dally's sister, Charlotte—who was moving across the room to perch on the cream couch, which looked fucking uncomfortable.

"I took her to Dante's." I named a restaurant in Glenville, where we both lived. "Do you want to know what we ate?" I arched an eyebrow, letting her know I was aware she didn't believe the story. She looked away. "I thought we were here because it's Dally's birthday?"

"We're here because twenty-four years ago, I gave birth to a daughter I didn't expect to be carrying." Her mother's voice was sharp. "We celebrate the fact I didn't *die* during labor."

I stared at the older woman. *Had she really turned someone else's birthday into being about her?* She glared back at me.

"Why do you call her Dally?" Her sister said into the ensuing silence.

"It's less of a mouthful than Magdalena every time I want her attention. It's cute and suits her. Do you want to know the other things I call her?" I softened my voice, injected a hint of intimacy into it that had Charlotte's cheeks turning pink and their mother's mouth pursing further. The questions were beginning to irritate me. The tone of them didn't give me the impression they were asking out of concern for the woman beside me, but because they wanted to find something to complain about or criticize. "Maybe you'd like to know what I bought for her birthday?" I cast a glance around the room, unreasonable irritation rising at the lack of cards or gifts waiting for her. "Judging by the lack of envelopes and brightly colored boxes, I'm guessing more than either of you did."

"Rook, stop." Magdalena's request came with her hand touching my arm.

"*Stop?* Darlin', I haven't even started yet." I tightened my grip on her waist. "She said we had to come here because it's tradition to come home for her birthday. I wanted to take her somewhere else, somewhere *special*, but she insisted. So here we are. I'm wondering whether I should have been more insistent, because I don't know who the fuck would willingly put themselves through this." I let my arm drop from Magdalena's waist. "Let's get out of here." I turned toward the door.

"You know I can't do that."

I swept another glance around the room. "Well, I fucking can." I walked out. Less than ten minutes with her mother and my trigger finger was itching. And when I wanted to pull a gun, things had a tendency to go all kinds of crazy. I stalked out of the room, the reason I was here forgotten in favor of anger over how the woman, my fake-girlfriend I had to remind myself, was being treated.

"Rook, wait!" She came after me.

"It's your birthday. This isn't how you should be celebrating. Your mother is a fucking psychopath. Come with me."

"I *can't*. And you don't know her. She almost died giving birth to me. She was fifty-two and didn't think she could have any more children. Can you imagine how hard that must have been?"

I glanced around the house as we walked through it. The house screamed wealth. "So difficult," I murmured. "Didn't you say you were raised by a nanny? What part did *your mother* play in your upbringing?"

"Rook, *please!*" She caught my arm just as I reached the main doors leading outside. "I need you to stay."

"And I need to get out of here before I say or *do* something that we'll all regret." I didn't think she'd appreciate me going out to get my gun from the car and shooting her mother.

Her hand fell away, and she moved to stand in front of me. "I hired you to be my date for the evening. Have you any idea how it must look to my mother right now? You're storming off while I'm running after you. She's going to think—"

"Think what? That she might have fooled you, but I can see right through her? Fuck, Dally, I've been here less than an hour, and I already have her fucking number. This gathering on your birthday isn't for *you*, it's for her. How do you not see that?"

"Why do you think I *don't?* This might be for her, but she's still my *mother!*"

I shook my head. "It's' your fucking *birthday*." I couldn't even explain why her acceptance of her mother's behavior made me angry.

"It doesn't matter. She needs this. Needs to see that I know how difficult it was for her."

"Fucking *difficult?* What was fucking difficult? Look around you! Are you so blinded by the money dripping from the walls that you can't see the truth? Fuck's sake!" I raked a hand through my hair. "I almost fucking pity you."

"*Why?* It's just a dinner. You'll never have to see her again after tonight. You can drive me home, and go back to … well, whatever it is you usually do, and never give me or my family another thought." She stiffened her shoulders and threw her head back, meeting my eyes. "I *paid* for your services."

I stared at her. Now would be a good time to tell her she paid the wrong guy, but the way her eyes were pleading with me, at odds with the defiant tilt of her chin, kept me silent.

"I'll give you a refund."

The fire bled out of her eyes, and she sagged. She slowly turned away.

I ignored the way it felt like a knife was twisting in my gut and blew out a breath. "Fine."

"Fine? You'll stay?" Her smile when she spun back to face me was like the sun rising.

"It's a fucking bad decision, but yes, I'll stay. I'll make nice, I'll play the role you've paid for, and then I'll take you home." I paused and cocked one eyebrow. "On one condition."

"Condition? You made no conditions when we agreed to this." Her voice rose. She caught herself and glanced around. "What condition?"

"We do this *my* way. I'm not a gentleman, Dal. I can't pretend to be cute and fluffy for you."

She blinked. "You think you've been *cute and fluffy* so far?"

"Compared with my natural behavior, absolutely."

"That's ... terrifying."

I let a grin stretch my lips. "Maybe. But you agree to that, and I'll stay."

She didn't answer straight away, her eyes tracking over my face, her teeth gnawing at her lip, then she gave an abrupt nod. "Okay, fine. Your way. But can you please remember, *I* have to see them again. *You* don't. I don't want to be completely thrown out of this family."

I chuckled, my temper easing. "I'll keep that in mind." I held out a hand. "Come on, then. Let's go back."

She glanced down, then slowly placed her hand in mine. "I just know I'm going to regret this," she muttered.

I squeezed her fingers. "But I'll make it fun for you, all the same."

The conversation was stilted, the atmosphere chilled, when we returned to the Summer Room—a fucking stupid name for a room as cold as the one we were sitting in, if you asked me. Magdalena, her sister, and mother behaved like my earlier outburst hadn't happened, and the conversation turned to Charlotte's husband

and kids. Dally barely spoke, seated beside me on the two-seater, clutching a fine china teacup, which clattered against its saucer any time she set it down.

Her mother said nothing further about my presence. In fact, she completely ignored me in favor of talking to Charlotte. When her gaze passed over me, or more accurately on the hand I had resting on Dally's leg, her lips pursed and her fingers tightened their grip on her own teacup. I was relieved when the bell rang for dinner, because it meant there were only a couple of hours left before we could get out of here.

The bell.

I laughed internally at that. This whole fucking household was trapped in the past—one where they were waited on by servants. Women had their place, and men seemed to be allowed to behave any way they damned well pleased. My mother would have chewed me up and spat me out for the attitude I'd displayed when I walked out, but Magdalena's mother appeared to accept it as normal. She didn't *like* me, that was obvious, but she also didn't say a word against my behavior or the way I'd spoken to her.

It was fucking weird.

After the bell rang, all three women rose to their feet. Dally turned to look at me.

"We have dinner in the main dining room. Father will be in there already." There was a note to her voice that I couldn't decipher, but I stood and held out my arm. She looked at me.

I took her hand and placed it around my forearm, patted her

fingers, then followed her mother and sister out of the room. The dining room was like something from a period drama. Dark paneled walls, and a long dining table taking up the center of the room.

A man sat at the head of the table, his dark hair peppered with gray, and one hand toying with a butter knife. He looked up when we entered, his eyes landing on me and staying there. Dally's mother moved around the table to sit opposite him, while Charlotte took the seat to her mother's right. I looked at Magdalena, who led me to the left side and waved a hand at the seat closest to her dad.

When she turned to the seat at her mother's left, I stepped up behind the chair and pulled it out for her. She murmured a quiet thank you and sank down onto it. All the while I could feel her dad's eyes on me, watching and, I'm sure, assessing. I took the seat Dally indicated and turned toward the older man, holding out a hand.

"Pleasure to meet you, sir. My name is Rook."

His eyes dropped to my hand and then back up to my face. "Magdalena hasn't said a lot about you, other than you've been dating for a couple of months." He reached forward and grasped my hand in a firm grip.

"That's right."

"How serious are you?"

"Daddy, we're still getting to know each other." Dally leaned past me to say, and I saw the other man's features soften slightly.

It seemed her relationship was clearly better with her father than her mother.

"I would still like to know his intentions, Mags." He released my hand and settled back on his chair.

Her mother tutted. "Do you *have* to call her that?"

"If you hadn't insisted on naming her Magdalena, I wouldn't have to shorten it, would I?" His voice was mild, as though this was an argument they'd had a thousand times before.

"It was my grandmother's name."

"And you *still* saddled our daughter with it."

I caught movement out of the corner of my eye and turned to see Dally covering her lips, but not quick enough to hide her smile.

"I think it's a pretty name," I said, reaching out to tug her hand down. "It's different. Unique … like the woman who bears it." They were idle words, an easy throwaway compliment, but her cheeks turned pink.

L. ANN

7

Magdalena

I knew he was playing a role I'd paid him for, saying things he thought a doting boyfriend would say, but it still didn't stop me from growing warm when he complimented my name. It wasn't even what he said; it was his *voice*. The way it softened, turned husky, gave hints toward an intimacy we didn't actually have.

He tipped his head and smiled at me. The action managed to give off the impression of affection and warmth. "Dally has brought an element of *unpredictable fun* to my life that I didn't realize I was missing. I never know what she will surprise me with next."

I narrowed my eyes. His smile turned into a smirk. My father chuckled.

"Mags has always been spirited. She needs someone who can keep up with that wild streak she tries to hide."

Rook's eyebrow rose. "Is that right?"

"No, it's not." My voice was firm, and Rook laughed.

"Enough chatter." My mother's crisp voice silenced us, as two maids appeared and silently placed plates in front of us all. A third moved around the table, filling glasses with red wine. Rook covered the top of his glass when she paused beside him.

"No thanks, honey. I'm driving later."

"Can I get you something else, sir?" she asked.

"Water's fine."

She gave him a nod and stopped next to me. I shook my head. "Thanks, Katy, but I'm still not drinking."

She smiled at me. "I brought you a cola instead, miss." When we were alone, Katy used my name, but I knew if she did that in front of my mother, it would be grounds for instant dismissal, so I didn't correct her.

"Thank you."

"I'd like to—" My mother broke off at a noise near the doors. A second or two later, it was flung open and my brother was framed in the doorway.

"I'm sorry I'm late. Traffic was bad." Fraser strolled across the room, and paused beside me to drop a kiss to the top of my head. "Happy birthday, sweetheart." He tossed a small, wrapped box onto the table, then continued moving until he was on the opposite side.

"Why *are* you late? The traffic isn't that bad coming into town." My sister turned to look at him as he took the seat beside her.

"No, but coming *out* of the city, it was." He stretched out a hand across the table. "You must be Maggie's mysterious boyfriend."

Rook shook my brother's hand. "Rook."

Fraser's brows creased. "You look familiar. Have we met before?"

"I don't believe so." Rook's voice was cool.

"You don't work in finance?"

"No."

"Huh, weird. I've *definitely* seen you somewhere. Do you work in the city?"

Rook shook his head. "I don't need to work. I'm ... " He glanced at me. "I'm independently wealthy."

"Oh?" Fraser's eyes brightened with interest. "What family are you from?"

"None that you'll recognize. My money didn't come from my parents."

I looked at him, then at my brother. I could see the burgeoning fascination, and knew the first chance he could get, Fraser would be off and searching for who Rook was. "Are you still dating Chantelle?" I spoke before my brother could ask any more questions.

He shook his head. "We broke up a while ago. She wanted marriage and babies and I ... Well, I didn't."

"Okay, enough chatter!" My mother stood, holding her glass of wine. "I'd like to give thanks for having another year of good health." She took a sip, waited until we all followed suit, then sat back down again. "Let us eat before the food gets cold."

Rook frowned. His mouth opened, and I dropped one hand beneath the table to grip his thigh and squeeze, hoping he understood I wanted him to stay quiet. He did, his head swinging sideways to look at me. I gave a small shake of my head.

When I was certain he wasn't going to speak, I loosened my hold on his leg. His hand covered mine and held it in place, and we held a silent battle while I tried to pull it free. Katy returned with a glass of water for Rook, saving me from saying something. Rook gave me an unrepentant smile and let me go.

Dinner was a quiet affair, with sporadic conversation revolving around my sister's marriage and kids, and my brother's job with a big-name bank in the city. I could feel the curiosity coming off Rook in waves as he tried to figure out why this supposed birthday dinner I'd brought him to wasn't mentioning or even celebrating my birthday.

When dessert was being served by the silent wait-staff, Fraser leaned across the table and tapped the box he'd dropped beside me. "Open it."

I glanced at our mother, who inclined her head, giving permission. I picked up the box and carefully peeled away the tape. Inside the colorful paper was a plain white box. I frowned at my brother. He smiled back at me.

"Keep going."

Wedging my thumb beneath the flap, I pulled it open and slid out the polystyrene package. "What is it?"

"Open it and find out."

I separated the two sections and caught my breath. "Oh!" The snow globe inside sparkled up at me. The scene encased in glass showed Persephone as she lifted a seed from a pomegranate to her lips.

"I love it. It's beautiful!"

"I saw it when I was in Athens last month and knew I had to pick it up for you." He leaned back on his chair, satisfaction clear in his smile.

"Thank you."

"I suppose since Fraser has broken with tradition, you might as well have your gift now." Mother's tone made it clear she wasn't impressed with Fraser *or* the snow globe. "Katy," she raised her voice. "Please retrieve Magdalena's birthday gift from my bedroom."

Katy dipped her head and slipped out of the room on silent feet.

"So they *do* get you something," Rook murmured in a low undertone beside me.

"It'll be a book. It's *always* a book."

When Katy reappeared with the book-shaped gift, I cast Rook a sidelong glance and took it.

"I know you don't like to read, but I thought this one might be interesting," my mother said as I unwrapped it. The book was thick, the words on the cover embossed. I traced over the letters, working them out in my head. The imagery on the cover gave me a clue—Greek statues of the various gods—but before I could say anything, Rook spoke.

"The Odyssey and The Iliad. Do you like Greek mythology then?"

"Yeah. I'm currently working on a sculpture of Zeus."

"You—" His mouth snapped closed, and I was sure he'd been about to say something that would have made it obvious we didn't know each other as well as we were pretending. Instead, he took the book from me and flicked through it.

"Thank you." I looked at my mother. I didn't mention the fact that there was very little chance of me reading it. I *couldn't* read it, not easily. But I'd match the cover to the audiobook and pick that up so that when she asked me about it, I'd be able to answer any questions she had.

Charlotte reached across the table with another parcel. "It's another book, I'm afraid. But I think you will really like this one."

When I ripped the paper off that one, it was to find a coffee-table book on Western Art. My smile was genuine. "I love it, thank you."

"And I bought you this." My father handed me an envelope. "Well, not bought but..."

I took it and opened it. There was a check inside for a thousand dollars. "You didn't—"

"Take it." His voice was firm, and I fell silent.

"Thank you."

I tucked the two books under one arm and held the snow globe Fraser had given me in my hand, and followed Rook out to the car. It was late, the moon high in the sky, and I gave brief thought to whether he would have preferred to leave in the morning. But

I hadn't paid him for that, so I didn't suggest it. The agreement had been Saturday only and, while I *could* have paid him more, I didn't want to overstep. I also didn't want to risk him being in the same room as my mother for longer than necessary.

"Call me when you're home safe." Unsurprisingly, it was my dad who spoke. My mother would probably celebrate my death. Maybe that was a little bitchy, but I was tired and keeping a smile fixed to my face all evening had been exhausting.

The lights flashed on Rook's car, and I heard the click as the doors unlocked. Before I could do it, he reached past me and opened the passenger door.

"Thank you." I climbed in, set down the gifts in the footwell and clipped my seatbelt in place. By the time I was done, Rook had joined me.

He didn't start the engine straight away, instead turning to look in my direction. "Your family is dysfunctional."

I glanced at him, then away. "I'm aware."

"Why do you put yourself through it? Is it worse when you arrive without a guy in tow?"

"It can be, which is why I wanted to avoid it this year."

"It would have been easier to avoid by not coming." He shoved the key in the ignition and fired up the engine.

"Until the phone calls started, demanding to know why I was treating her like she wasn't important."

"Has that happened?"

"Once, a couple of years ago. My twenty-first. I wanted to

go out with friends from school instead of going home. She was not happy."

"You're allowed to have fun, Dal."

I tipped my head back against the seat and sighed. "My mother had a hard time when she was pregnant with me."

"That's not your fault." He twisted in his seat to watch out of the back window while he reversed across the drive.

"I know, but—"

"Don't make excuses for her."

"I wasn't going to."

He snorted. "Sure."

I glared at him. He ignored me, turning back to face the front of the car, and drove down toward the front gates. He didn't speak again until we were on the highway.

"You have to look at the facts, darlin'. You were desperate enough to hire a stranger to pretend to be your date, just to avoid an uncomfortable situation with your mother. One my presence made even more awkward. You think she wasn't aware we barely know each other?"

"She has no idea."

He gave another derisive laugh. "Darlin', a wet fart has more chemistry than we showed back there. Any time I looked at you, you stiffened up. That's not the behavior of a woman in love."

"Then it'll make our breakup even easier to understand."

The boyfriend for hire thing hadn't been my idea anyway, it was Jasmine's. I was just relieved it was over and I could go back to my apartment and hide out for another six months—that's when I'd have to go back for Charlotte's birthday, which would be a completely different version of events. I wondered what Rook would say if I told him that, or took him to Charlotte's birthday—which would be a party with friends and family, and birthday cake and gifts. I gave a mental shake. He wouldn't ever know. After tonight, I wouldn't see him again.

L. ANN

8

Rook

The atmosphere inside the car was cool, the girl beside me clearly unhappy with my assessment of whether she had convinced her family we were dating. I didn't try to make her comfortable. She'd paid for my time, not my conversation. Plus, nothing I could say would make her feel any better. Her mother was awful, her sister not much better.

I had my suspicions about her brother's apparent affection toward her. Something about it had seemed off. Her father seemed to be the only decent one there, and my opinion of him wasn't high because of the way he allowed his wife and daughter to treat Dally.

Instead, I focused my attention on the road. It was reasonably late, eleven pm, and the road ahead was clear. Not that I'd expected it to be any different. This expanse of road was rarely busy, very few people wanted to drive to the town we lived in. It wasn't a small place, but with the city only an hour away, the town was mostly populated by those who commuted to work.

It was unusual for anyone to come *to* Glenville unless they lived there. That was the biggest reason I'd chosen to move there—that and the fact my brother lived there.

A flash of lights drew my attention to a car speeding up behind us, and I glanced back in the rear-view mirror as it drew closer. I crossed over into the other lane to allow it to pass, but it slowed down and kept pace behind us. There was nobody else on the road, no reason for the car *not* to overtake, and yet it stayed a few feet behind us, driving at the same speed. The hairs on the back of my neck rose, a surefire indicator that something wasn't right. I'd learned to trust my instincts a long time ago, and they were screaming at me now, telling me to pay attention.

I glanced at the woman seated beside me. " Is your seatbelt on?"

"Yes, of course. Why?"

"Because you might want to hold on."

She sat forward, peering out of the window—as though there was something to see. "Has there been an accident?"

"Not yet."

The car behind us moved closer, the beam from its headlights brightening the interior of my car, and making it impossible for me to see who was in theirs. "I need you to hold on tight."

"What is it? What's going on?" There was a shrill note to her voice, but I couldn't afford to take the time to ease her concern. Not when the car behind us was tapping on my tail lights in a bid to send me off the road.

Who the fuck was it?

I didn't have time to ask Magdalena if there was a chance anyone could be after her, because the car behind us hit again. This time it wasn't a gentle love tap on my tail lights, and it happened three times in quick succession. My car swerved towards the embankment. I had less than three seconds to make a decision—slam on the brakes and take a risk that whoever was coming after us wasn't carrying firearms, *or* aim for the embankment and hope for the best.

When my car was hit again, harder this time, the force of it took the decision out of my hands. Dally cried out beside me, and I threw out one hand across the center console to hold her in place against the seat as the car took a nosedive down the hill.

A few seconds of bouncing down the incline, and I had no choice but to release my grip on her shirt front and return my hands to the steering wheel. It was that or crash into one of the trees rapidly approaching. I gripped the wheel. It took every bit of strength and focus I had to keep it from spinning out of my hands and sending us headlong into the nearest tree.

Why didn't I slam on the brakes and stop the car? Because someone was intentionally driving us off the road, and there was a high chance they were going to come down after us, so I wanted to put as much distance as I could between us before we had to stop.

Dally moaned beside me, whispering words I couldn't quite catch. I risked a quick glance over at her.

"Are you religious at all?" I vented a quick laugh at her head shake. "Now might be a good time to find Jesus."

She shot me a terrified glare. "That's not funny!"

"It wasn't meant to be." I yanked the steering wheel hard to the left, narrowly missing a tree. I was more than aware that there was no way my luck was going to hold out forever, and it was only a matter of time before the car hit *something*. I just needed to make sure it was something we could walk away from. "Find something to hold on to," I warned her. "I need to stop the car before it stops itself and kills both of us."

I jerked the steering wheel left again and felt the back end of the car spin out sideways. It put the driver's side, namely me, in a direct line for the large tree coming straight at us.

"Hold on tight," I warned. " Brace for impact, darlin'."

There was a crunch as the tree hit the car. The door on my side bent inwards, and Dally screamed. My head snapped sideways, just as the window shattered, glass spraying inwards. I threw up one arm to protect my face. The force of the impact threw Magdalena forwards until her seat belt snapped into place and held her still. She reached across the seat and grabbed my arm.

"Oh my god. Are you okay? Did your head hit the window?"

I pulled my arm free from her grip, looking around. "I'm fine. Can you open your door?" There was no way mine was going to open. For one thing, it was trapped against the tree we'd crashed into and, for another, the impact had warped it out of shape. But we had to get out.

Whoever had hit us would be heading down the hill to grab

whichever one of us they were after—my guess was me. There was no reason the girl with me would have someone using such extreme measures to get to her. And *that* meant there was a risk of death being the end result of them catching up with us.

"Dally, concentrate!" I snapped when she didn't move. "I need you to get that door open. Can you do it?"

"I don't … I don't know." Her hands shook as she tried to unclip her seat belt, so I reached over and popped it free for her.

"Try the handle."

She did as I demanded, and the door swung open. I breathed a silent sigh of relief. "Good. Okay, now listen carefully. There's someone out there and we don't want them to see us. It's going to take them a couple of minutes to get down here. We need to move *fast*. Do you understand?"

"But who are they?"

"I don't know. But now isn't the time to talk about it. We need to get moving. Get out and stay low. Move to my side of the car, then wait for me." I caught her hand as she turned. "Dally, *stay low*. Do you understand?" I repeated my question.

After a second's hesitation, she nodded. I squeezed her fingers. "Good girl. Okay, go."

I wasn't happy with letting her go first, but I had no choice. I couldn't get out from my side, and I didn't think she'd appreciate me climbing over her. We had time on our side for the moment, a few minutes, but no more than that. It should be enough to get her out safely and under cover.

As soon as she exited the car, I checked to see if I could reach my gun. It was in a small compartment between the door and driver's seat. One glance was all it took to tell me there was no way I was getting it out, not with the way the door had warped inwards. I climbed over the center console and through the door. She glanced back at me, slowing down, and I pressed my hand against her back and pushed her forward.

"Keep moving. Don't worry about keeping quiet. Focus on getting to the other side of the car."

She nodded and stumbled forwards, reaching out one hand to lean against the hood as she rounded the car to keep her balance. Once we were safely on the driver's side, I pulled her down into a crouch.

"I need to know how many people are coming after us. *Stay* here. Do not move. Don't lift your head. Don't show yourself. Stay here until I come back. Got it?"

"But—"

"Don't argue with me."

I had a quick glimpse of pale features, and then she ducked her head down and crouched low. "What if you don't come back?" Fear drenched her voice.

I gave her a tight smile. "I promise I'll come back. Stay put and keep quiet." I moved past her and round to the trunk of my car, noting the damage to the driver's side as I went.

Whoever had caused us to crash was going to pay for the damage they'd caused. I fucking *liked* this car.

Staying low, I used the shadows cast by the trees to hide my movements and made my slow way back up the hill. We hadn't actually gone down as far as I'd initially thought, and I'd only moved a few yards before I heard a quiet voice.

"With any luck, he's dead and we can grab her and get out of here."

I frowned. So it *was* Magdalena they were after, but *why?* It was just my luck to get caught up in something twelve months into my retirement. Bad luck for the two guys making their clumsy way down toward my car, though. *They* should have made sure I was dead before even attempting to grab the girl I was with.

I pressed against the tree and watched as they walked past me, their eyes on the ground as they watched their footing instead of their surroundings.

Big mistake. I slipped out of the shadows and kept pace behind them. Unlike them, I focused my eyes exactly where I needed them to be—on the men ahead of me.

I stooped and picked up a small branch, then threw it. It hit a tree, bounced off, and fell into the nearby bushes with a rustle.

"What was that?" One man stopped, and I rolled my eyes. He was so green he fell for the oldest trick in the book.

"Keep moving. I can see the car up ahead." The other didn't even look in the noise's direction, which told me that at least one of them was semi-professional. "We're surrounded by trees and undergrowth. It's nighttime. Animals will be out. Stop being so fucking jumpy."

I chose that moment to curl my fingers into the collar of idiot number one's shirt and pull him around. My fist hit his face before he registered what was happening and he dropped like a stone. He landed with a thud, which caused asshole number two to turn.

His eyes widened, but I didn't catch him unawares like his friend, and he immediately swung a punch. I ducked and countered with a right hook of my own. He avoided it, stepping out of reach, and then came at me.

His head hit my chest, arms wrapped around my waist, and we fell to the ground, trading blows. I rolled, straddled his hips, and nailed him with a punch to the jaw. His hands slapped against my chest and shoved, sending me backwards.

I shot to my feet a second before his foot connected with my ribs and went for him again.

"Fucker." He grunted when I buried my fist into his stomach. I didn't wait for him to catch his breath, wrapped my fingers into his hair and slammed his face against my knee. He dropped to his knees, hands lifting to cover his nose.

I spun away, in time to get a fist to my jaw from idiot number one, who'd regained his feet.

I staggered backwards, then pressed forward, throwing punch after punch.

9

Magdalena

The sounds of fighting drew closer, and I leaned up to look through the window of the car. I could see Rook and two other men. One was on the ground, but the other was facing off with Rook. Punches flew, legs kicked out, and I couldn't tell which one was winning because whenever one gained ground, the other pushed back.

I was tempted to run. My mind *screamed* at me to run—escape while their attention wasn't on me. But I didn't want to leave Rook. What if he was hurt? What if he needed help? What if they *killed* him? What was I supposed to do?

He'd told me to stay here, not allow myself to be seen, but could I really just watch while they beat him up? And what if they killed him and then came for me?

I lost sight of them through the car window. Should I check and see where they were? Maybe I could call 911 and get help? My eyes fell on where my bag was in the car's footwell. I'd have to go back around to reach inside to get my cell out. I couldn't do that without being seen. What if I ran back to the road and flagged someone down to help? If I stayed low and crept up the hill, surely no one would see me?

I risked peeking over the roof of the car. None of the men were facing me. The one Rook had knocked to the ground was still on his knees with his back to me, while Rook and the other man circled each other a little way past the car.

If I ran now, maybe no one would see me.

My heart beat so hard, I could *feel* it in my throat. It was now or never. While they were distracted. I stood, looked once more at where the men were fighting, then ran. I scrambled over the undergrowth and reached the closest tree. Leaning against it, I looked back. No one had seen me. *Good*. That meant I could make it. I set off again, trying to keep to the shadows.

My breath was harsh in my ears as I scrambled up the embankment. I could see the lights lining the road above. I was almost there. I put on a burst of speed and then skidded to a stop as a figure detached itself from the shadows and stood between me and the road.

"Did you really think one of us wouldn't stay up here in case you ran?" He lifted one hand, and my eyes widened at the gun pointed at me.

"What do you want?"

"Well, that's the question, isn't it? I want you to come and get in the car and I want you to do it without argument." He waved the gun, and my eyes followed the direction he indicated to where a car was parked at the side of the road. "Ideally, before some well-meaning traveler drives past and decides you need help. You don't want an innocent's death on your hands, do you?"

I swallowed, mouth dry. "Who are you?"

"That isn't something you need to know. Get in the car, Ms. McCarthy."

"You know my name ... *how?*"

"I know everything about you. The only thing we didn't account for was you bringing the wrong person with you today. It's unfortunate, but we adapted the plan."

A shot rang out, and I flinched, a scream tearing from me. The stranger took advantage of my distraction and lunged, grabbed my arm, and dragged me toward the car. I struggled, twisted, tried to free myself from his grip, but his fingers bit deeper into my arm . He pushed the gun into my cheek and I froze.

"Don't make me kill you, Ms. McCarthy. I would prefer for you to stay alive for now—that's our plan. But I can change that. Get in the car quietly."

Terror turned my bones to jelly. I was shaking. Tears filled my eyes, spilled over and down my cheeks. I couldn't stop them, couldn't hide my fear. I'd never been this close to a gun, never thought I'd be in a situation like this ... and I didn't know what to do.

Where was Rook? Had they killed him? Was that what I'd heard?

A sob broke free, and I sagged, allowing the man to drag me the rest of the way to the car.

"Put your hands behind your back."

I didn't argue, and a second later, something bound my wrists together. "Turn around." He pulled me back to face him and taped my mouth closed. He leaned past me and took a bunched up piece of material from the car, shook it out and put it over my head. It smelled sour, the sharp tang making my eyes water. "We can't let you see where we're taking you." He pushed me, and I fell back onto something hard and cold. "Sit tight. We'll be there soon."

I woke up with a scream, sitting bolt upright, my heart pounding in my ears. Darkness enveloped me. I could feel material under my fingers, but couldn't *see* anything. My hands were free, my mouth uncovered.

Had it been a dream? A nightmare? Was I in my bed? Maybe I fell asleep in the car, and didn't remember going home?

My heartbeat slowed to a normal rate as my mind convinced myself that I was back in the bed in my apartment.

It had to have been a dream. Nothing else made sense ... right?

I sucked in a shuddering breath and reached out for the switch on my bedside light. Emptiness greeted my fingers where my nightstand should have been and my heartbeat cranked up again. Carefully, fingers shaking, I felt along the edge of the bed. Cold metal pressed against my fingertips.

My bed wasn't made of metal. It was wooden.

Oh god.

It hadn't been a dream.

"Magdalena ..."

10
Rook

Asshole number two pulled a gun and fired wildly in my direction. It went wide, but a scream rang out across the ensuing silence, and I spun in the direction it came from.

"Dally?" I shouted her name, ran forward a step and was hit in the side by the guy I'd left on the ground earlier. "Fuck." I swung an arm and caught him on the side of the head with my elbow. I took another three steps before asshole number one tackled me.

The three of us went down in a tangle of limbs, more punches missing their mark than making a connection, and we rolled around in the dirt. And then there was the recognizable click and the kiss of cold metal as one of them placed a gun against my temple.

"Stand up."

I scowled up at guy number one. "Shoot me."

"Don't think I won't."

"I *know* you won't." I turned my head until the gun pressed against my forehead. "Fucking pull the trigger. Do it. Shoot me."

His finger wavered, shifted to the trigger. I held his eyes with my own.

"Shoot me. It's the only thing that'll keep you alive. Fucking *shoot* me." I meant it. *Every word.* And he knew it. It was there in his eyes. The way they flickered away, searching out his partner, his uncertainty clear. I rose to my feet without looking away. "If you shoot me, my brothers will come for you. If you don't, I'll kill you."

"We can't kill him." The other guy spoke from behind me. "We need to take him with us. It'll keep the girl docile."

The man in front of me let the gun drop away. My lip curled up. "Coward."

That was the last thing I remember before pain exploded at the back of my head and the world went black.

I came to face down, my head throbbing and nausea threatening. Lurching to my feet, I stumbled sideways and crashed into a wall … a wall that made a distinct metallic thud when I hit it. My hand lifted and gingerly touched the back of my head. It was tender, but there was no lump or break in the skin. Flattening my palm against the wall, I walked forward, waiting for my eyes to adjust to the darkness.

My fingers touched something, and I stroked over it, feeling the shape of a light switch. I pressed it and light flared around me. My eyes watered at the brightness, and I closed them, waited for half a second and then slowly opened them again.

I was in what appeared to be a bathroom—it contained a toilet, sink and basic shower. A bar of soap, a washcloth, and a towel were on the floor. The floor, walls and ceiling were metal, and the shower cubicle was rudimentary, at best. Nothing more than a section of the floor, with a small lip to contain the water, and a hole—only an inch wide—for drainage.

The shower system itself was a simple dial for cold/hot and an on/off pull-switch. The shower head was embedded into the ceiling. A cheap white shower curtain gave a little separation from the rest of the room, but not much. If I stretched out my arms, I could almost reach either side of the small room in any direction. There was maybe a five-inch separation from the tips of my fingers to the wall.

I turned in a slow circle. There was a small medicine cabinet fixed to the wall above the sink, a mirror on the doors. I slid it open and found toothpaste and a toothbrush inside, still in its packaging. Closing the door, I studied my reflection. Setting aside the fact we'd been run off the road, attacked by strangers and I'd woken up in an unknown location, there was something weird about this situation.

Like they had prepared the room in advance for someone.

Like the entire thing had been *planned*. And that took me back to the day Dally approached me in the diner... and the man who had been watching the door. The one who I was sure was the one she was meant to meet.

I turned and took the few steps necessary to reach the door.

Time to see what was beyond door number one. It swung open at a gentle push, but gave out an unholy screech as it did so. A scream pierced the darkness beyond. One that sounded familiar.

"Magdalena." I shoved the door open wider, so the light from the bathroom spilled through, and let my eyes scan the room.

There. At the opposite end of the room, a figure huddled in a small ball. I strode across to her.

"It's me." I caught her hand as she threw it outwards to ward me away with another high-pitched shriek. "Dally, it's me. It's Rook. Stop screaming."

"What did you do? Why am I here? Who *are* you?" She struggled against my grip, pulling her hand free, and shoved at me. "Where are we?" Each question was shriller than the last.

"Calm down. Panicking won't get us out of here." I caught her arms and shook her. "Dally, I need you to calm down and *think*. Did you recognize any of the men?"

"No!" She hit me again, her fingers curling into fists as she slammed them against my chest.

"Stop it! Can you think of anyone who would want to hurt you?"

"Of course not! " She wrenched out of my grip and tumbled backwards onto the mattress. "What kind of person are you to even think of that?"

"The kind that wakes up in a place like this and knows we're in trouble. *Think*, Dal."

"How do you know they wanted *me* and not you?"

"If they were after me, it would have been to kill me, not capture."

Her jaw dropped, lips parting, my words cutting through her panic. "What does *that* mean?" she whispered.

"It doesn't matter. Not right now."

I saw the fear of the unknown slowly get replaced by the fear of who *I* might be in her eyes, and she scrambled further across the bed, putting distance between us. I stepped back, giving her space, and waited for her to gain control of herself. When her spine stiffened and she threw her shoulders back, I gave a nod.

"Good girl. Okay, first thing we need to do is find the light switch. There was one for the bathroom. There has to be another in here. Let's see what we're working with."

"Why are you so calm?" Her voice held a slight tremor to it.

"There's no point in panicking until we know if we should. Come on, focus. Let's get some light in here."

She took a deep breath, then nodded and stood so she could walk across the room and lay her palm against the wall. "It feels cold. It's not a brick wall. What is it?"

"From what I could see in the bathroom, I think we're in some kind of converted container. It's been prepared in advance. Whoever these people are, it wasn't a spur-of-the-moment thing. They targeted us."

"Targeted," she repeated quietly. "Wait. I remember … You were fighting, and I thought I could sneak back up to the road and get help. There was another man there, waiting for me. He said …" She stopped, swallowed, and began again. "He said that he knew who I was … that I didn't have the right person with me." Her eyes widened. "That means he's been watching me for a while. Oh my god, they were *watching* me!"

I caught her shoulders and spun her back to face me. "Look at me." I waited until her head tipped back. "Don't let the panic drag you under. Take a breath." Her chest moved as she did as I said. "That's it. And again." Another deep breath. "Good girl. Can you remember what else he said?"

"He said …" She bit into her bottom lip. "He said that they knew everything about me, and that it was … was unfortunate that you were with me. But that they'd adapt. What does that mean? Adapt how?" Tears filled her eyes.

I ignored her questions. "How do you usually get to and from your parents?"

"I travel by train."

"They must have had to improvise when they realized you were with me. That's good. We can use that. They didn't want to kill you, that much is obvious. They're not killers, otherwise I wouldn't be here."

"How do you *know* that?"

"There's a single toothbrush and towel in the bathroom. They expected to grab you alone and keep you here. If they wanted to kill you, they wouldn't have left supplies for you to use."

"But—"

"Enough talking. Find the light switch and let's see what we're working with." I was being abrupt, but I didn't want her to spend too much time thinking about the situation we were in.

Not until I had more information, and could make a plan. "You take this side of the room, I'll take the other. Feel along the wall for a light. There's enough light from the bathroom to see more on the other half of the room, so start by the bathroom door."

L. ANN

11

Magdalena

I couldn't stop shaking, but Rook's calm voice settled my nerves enough that I could do as he said and slowly worked my way along the wall, searching out a light switch. The light from the bathroom gave enough visibility to show there was nothing near the door which led inside, so I inched along the wall, further into the darkness. My fingers hit something.

"Rook?" My voice trembled, and I sucked in another breath before speaking again. "I think I found something." I felt around the shape. "Oh my god, it's a *door!*" I searched for the handle and sagged with relief when my fingers curled around it. That relief was short-lived when it didn't move. "It won't open."

"Of course it won't. It'll be locked from the outside." His voice, close behind me, made me jump. "But I bet the light switch is close by." He brushed against me as he walked past, and a second later, light filled the room.

"Oh!" The startled exclamation left my lips before I could

stop it. Rook stood inches from me, a far cry from the neat and tidy man who'd driven me to my parents. His shirt was filthy, hair a disheveled mess, and at least twenty-four hours' worth of stubble coated his jaw, along with a bruise on his cheek.

"Are you hurt?" My question was joined by my fingers reaching out to touch his cheek. He jerked away with a hiss.

"No. It's nothing." But his reaction told me his words were a lie. "Look, there are cabinets over there and a stack of paper plates. I bet they've stocked up with food you can eat cold."

At the mention of food, my stomach made an ungodly noise. He quirked an eyebrow and laughed. "Hungry?"

"I *wasn't* ... not until you mentioned it. I shouldn't be, though. The last thing I should be thinking about is food right now."

"Why?" He crossed the room and crouched to open one of the cabinet doors. "Just because we're stuck here doesn't mean your body isn't going to want sustenance. In fact, *not* eating would be stupid. We need to keep our strength up."

"But we don't know how long we're going to be here." I finished the sentence softly, all the fears of earlier returning. "I don't understand. Why? Why have they done this?"

Rook didn't reply straight away, busy rummaging through the stockpile of tins.

"Rook, don't you want to know what's going on?"

He stilled, then rose back to his feet and turned to face me. "We'll find out soon enough. My guess is it's a ransom situation. They're going to demand money for your safe return. Your family is rich, not high profile rich, but they're obviously not short of money. If you're not the one with enemies, then one of your immediate family is, and you're their method of revenge."

I gaped at him. "You think they're going to ask for *money* to let us go?"

"Let *you* go." Walking past me, he wedged his fingers beneath the mattress on the small bed and lifted it. "Hmm."

"Hmm? What does *that* mean?" I hurried over to stand beside him and followed his gaze. "What?"

"The bed frame is metal, and it's been welded to the floor so it can't be moved. They built the entire thing in such a way we can't break any of it off to use as a weapon."

"A weapon?" My stomach twisted. "You think we'll need to protect ourselves?" God, how stupid did I sound? Of course we needed protection. Strangers had *kidnapped* us!

"Protection, no. To aid in our escape, yes." He dropped to his knees and ducked his head to look beneath the bed. "Yeah, this thing isn't going to be useful." He sprang upright, and I jumped backwards. "Plan B."

"Plan B?" I trailed after him as he strode to the door near the light switch. "Wait. What was *plan A?*"

He glanced at me over his shoulder. "Plan A was using part of the bed to knock one of the men out when they came in."

"What's Plan B?" I whispered.

Rook raised one hand, made a fist, and banged on the door. "Fucking show yourself!" he shouted.

He stood, waited for the echo to die down, then banged again … and again … and again. I clamped my hands over my ears as the din echoed around the interior of the room. For at least five minutes he stood there, hammering on the door and shouting curses, and then silence reigned when his hands dropped.

"This would be louder if you joined in," he said.

"Me?"

"Do you see anyone else here? Hit the walls, shout. Do whatever you can to attract attention."

"You think someone might hear and rescue us?"

He snorted a laugh. "No. I think one of *them* will hear us and come tell us to shut the fuck up."

"Then what's the point?"

His smile sent a shiver down my spine. "One thing at a time, darlin'." He raised his hands again. "Ready?"

I stepped forward, closer to the wall, and nodded. "Ready."

We'd been at it for *hours*.

Banging and kicking the door and walls.

Shouting until I was hoarse.

My throat hurt, my ears ached, my head pounded, but whenever I dropped my hands or lowered my voice, Rook turned to look at me and told me to keep going. The third time I stopped, I refused to start again. Instead, I turned and slid to the floor with my back against the wall, and glared at him.

"No one is coming!" I snapped in response to his scowl.

"That right?" He resumed banging and shouting and … I couldn't stand it any longer.

I jumped to my feet and shoved him. He didn't move, not even a small step sideways. He just glanced over at me, frowning.

"Stop it! *Stop it*! I can't stand it anymore. The noise, the yelling. Please … I need you to stop!" I screamed the words at him. "No one is listening! They're probably far away from here, trying to decide when to kill us. All you're going to do is make it happen faster because you're trying to draw attention." I shoved at him again.

He turned slowly until he was facing me. "You're being hysterical." His voice was flat.

"I'm being … I'm … I …" I laughed, and sure enough, even I could hear the hysteria in it. "I'm *not* hysterical!" I denied it anyway.

"Sure." He lifted a hand, fingers curled into a fist.

"Don't you dare."

He rolled his eyes at me … *rolled his eyes* … and pounded on the door and … *I … lost … it!*

I threw myself at him, wrapped my hand around his arm, and pushed it down.

"*Stop! Stop! Stop!*" I clutched at his shirt, twisted it in my fingers. "*Please!* I can't do this anymore."

His sigh was distinctly irritable. "*You can't do this anymore? We've been locked in here for less than a day and you can't do this anymore? I don't know whether you've noticed, darlin', but you haven't got any choice in the matter. We're stuck in here until one of them comes back and either kills us, lets us go or explains why we're here. Until then, we have to do everything we can to try and find a way out."

"What if they decide to kill us because *you* won't stop making all this noise?"

He laughed. "That's not the way it works, Dal. They want *something*, otherwise they wouldn't have put in this much effort. There's enough food and water here for us to survive for at least a week, if we ration it properly. Their intention was only to grab one person ... *you*."

I'd been trying to avoid thinking about that. My stomach churned, nausea a solid lump in my throat. "But why?"

His expression softened slightly, which wasn't much—it simply turned the iciness in his eyes to minus five degrees instead of minus ten. "Like I said, my guess is a ransom demand. Your brother works in finance. So did your father. If they've caused someone to lose money or their business. If they suggested a poor investment, then it could easily be an act of desperation. Although, the amount of care they've taken suggests otherwise."

"What do you mean?"

"I *mean* this looks like it was a controlled hit. That the people behind the grab have taken their time to research you *and* your family. This could have been in the planning stages for years."

"But—" Someone banging on the door from the other side interrupted me. My eyes widened and darted to Rook. He said nothing, turning to face the door.

"Move back against the far wall. I'm coming in. I have a gun and *will* use it. You have thirty seconds."

"Rook?" I whispered his name.

His hand reached back and touched my arm. "Just do as they say. We need to find out who they are and what they want."

"Twenty seconds," the voice called out.

I scrambled backwards, almost tripping in my haste to get to the far side of the room. Rook was slower, taking his time and never turning his back on the door.

"Good. Now face the wall."

"How do they—?"

"There must be hidden cameras in here." Rook cut in before I could finish my question. "They're watching, and probably listening, to *everything*."

L. ANN

12

Rook

Magdalena breathed beside me—quick and frantic. She was on the verge of panic again. I *knew* that, but I couldn't afford for her to do something stupid. I could have been gentler on her, tried to calm her, but right now we didn't have time for that. Hopefully, she would follow my lead, stay calm, and not get us both killed.

"Keep facing the wall." The voice was inside the room now. "I have a gun trained on the pair of you. If you try anything, I will kill one of you. Don't fuck with me."

"You're making a mistake," I said.

"Link your fingers together on the backs of your heads." He ignored my comment. "*Slowly.*"

"Rook?" Dally's voice was a scared little whisper.

"Just do as he says, darlin'."

I lifted my arms, placed my palms against the back of my head, and linked my fingers together. From the corner of my eye, I could see her doing the same.

"Good. Now don't move. We searched you when we brought you in, so I know you don't have any weapons on you."

"If you took my wallet, then you also know my name. If you have any sense, you'll Google that, and then reconsider whatever plan you have here."

"Shut the fuck up." He pressed the gun to the side of my head. "I could blow your brains out now."

"You could," I agreed, my voice pleasant. "And then you'll have my brothers to deal with. Trust me when I tell you *I'm* the nicest of us all. Killing me will make your life a lot harder."

"We'll be long gone before they find your body."

"You'd think that. But the chances are, my brothers are already tracking me. As soon as I didn't check in after dropping her back home, they'll know something was wrong and will track my movements. You have no more than two days before they'll find you." I was bluffing. They wouldn't think there was anything wrong unless a week passed without me checking in.

"Bullshit."

"Keep telling yourself that." I turned my head slightly, and he pressed the gun more firmly against my temple. "What's the plan? I assume you're looking for money in return for our safety?"

"*Her* safety. You shouldn't have been there."

"I know." I let one corner of my lip curl upwards. "I saw your guy in the diner. What was the play? He was supposed to pick her up, and then what? Was he actually going to take her to the dinner or was the grab supposed to go down before then?" That was a guess, but the more I thought about it, the more sense it made.

"Last warning to shut the fuck up before I blow your head off. Who are your brothers?"

"Not your best idea, gotta be honest." I ignored his threat and his question. He wasn't going to kill me. It was in his voice, the concern over what I'd said about my brothers. He was already questioning whether he was on borrowed time, worrying over who I was and why I wasn't displaying any of the normal reactions that someone who'd been grabbed and held at gunpoint should do. "Google my name, asshole. Rook Chambers. Then come back and we'll talk."

"You have no control over this situation. Shut *the fuck* up."

"What's taking so long?" A second voice called out. "Just bring the girl out, for fuck's sake."

"Don't fucking move," he warned me again, wrapped his free hand around Dally's arm and pulled her backward. The gun's aim transferred from me to her. "Stay facing the wall until you hear the door close."

"Rook!" Dally's fearful cry almost had me turning, but I forced myself to stillness. I couldn't afford to make a move yet, not until I knew more. I'd have to gamble on the fact they would not kill her until they'd sent a ransom demand. I couldn't be sure they wouldn't do anything else to her, but she'd be alive when she came back. Killing her before they got what they wanted would be foolish and too much effort had been put into turning this place into somewhere she could survive for a while.

The thought of her being forced into a situation I couldn't protect her from sent an icy chill through me. I forced it away. She was nothing to me other than a foolish decision made when I was bored. One that might work to her benefit. She didn't know it, but I was her best chance of getting out of this alive. She might be a little damaged in the process, but she wouldn't be dead.

It was better than nothing.

When the door clicked shut behind me, I wasted no time and spun round. First, I stripped the bed, tossing the thin mattress to the floor and shaking out the covers. I ran my fingers over the frame, searching out anything that could be a hearing device. There was nothing attached to it, so I climbed up onto the bed and checked the ceiling. There was a small camera in the corner and I pried it out, then ripped it out of the wall. There was another in the small area where the cabinets were. I destroyed that one. The third was in the bathroom—dirty fuckers. It was pointing at the shower, so I knew the reason *that* was there.

Once I was certain there was no more to be found, I replaced the mattress on the bed, tossing the covers on top in a haphazard pile, and waited for them to return Magdalena.

13.

Magdalena

"Where are we going?" My question was shrill and ignored by the man who pulled me across the floor. I glanced around. *Nowhere anyone could hear us.* Rook had guessed right about us being inside a converted container, and it appeared to be in an old, abandoned warehouse. It was big enough that I couldn't see the walls, only the immediate area ahead, which had three floor lamps shining light into a large circle.

He pushed me down onto a plastic chair, pulled my hands roughly behind my back, and wrapped something around them.

"Who are you?" I tried again, twisting around to see the face of my captor.

"Don't be stupid, girl." The voice of the man who had caught me by the roadside came from out of the shadows.

"Please. I don't know why you've taken me. I haven't done anything. Why am I here?"

"It's nothing personal."

"Not personal? You've *kidnapped* me! Of course it's personal."

"Not for anything *you've* done. Now do I have to gag you or will you shut up and let me explain to you what happens next?" Legs appeared in my line of sight.

I fell silent, my heart pounding so loudly in my ears, I could barely hear him talking.

"Are you paying attention?" His snapped words brought my eyes up to meet his.

Why wasn't he concerned about me seeing his face? Didn't they always say if your captor lets you see them, it means they're planning to kill you?

"Are you going to kill me?" I blurted the question, unable to stand not knowing.

"Not if the ransom is paid."

I swallowed. "So you *do* want money?"

He nodded. "That's right." He moved closer and crouched down until we were at eye level.

"But I can see your face. I can tell people what you look like. That means you're going to kill me, doesn't it?" I whispered.

"We'll be out of the country before you can describe me to anyone. I don't plan on killing you, not if you do as you're told. I can't make the same promise for your friend. That depends on—" He glanced behind me. "Are we ready?"

I tried to twist around to see who he was talking to, but I was too firmly attached to the chair to do more than try to crane my head around. The man in front of me sprang back to his feet.

"Good. Okay, here's what I need you to do." He placed a sheet of paper on my lap. "When I say, I want you to look straight ahead and read out what's on that sheet."

I glanced down, the words swimming in front of my eyes. A jumbled mess that I couldn't decipher. "I ... can't."

"This isn't the time to be heroic. Read the message, then I'll take you back to your room."

"I *can't*." I wasn't trying to be awkward. I *couldn't* read it. My dyslexia was worse if I was stressed or panicking—and I was *both* right now.

"Try!" He barked.

I blinked, my throat aching around the lump building there and my eyes burning with the need to cry. They were going to kill me because I couldn't read it. I was going to *die* because I was stupid.

"I ... I ..." I stammered, wanting to explain but unable to get the words out. I'd spent years avoiding the reason I struggled with words and writing. My mother refused to believe I had an actual problem. She thought I was just lazy, or had a low IQ, so I learned to avoid the subject of my struggles as much as possible. But now, *here*, my inability to read the words on the sheet was going to get me killed.

Think about how you deal with this when you're not stressed! Concentrate on that.

I gnawed on my lip, staring down at the paper, willing the words to take on a more understandable shape. The more I focused, the more jumbled it looked. I closed my eyes, and took in a deep breath, then tried again. "I ... I'll try."

He moved back two steps, and then the lights brightened as he switched on another lamp. In front of it was a video camera, pointed directly at me. When he came out from behind the light, he had a mask over his face. My heart beat wildly as he came toward me, a gun in his hand.

This was it. He'd lied. He was going to kill me on camera!

Instead, he moved past me. I jumped when a hand landed on my shoulder. "Look at the camera, girl." His voice changed, became cooler. "Turn it on." Movement near the light told me someone else was there, then a little green light flashed on the camera.

"We're recording." Another voice said.

The hand on my shoulder squeezed. "We have your daughter. For her safe return, we want five million dollars. This is your proof of life video, which I'm sure you will want to show to authorities." The fingers flexed again. "Tell them today's date."

I did.

"Now tell them what we want."

I glanced down at the sheet, and relief coursed through me when some of the words came into focus.. "They ... They w-will kill me if you try to f-find me." I stammered over the words, tears spilling down my cheeks. "I ... I can't read it."

"I was told you were stupid." He cuffed the back of my head, voice irritated. "Believe me when I say that if you try to find her, she will be dead before you reach her. Five million dollars. We will be in touch with the location for the drop in twenty-four hours."

The green light on the camera turned to red.

"Untie her." The man who appeared to be the leader instructed, and the one who'd been standing in the shadows behind the camera, stepped forward.

"What's the rush? Maybe we could have a little fun first." His smile was a leer, and my blood ran cold.

"They paid us to keep her alive and untouched." The other man's voice was crisp. "If they don't pay, *then* you can have some fun ... before we kill her."

Paid? Someone had paid for them to take me?

"What about the other one? He wasn't part of the job."

"I'm waiting to hear back. If they want him dead, they'll have to pay more. For now, keeping him alive might ensure her compliance. You understand, girl? If you refuse to do what we say, we'll start breaking his bones while you watch."

The man hauled me to my feet by whatever was binding my wrists, and pushed me toward the other man.

"Take her back. No detours on the way. If I find out you've touched her, I'll kill *you* for free."

The second man caught my arm and pulled me forwards, muttering in a language I didn't understand under his breath. We took the same path back, and the container loomed into view.

"Such a shame to throw you back in there. Maybe we should wait out here for a little while longer. If you're quiet, Rushka will never know."

"I'll scream." I fought to keep my voice stable. "He'll hear me."

"Not if I gag you first. I like a little fight in my women. It makes the conquest much sweeter." His hand covered my breast and squeezed. "And you're not in any position to stop me."

I sucked in a breath, my intention to scream as loud as I could, and pain exploded across my lip as he backhanded me. The taste of blood filled my mouth, and I flinched when his thumb pressed against my lips. "A little blood is even better." He kissed me, sinking his teeth into the split in my lip, and laughed when I cried out.

"What are you doing over there? Get back here. We have things to do!" The shout echoed around the warehouse.

"Until we next meet, sweetheart." He unlocked the door and pushed me through.

I tripped, stumbled and crashed to my knees.

14

Rook

The metallic clang of the door unlocking was my first clue someone was about to come inside. I unfolded myself from where I was lounging on the bed and was halfway across the room when Magdalena was shoved through. The door closed on her back without anyone else entering, and she dropped to her knees, head bowed, and her hair covering her face.

I waited for her to stand, but when minutes passed and she didn't move, I crouched in front of her. "You okay?" I reached out and pressed a finger to her chin so I could tip her head up.

Brown eyes—huge, round, red-rimmed and wet with tears—pale pinched features and a splash of blood on her mouth. I cataloged it all in one glance. I touched her bottom lip with my thumb, and she flinched back, eyes focusing on my face.

"Who did that?"

"One of the men."

It was the obvious answer. I wondered if she'd heard any names, whether she'd been in a calm enough state to take them in.

"Why?"

"Because he wanted to ..." She paused and swallowed, then licked her lip, frowning when her tongue touched the blood coating it.

I nodded, not needing to hear the rest. "Let's get it cleaned up." I held out a hand. She didn't move. "Dal?"

"I can't move my hands. There's something around them."

I scowled, stood, and strode around to find a cable tie wrapped around her wrists. "This is going to sting." I warned, gripped her wrists and yanked them apart. The cable tie dug into her skin, then snapped, leaving red indents on her wrists. She immediately rubbed at them.

"Come on." I led her over to the bed and then walked back to the other side of the container to grab a bottle of water. Returning to where she sat, I tore the corner from the blanket, soaked it in the water and lifted it to press against her lip. "Tell me what happened out there."

I wrapped my fingers around her wrist and brought her hand up to hold the wet cloth to her lip. She looked at me, dabbing at her lip, but didn't reply.

"I found four cameras. There might be more. If there are, I haven't located them yet. This isn't a cheap operation. What did they say to you?"

"They want five million dollars or they'll kill me." Her voice was little more than a whisper.

"Five million. That's what they said?"

She nodded. "But they're not the ones who organized it."

My interest sharpened. "How do you know?"

"One of them wanted to kill you. The ... the other one said he had to wait for orders. And if *they* wanted you dead, they'd have to pay extra."

I grunted. "That confirms it's a paid job, which makes sense."

"*How* does it make sense?"

"They're mercenaries for hire. That means they've been paid to take you, hold you here, and collect the ransom. Any extra kills will cost more as it increases the risk of them getting caught. But that raises a bigger question. *Who* wants your parents' money enough to hire them to take you? And why you and not one of your siblings?"

She stared at me.

"Think," I prompted.

"How do you know what they are?"

"It's not important."

"Do you know them? Are you involved? Is that why you agreed to come with me? *Wait*, are *you* part of this?" She scrambled back across the cot, putting distance between us.

I let her. There wasn't anywhere she could go and if she felt safer a few feet away from me, I could give her that.

"I'm not involved, and no, it isn't why I agreed to come with you."

"Did you set up the ad? Oh my god," she whispered. "That's it, isn't it?"

She was quick, but on the wrong track. "I didn't set the ad up, Dal." I sat on the edge of the mattress. "But you're right in that it *was* a setup. I think the guy you were supposed to meet was the one who was meant to grab you ... you were never supposed to make the dinner."

The remaining color bled from her face.

"But you were the one I was meeting." Her protest was weak.

I shook my head. "No. The guy at table twenty-one was your fake date. *I* was at table twelve."

"I don't believe you. Why would you agree to do it, if it wasn't your ad?"

I shrugged. "I was bored and looking for entertainment. Your plan sounded crazy, and I wanted to see how it played out."

Her hand dropped from her lip. "You weren't ... I wasn't ... you ..."

"I wasn't the person you were supposed to meet. I had no idea what you were talking about. I was going to give you your money back after I dropped you home."

"And now you're here ..."

I risked reaching out to take her hand. "Darlin', trust me. *That* is going to turn out to be the best mistake you ever made."

"You told them to search for your name. What will they find?"

I rubbed my jaw. I didn't want to tell her the full truth. I wasn't sure how she'd take it, especially after the shocks she'd already had. Not to mention we were trapped together, and she had nowhere to run.

"I was wrongly jailed a few years ago. The retrial was splashed across the papers last year. The jury dismissed all charges and had me released and compensated for the time I was incarcerated."

"Wrongly jailed? For what?"

"Murder."

"You murdered someone."

"You remember that part where I said I was wrongly jailed and then released?" I injected a hint of humor into my tone.

"How long were you in prison?"

"Five years."

"Five years." Her whisper was horrified. "They locked you away for *five years* for something you didn't do."

I hesitated. That was something I didn't want to get into ... not right now ... "It's not important. What *is* important is that you mistakenly came to me, and I can keep you alive *and* get us both out of here."

That got her attention. *"How?"*

"You're going to have to trust me, okay?" I took the now-dry scrap of material from her and tilted her head up to look at her lip. "The bleeding has stopped. It's no worse than if you'd bitten your lip. Be careful not to break it open again."

I stood and walked over to where the tinned food was stored.

"Rook?"

"Yeah?" I looked back over my shoulder at her.

"What if my parents don't pay the ransom?" Her voice was small, worried.

"Why would you think they won't?" Was her relationship with her parents that fucked up that they wouldn't *try* to raise the money to get her back?

"It doesn't matter. We'll be gone before that happens." *And if we weren't, it still wouldn't matter because we'd both be dead.* I didn't voice that, though. She didn't need to hear it. "You should have something to eat. Keep your strength up. And then get some sleep."

"*Sleep?* I can't sleep. What if they come back in?"

I pulled out a can and examined the label. "I'll keep you safe, darlin'. How do you feel about cold spaghetti?"

15

Magdalena

I was sure I wouldn't be able to eat a thing right up to the moment Rook placed a plastic bowl filled with the cold spaghetti bolognese in front of me. My stomach grumbled, telling me I was hungry.

"There's no point in starving." He slid the plate closer to me. "Eat up and drink some water. Then get some sleep."

"Sleep? How am I supposed to sleep?"

He smiled. "You go over there, lay yourself down, and close your eyes. Your mind might be scared, but your body needs sleep. Trust me."

"What about you?" I picked up the fork and twirled the spaghetti around its prongs.

"I don't need to sleep just yet. I'll keep watch in case one of them comes back."

I frowned, chewed the mouthful of food, trying to ignore that it was cold and not at all good-tasting, swallowed and then pointed my fork at him. "Surely the argument you're using on me works for you as well. Shouldn't *you* rest?"

"I will."

"When?"

He shrugged.

"Why *are* you so calm?" I couldn't deny that his lack of panic and fear settled my nerves, made me almost confident that we *would* get through this alive. But it also kinda scared me. What had he done in his life for this to seem so ... so *normal*?

"We'll achieve nothing with wholesale panic. Staying calm and thinking everything through is our best means of survival. That's all."

There wasn't a lot I could say to that.

"Why were you arrested for murder if you were innocent?"

His smile was a quick flash of teeth. "I never said I was innocent, darlin'."

"But—"

"I said I was imprisoned for murder, and set free later. I never claimed I didn't do it, the courts did."

My fork clattered to my plate. "You mean ... you *did* murder someone?"

His head tilted, eyes on me. "I *killed* someone. I *didn't* murder them."

Bile rose in my throat, and I lurched to my feet.

"Where are you going to run, Dal?" His voice was soft, calm. "If I wanted to kill you, I'd have done it already. Sit down and finish your food."

I stared at him. He leaned back against the wall, the picture of relaxation, and held my gaze.

"If there was enough evidence to send you to prison for five years, why did they do a retrial?"

"Because more evidence came to light to prove it was self defense and not murder. It was kill or be killed. I was faster and luckier. He wasn't."

I was sure there was way more to the story than what he was telling me. There *had* to be. People didn't just *kill* other people and act like it wasn't important.

"Come on, sit down and eat. I'm not a serial killer. I don't randomly walk around and kill people because I'm in some kind of mood." A smile curved one side of his mouth up, as though he was laughing at some private joke.

"Why *did* you kill someone, then?"

"I told you. It was self defense. I won't lie to you. I *am* trained to kill. And when someone comes at me with a knife, I will do what I need to do to take them down. If I hadn't killed him, he wouldn't have stopped until I was dead. I swear, it really was self-defense. They incarcerated me for second-degree murder. A couple of years into my sentence, my lawyer found evidence that could prove my innocence. He appealed to have the case reopened. The judge agreed, and the jury found me not guilty. My sentence was repealed, and they compensated me for my time inside."

"Compensated?" I eased back down on the floor opposite. The calm way he spoke eased the rapid beating of my heart and the fear of being in just as much danger from the man locked away with me as I was from those who had kidnapped me receded.

A smile flashed across his face. "They paid me a *lot* of money as compensation. The whole thing was across the news for around six months."

I ate a mouthful of spaghetti, then stopped as a thought occurred to me. "But you told them to search for you. Finding out you were released after being found not guilty will not scare them."

He gave a soft laugh. "Don't think that because a jury found me not guilty *one* time it doesn't mean I haven't got blood on my hands." He leaned forward. "People like them …" He waved a hand toward the door. "In the business I was in before I went to jail … they'll recognize my name and those of my brothers."

"What's stopping them from coming in and killing us both at that point?"

"Killing me would put them on the most wanted list of my brothers and, trust me, Dal, *no one* goes onto that willingly. *I* have a reputation, but my older brother makes me look like the Easter Bunny."

I stared at him. "Who *are* you?"

He shook his head. "Someone you should never have met or know about. You don't move in the circles of people who need to be aware of my name. Let's leave it at that."

His tone told me the discussion was over, but I had too many questions. I *couldn't* let it go.

"It doesn't make sense. You've done nothing to make me believe you're dangerous or scary." *Aside from taking on two men alone down the side of an embankment after crashing the car.* "You said yourself that they found you guilty of a crime you didn't commit. You don't *look* how I'd imagine some big, bad bogeyman would appear."

He chuckled at that. "And how would you know what the bogeyman looks like? Do you think they walk around with a sign warning people of how dangerous they are?"

"I've seen the news, television shows. The bad guys *always* look bad."

"Do they now?" His voice was an amused drawl. He rose to his feet and used one hand to unbutton the cuff of his sleeve. He folded it back, revealing bold tattoos covering his arm. "Come here."

I frowned, but scrambled to my feet and moved to stand beside him. "This ..." He pointed to the shape on his inner wrist.

At first glance, it looked like a clock face, but when I looked closer, there were no hands or times on it. Instead, it was a circle filled with lines. Some intersected ... almost like a ... a counter. "What is that?"

"Count the lines." He held his arm steady, and I reached out to touch it with one finger, stroking over each line as I counted.

"Fifty-five ... no wait ... fifty-six." I looked up at him. "What does it mean? And why are three of them in red?"

He didn't answer right away.

"Rook? Why are there three in red?"

"Because out of all the deaths I've dealt, those three didn't deserve it."

My lips parted. *Had he just admitted to killing fifty-six people? That's what he was saying, right? Fifty-six people!* And only *three* didn't deserve it? My tongue swept over my lips, dry with sudden fear.

"You...that can't be right. Are you telling me you kill people?"

"Killed, past tense."

"*Why?*"

"That's a complicated question to answer. I could say for money. People ... *rich people* ... often want their competitors removed in any way necessary and will pay well for it. Some people have other reasons to want someone dead. There's a thriving market for someone with the skills to achieve it and make it look natural."

I took a step backward. "You kill people for money? You're a... a *hitman?*"

"*Was.* I retired shortly before they arrested me for murder."

"You kill people. I'm trapped in here with someone who kills people." I shied away from the word *murderer*. That's what a hitman was... *a murderer.* Someone who killed people for money. And *I'd* joked about Jasmine hiring a hitman to kill my mother.

"Oh my god." I wanted to throw up. My stomach churned, my skin was clammy, and I wanted to run, escape from the man staring at me, his face expressionless.

"Are you okay?" His question drew a shrill laugh from me.

Was I okay? I'd never be okay again!

"You're very pale, darlin'. Are you going to pass out? Come on, sit down." A hand closed over my arm and I stared down at it. *A hitman was holding my arm, showing concern.* I laughed again.

"You *kill* people." It was the only thing I could say, repeating it over and over. "*You. Kill. People. For money!*"

His sigh was irritable. "I shouldn't have told you, but we're stuck in here together and I need you to trust me."

"*Trust* you." Another laugh broke free, and I pulled out of his grip. "I'm supposed to trust a hitman." Another thought occurred to me. "Or are you just crazy? Are you having a psychotic break because of the situation we're in? Do you even *know* what is real?"

He rolled his eyes. "Don't be dramatic, Dal."

"*Dramatic*. Me? *I* shouldn't be *dramatic*? Have you even *noticed* what's going on right now? I've been kidnapped, forced to record a video demanding ransom money, and *now* I'm locked in a room with a *hitman*! *A. Hit. Man!* Do *not* tell me not to be dramatic!"

His head canted, lips pursing. "You make a fair point."

"I'm glad you agree," I muttered, and he laughed.

Spinning away, I walked across the container to where the bed was located.

"What are you doing?"

"I need to process this. Process *everything*. Just ... don't talk to me right now." I couldn't wrap my head around what he'd told me. He was a hitman. A *hitman*! The words went round and round in my mind.

He'd killed... *murdered*... fifty-six people. In cold blood. *For money*! And I'd walked right up to him and asked him to pretend to be my boyfriend.

And he'd agreed.

He. Had. Agreed!

Why? Why would someone who did what he did agree to that?

I risked a glance at him. He'd cleared up the remains of our food, then moved to stand propped against the wall, arms folded, head tipped back and his eyes closed—a picture of relaxation. Who relaxed when they had been kidnapped?

A hitman, that's who!

16

Rook

I kept one eye on Magdalena as I cleared up the remains of our dinner. She paced up and down, muttering to herself and gnawing on a thumbnail. I let her do it. It beat the alternative. At least she wasn't screaming and crying. Telling her *what* I was had been a calculated risk. I needed her to know I had the abilities to get us out of here and until she had a reason for that, she was going to continue questioning me about it.

Of course, the flaw in that theory was that she might now refuse to trust me at all, might even convince herself I was part of the situation she'd found herself in. And, currently, I had no way of proving otherwise. But my gut was usually pretty good with people, and something told me this girl was stronger than she appeared. She might need a little while to digest, but I was confident she'd be able to overcome her natural fear of what I'd admitted. I caught her glancing over at me more than once, but I said nothing. The best thing to do right now was let her come to me.

Once I had cleared everything away, I positioned myself next to the door and leaned against the wall. That way I was ready for if anyone tried to come in. It would also give Dally a chance to calm down and see I wasn't a threat to her.

My patience was rewarded about an hour later. I'd gone from standing to sitting near the door, head tipped back, eyes closed, snatching a quick catnap. A soft footfall opened my eyes to find her standing no more than a foot away.

"You said you think you can get us out of here." Her voice was hesitant.

"I said I *can* get us out of here, not that I *think* I can."

"How?"

I patted the floor beside me. "Come and sit down."

She settled on my left, on the opposite side of the door, drawing her knees up against her chest and looping her arms around them. "I've been trying to figure out why they targeted me. It would have made more sense to take Charlie."

"Why do you say that? You're just as much your parents' daughter as she is."

"But she's also married to a man with his own money. They could have asked for more."

"Maybe they don't *need* more. Sometimes things like this aren't about getting as much money as you can, but as much as you *need*."

"Who *needs* five million dollars?"

I laughed. "You'd be surprised at what people think they need." I stood, stretched, and turned to face her. "Okay, let's go through what we know."

"We don't *know* anything!"

"Of course we do. We know someone else hired them. We know they've been tracking your movements for a while. We have to assume they set up the boyfriend for hire ad specifically for you to find. Could your friend be involved?"

"Jasmine?"

"She was the one who pushed for you to hire someone as your date, wasn't she?"

"Well, yes, but ..." She shook her head. "No, there's no way Jasmine would do something like this. We grew up together. We've been best friends since kindergarten." But there was doubt in her voice.

"You're sure?" I pushed.

She nodded. "Yes." She sounded more confident that time. "I don't think Jasmine is involved. So that takes us back to knowing *nothing!*"

"No, it doesn't. We still know someone hired them. They haven't killed me because they need to see what their employer wants them to do. They're not thinking for themselves, or adapting to the circumstances."

"Is that what you do? Adapt to the circumstances?"

"Absolutely." I paused, considered my options, then continued. "That's why I ended up in prison. The guy I killed ... I thought he was a friend. He asked me to go with him on a hit, begged me to go along. Said he thought something was off about it and wanted back up. I'd retired six months earlier. I was tired of the lifestyle and wanted out of the game. There comes a time when ..." I broke off. She didn't need to hear about my crisis of morality.

"When we got there, there was a young family living in the house." I shook my head. "There's a line I wouldn't cross with the contracts I took. Killing women and children is not something I do. I got the kids and wife out, then returned to find my *friend*. Turns out, I'd fucked up because *I* was the mark, not the family. They were just the cover story. He took me to that specific house because he *knew* I'd focus on getting them out of there. Some powerful people decided that my retirement was dangerous to them and painted a target on my back. We fought. He wasn't going to stop until I was dead, so I ended up having to kill *him*. When his employer found out the contract on me had failed, they planted evidence to prove I was there, then threatened to kill the family if they spoke on my behalf. They refused and went into hiding. A few months after I was incarcerated, they were found and killed."

"Are they ... the red marks on your arm?"

I nodded. "That's right. If they had taken the stand and said I was responsible, they'd still be alive. But because I protected them, they didn't want to lie. Their blood is on my hands." I shrugged. I'd dealt with the guilt over those deaths a long time ago. "None of that matters right now. What *does* matter is my experience gives us insight into what we're dealing with. What else can you remember?"

"Nothing."

"Concentrate. Think. The man who took you out of here. Can you remember what he looks like? Was he the one who ran us off the road?"

"I don't know. I don't think so? I didn't see the faces of the men you were fighting. He wasn't the one who was waiting at the top."

"Okay, after he took you out of here, then what? What did you see?"

She licked her lips. "It was dark…" Her eyes closed, her brows pleating together as she concentrated. "His voice echoed when he spoke. I remember thinking we were in some kind of warehouse, maybe. I couldn't see the walls or the exit. There was no natural light. We didn't walk for more than a couple of minutes. I couldn't see anything more than a couple of feet around me. There were three tall lamps in a circle, and a chair in the center. They put me on a chair, then pointed a video camera at me."

"They? There was more than one out there?"

"Y-yes. The one who was waiting by the road was there. He was the one who spoke to me."

"What did they have you say?"

"I … I couldn't read it."

"There was a lot?"

"No." She lowered her lashes. "There were only a couple of lines, but …" She took in a breath, squared her shoulders and lifted her head to look at me. "I panicked. I couldn't read it. When

I'm stressed or…"

"Or scared," I added softly.

She nodded. "Yes, or scared. Well, I couldn't read it."

She was trying to avoid telling me something. Her eyes shifted away, there was a look of almost embarrassment on her face. I filed it away as something to look into later … when we were less likely to die.

"What happened then?"

"They made me say the date and that they want five million dollars. When I couldn't read the rest, one of them—the one from the road. He is the leader, I think—took over. He said they would contact my parents in twenty-four hours with a drop-off location and further information."

I scratched my jaw, thinking. "That seems standard. Can you remember anything else? Names?"

"No …. Wait, yes. The one who came into the room called the other one—the leader—Rushka."

"Good. That's good. Okay, here's what's going to happen." I held out a hand and pulled her to her feet. "You're going to get some sleep."

"I told you, I *can't* sleep."

"Sure you can." I drew her over to the narrow cot. "Lie down." She did, frowning in my direction. "Roll onto your side, facing the wall."

"Why?"

I chuckled. "So suspicious. Just do it. You're at no risk from me."

She shifted on the mattress, and once she was on her side, I sat beside her. "Don't freak out." I stretched out, turned onto my side, and looped an arm across her waist. She immediately tensed. I moved closer and dropped my voice to a whisper. "This way, if I've missed any cameras, it'll look like we're sharing the bed and getting some sleep. This is my plan ..."

L. ANN

17
Magdalena

My eyes snapped open, the tail-ends of a dream jolting me awake, and I lay still, blinking until my vision focused. There was a heavy weight across my waist, and the memory of the day before flooded back.

I'd fallen asleep? I'd actually fallen asleep with everything that had happened?

I shifted onto my back and discovered the weight was Rook's arm. He was deep asleep beside me. His breathing was quiet, lips slightly parted and his lids shielding that piercing gaze. I twisted further, so that I was on my side, facing him.

Looking at him, I found it hard to believe he'd killed people, *lots* of people.

How old was he?

I hadn't really thought about that before now, but looking closely, I could see a slight peppering of gray mixed in with the raven black hair at his temple and in the stubble coating his jaw.

He had to be in his late thirties, at the very least.

"I can feel your eyes boring through my head."

I jumped at the deep sleep-thickened rumble, then I found myself staring into dark eyes.

"I thought you were asleep."

"I guessed that. Do you often stare at people when they're sleeping?"

"I do when they've admitted to killing hundreds of people for money."

One sleek dark eyebrow rose. His chuckle vibrated through me, and I realized how close we were on the small cot. "I haven't admitted to killing *hundreds*, only fifty-six."

"Only…"

"I'm sure my brother has more blood on his hands."

"Is it a competition, then?" My question was tart, and he laughed again.

"Not anymore." He propped up on one elbow. "You seem less … scared of me now you've slept."

Was I?

I hadn't really thought about it. "I guess you're not as terrifying as the men on the other side of this container."

His smile was faint. "I can assure you that I'm *far* more dangerous than they are. Just not to you." His hand lifted, and he tucked a stray lock of hair behind my ear. "I don't think it'll be long before one of them comes for you again. They'll want you on film when they send instructions for the money-drop. Having their captive there gives a bigger impact. Are you ready?"

I nodded.

"No hesitation, Dal, remember?"

Dal—he'd been calling me that since the party. *Dal and Dally*. I liked them more than *Mags*, which most people used.

"I think so."

"Do you want to go through it again?"

I shook my head. "Are you sure it'll work?"

"As sure as I can be. There's always room for error. But if you do as I say, we should be okay. Be ready."

"Be ready? How can you ever be ready for something like this?"

He chuckled again, his fingers brushing my cheek. "I forget that for normal people, life isn't like that. It's second nature to those in my business."

I licked my lips, and his eyes dropped to follow the movement. "Your business? You mean killing people?"

One finger touched my lip, just over where it had split. "I'm not ashamed of what I've done, Dal. I am very good at my job."

"But who are you to decide who lives and who dies?"

His lips tilted into a faint smile."I don't. Whoever pays me makes that decision. But if someone is hiring me to kill you, then it's unlikely to be because you've lived the life of a saint. You've done *something* bad somewhere."

His finger moved, stroking lightly over my bottom lip, and something flickered in his eyes, gone before it really registered.

"How do you *know* all the people you've killed were bad?"

"People rarely take out a contract on another person because they shoplifted a two-dollar bag of chips. The people who hire me do so because whoever they want taken out has hurt them ... badly enough to want them removed from the world. *Or are in competition.*"

"That doesn't make them deserve death."

One side of his lip curled up. "True. But these people are typically all as corrupt as each other and it's simply a matter of who gets taken out first."

Was I really lying here discussing why someone deserved to be killed? Although, at no point had he said the people he killed deserved it, only that they weren't innocent of any wrongdoing themselves.

His fingers moved from my lips and stroked along my jaw. "Most of my contracts were from various government departments. Deaths they didn't want traced back to them. One of them was behind the one taken out on me."

"What's stopping them from trying again?"

His expression hardened, but the touch on my skin remained gentle. He ran the back of his fingers down my throat. "I tracked down the man who issued it and ..." His lips twisted and *not* into a smile. "Well, let's just say I made it clear I wouldn't be happy if they tried to repeat the assignment. They canceled the contract."

"Just like that?" The light caress was relaxing me, almost sending me back to sleep, and I let my head drop back against the thin pillow, my eyes sliding closed.

His laugh was soft and warm ... *intimate.* "It may have taken a couple of broken bones, but the message was received, eventually."

"You didn't kill him?"

"No. That wouldn't have achieved my purpose. If I'd killed him, someone else would have taken his place, and I needed him alive to void the contract. Keeping him alive ensures the contract doesn't get reissued again any time soon. Because he *knows* I will come after him again."

I sighed. "You talk like it's the most normal thing in the world."

"For me it is." His fingers stopped moving, resting against the top of my arm. "On a scale of one to ten, how freaked out would you be if I kissed you right now?"

My eyes popped open. His face was close to mine, dark eyes intent on my face.. "I ... umm ..." My heartbeat picked up speed and I licked my lips. "I wouldn't be against it," I whispered.

"No?" He moved closer, the hand on my arm sliding up to curve over my cheek. His thumb brushed over my lips, and then his head lowered, mouth hovering above mine. "The one that hit you ... that was the same guy who took you out of here, yes?"

I nodded.

"I'm going to kill him for that."

His mouth cut my intake of breath short by covering mine. His lips were firm, yet he kissed me with a gentleness I didn't expect. It was nothing like the kiss we'd shared outside my parents' home. That had been a display, a message to anyone watching that we *were* really in a relationship.

This was different.

There was no one watching, no one to convince ... and no interruption. The hand on my cheek moved, cupped my jaw and held me still, while he pressed small closed-mouthed kisses to either corner of my mouth, avoiding the split in my bottom lip.

He kissed me again, and I parted my lips at the touch of his tongue. The pressure of his lips changed, became hungrier, and his tongue slid along mine.

I lifted my hands, wrapped my arms around his neck, pressed closer to him, and he rolled, until I was beneath him and he was pushing one leg between mine. His erection was hard against my thigh, and the contact startled me. My eyes flew open, my mouth pulling from his.

He dropped his head against my shoulder, releasing a quiet groan.

"No, you're right. This isn't the time or the place to take this where I'd like it to go," he murmured, "but I had to see if my memory was flawed. I wanted to remind myself of how soft your lips are, of how you tasted."

He rolled away and stood, stretched, and crossed the room. Picking up two bottles of water, he turned and tossed one to me.

"We should eat and drink." His voice was husky, rough, and I blinked, fighting to calm my racing heart.

"In case it's our last meal?" I forced the words out, tried to make a joke out of it, but now he'd reminded me of where we were, the reality was I was terrified that was exactly what this was going to be. Water and a can of something random—that's what they'd find in the contents of my stomach when they discovered my body.

"Someone might die today, but it won't be us." Arrogance had returned to his tone.

"You can't know that."

"Trust me, Dally. That's all you have to do." He busied himself opening a tin of … *something* and emptied it into a bowl. "Cold soup for breakfast."

He set it down and handed me a spoon. "Eat up," he instructed.

I don't know how long passed—it could have been hours, it could have been days. I know we slept twice and Rook insisted we eat another four meals. But with no accurate way of tracking the time, seconds felt like minutes, and minutes felt like hours.

For all I knew, only one day had passed, but it *felt* longer. Especially because there was nothing to do to pass the time—well, other than laying with Rook on the bed where he took my breath away with long, passionate kisses. Kisses that, the second they became too hot, too hungry, had him breaking away and putting space between us.

I think it was the second day when we were laying together, my head resting against his shoulder as I dozed when Rook's head tilted, and his entire body stilled. My head lifted, eyes searching his out.

"It's time," he murmured. "Remember what I told you."

My heart sped up. This was it. This was what he'd told me to watch for.

"Deep breaths, Dal." Warm hands cupped my face and tipped

my head back until I stared into dark eyes. "Just stay calm, okay?" His voice was soft.

I nodded, swallowing. His eyes tracked over my face, and then his head dropped, lips covering mine in a quick kiss, over before I could react. He lifted me off him, stood and crossed the room to stand out of view of the door.

"Move across the room." The same man who'd instructed us last time yelled. "Stand against the wall."

I looked at Rook.

"They can't see us. They're only behaving like they can," he said.

"How do you know?"

"You think they wouldn't have come in or said something when we were fooling around on the bed?" His eyebrow rose. "Dally, you need to do what I told you." His voice was firm.

I bit my lip and climbed off the bed. "It's done." I called out. Rook had told me to behave as though we were doing as they said. Well, in actual fact, *I* was. He'd said to make sure I was far from the door when everything happened … *Everything* … my mind shied away from what *that* entailed.

"Face the wall." The voice called again. "I'm coming in. Put your hands behind your back."

"Don't turn back around, Dal. Keep your eyes on the wall. Wait for me to say it's safe." Rook's voice was a low warning, and I swallowed, put my hands behind my back, and closed my eyes.

I knew what he was about to do, and he'd told me to stay far away so that if it went wrong, I wouldn't be …

Stop it!

It would not go wrong. I just had to stand here, keep my eyes focused on the wall, and wait.

The door creaked open. I bit down onto my lip, trying to control my breathing, and squeezed my eyes closed. My heart was like a loud drum beating in my ears. I curled my fingers into my palms; the nails digging into my skin; and I tried to focus on that instead of the noises and shouts that erupted behind me.

The fear of the unknown skittered like ice down my spine. I wanted to turn, to see what was happening, but Rook had said to stay exactly where I was until he spoke to me. But what if he didn't speak? What if he wasn't as good as he claimed?

What if he was ... *dead?*

There was a yell, followed by a thud that sounded sickeningly final and then ... silence.

My mouth dried up.

What had happened?

Should I look?

Should I wait?

What should I do?

I tried to swallow past the lump in my throat, forced my fingers to unclench, and opened my eyes. I listened ... hard ...

I should turn around. I needed to know what was happening.

Almost as soon as I decided to look, a hand fell onto my shoulder.

L. ANN

18

Rook

I took up position against the wall on the side of the door where it would open toward me. It was the perfect way to conceal my location. While I waited, I tossed my jacket to one side, then unbuttoned my shirt and removed it. I needed to do what I'd planned as fast and effectively as possible. Removing the jacket gave my incoming target one less thing to hold on to. My shirt ... well, that I was going to use as a weapon.

The door swung open, and I waited. The guy's shadow appeared before he did, and I took a silent step forward. The second he was inside, I flattened my palm against the door, shoved it shut and wrapped my shirt around his neck from behind.

He threw his arms up, reaching back to grab my wrists, nails digging in as he attempted to break my hold. I tangled a hand in his hair and wrenched his head back. His body bucked and twisted, but I was bigger and stronger, and he clearly hadn't been trained the way I'd been. I twisted the two ends of my shirt around each other, tightening its hold on his neck, then wrapped my arm around his throat, bringing my hand up to lock against my other arm to keep my grip in place around his neck, and *squeezed.*

He grunted, and renewed his struggles to get free, one hand dropping to grope for the gun tucked into his waistband. I held steady, squeezed harder, until his struggles reduced and and he forgot about his gun in favour of clawing at my arm, fighting to loosen my grip so he could breathe.

And then he stilled, relaxing his body, probably thinking I would loosen my grip.

Big mistake.

In a move too quick for him to stop, I dropped one hand, shifted my arm, grabbed both sides of his head and twisted... *hard and fast.* The snap as I broke his neck was loud in the small room.

His eyes widened, mouth dropped open, and he tried to speak. When nothing came out, *that's* when he realized he'd made a mistake by not checking his surroundings as he walked in. An over-confidence that had resulted in his death—because although he might still be conscious, his body was already dying.

I let him go, and he dropped to the floor, mouth gaping like a fish. I crouched beside him. "That's for making her bleed, asshole." I whispered, then stood, stepped over him, crossed the room and touched Magdalena's shoulder. She jumped.

"Let's go."

She twisted, her eyes falling onto the man twitching on the floor. "What did...? Is he...? He's not dead..."

I glanced at him. "Not yet, but soon enough. We need to get out of here before someone else comes looking for him." I looked down, frowned, then nodded toward her feet. "Leave the shoes behind. If we need to run, you'll be better off barefoot than in those."

"Is that why you're shirtless?" She hadn't taken her eyes off the guy flopping around like a fish.

"No, that was because I needed something to hold him with while I dealt with him."

"Dealt with him," she repeated in a whisper.

"What did you *think* I was going to do? Invite him for lunch?" I curved a hand around her arm. "Get moving, Dal. We don't have much time."

"Much time … " She couldn't seem to look away from the idiot on the floor. "Shouldn't we call a doctor?"

"What? Fuck, no." I dropped to a crouch beside him and searched his pockets for his cell, then took his gun. I checked his cell for network coverage. It showed zero bars, which meant we needed to get outside before I could call anyone.

I returned my attention to the man on the ground. His eyes were on me, screaming silently as his body short-circuited because it couldn't receive instructions from his brain anymore. I studied him, debating what to do, then nodded to myself, rose to my feet, and pointed the gun at his head.

"Rook, what are you—?" Her words turned into a scream when I pulled the trigger.

"Let's go."

"No! *No!* You killed him."

"He was already dead." I caught her arm again and pulled her toward the door.

"He wasn't. He was moving. He *looked* at me."

"He was suffocating. He'd have been dead in a few more minutes. I gave him a quick ending instead of the long, painful death he deserved." I stopped beside the door and swung to face her. Her face was white, eyes huge and full of terror. "Listen to me, darlin'. If I hadn't killed him, he'd have eventually killed us. We weren't getting out of here alive. You saw their faces. They'd have taken the money, killed us and gone on their merry way."

"You *killed* him!"

I sighed. "I know that this isn't something you're used to, but you need to get it together. We have to go *now*, and if you don't shut the fuck up, someone is going to hear you and come to find out what's taking him so long."

"*You shot him in the head!*" she screamed at me. "Someone will have heard *that*."

I tapped the gun. "There's a suppressor on it. Unless they're standing right outside, they won't hear it." I made sure the safety was on, checked the temperature of the barrel, then tucked it into my belt. "Unlike *you*. Close that pretty mouth and pull yourself together."

She slapped me.

Probably should have expected that.

When she raised her hand to do it again, I caught her wrist. "We really don't have time for this." I spun her to face the door and wrapped my other arm around her waist, pulling her back against me when she struggled. Dipping my head, I placed my lips close to her ear. "Listen to me, darlin'. You can beat on me all you want when we're away from here. But for now, *concentrate*. I'm going to open the door. You stay behind me and keep quiet. We move slowly until we find a way out. If we're seen, you fucking run. Do you understand me? Do *not* look back. I'll catch up to you."

She didn't speak. I tightened my grip, squeezing her waist. "I said, do you understand me?"

"*Yes!*"

"I'm going to let you go now. Do you have control of yourself?"

She nodded. I released my hold, and stepped back, watching for any sign she was going to freak out again. She didn't move, stayed facing away from me, her arms lifting to wrap around herself.

I stooped, untangled my shirt from the dead guy on the floor, pulling a face at the blood spatters, then dragged it on.

"Take your shoes off." I pulled the gun out from the waistband of my pants, and reached for her hand with mine. "Hold on to my shirt or my belt and stay close." As I spoke, I guided her hand around to my back.

She didn't argue, her fingers curling into the material of my shirt. I released the magazine and checked how many bullets it held. Ten. Hopefully, that would be enough. I shoved the clip back in, flicked the safety off, and held the pistol close to my thigh.

"I'm going to open the door. Can you remember what direction you were taken in?"

"S-straight ahead." Her reply was low and stilted.

"We're going to turn to the right and move along the side of the container until we reach the end, okay? ... On three." I reached for the door.

"Wait! What if someone is outside?"

I lifted the gun slightly. "That's what this is for."

"You'll kill them ..."

"It's them or us, darlin'. Ready?"

"No?" Her voice wobbled.

I chuckled. "Take a deep breath. One ... two ..." I moved to one side, flattened my palm against Dally's stomach and held her back against the wall, then opened the door. No one came in or spoke. "Stay quiet. Let's go." I eased forward, felt her grip tighten on my shirt, and then she followed me through the door.

19
Magdalena

My heart hammered in my throat, my mouth was dry, and the fingers I'd wrapped in Rook's shirt shook as we crept along the side of the container. The slightest noise, the quiet scrape of Rook's boot along the floor had me tensing. I expected someone to loom up out of the darkness and see us, *shoot* us, but no one appeared. Not even when we reached the end of the container.

We turned the corner, and I collided with Rook's back when he stopped.

"Duck down here," he whispered and reached back to tug me down into a crouch. "Something isn't right."

"What do you mean?"

"No one came to investigate why he was taking so long. He was supposed to grab you and take you back out. It's been at least ten minutes and *no one* came after him. Why?"

"I don't—"

"I wasn't asking you." He spoke over me. "Stay here. Do *not* move until I come back for you."

I reached out to grasp his sleeve. "Where are you going?"

"To find out what the trap is."

"Trap?"

"They expected us to escape. I'd even say they sent him in for me to kill. Stay here. I'll be back."

"Rook!" I whispered his name, but he disappeared into the darkness and left me there ... alone.

The silence stretched. All I could hear was my breathing and the sound of my heart. Both were so loud I was sure *someone* would hear them and discover me. Time passed, and I wasn't sure if it was minutes or hours. My thighs burned from crouching, but I didn't dare change position in case someone saw me. My eyes were dry from straining to see through the darkness. I was cold—my bare toes trying to curl in on themselves to reduce the chill rising from the ground. I rubbed my hands up and down my arms, trying to generate some warmth, with very little success.

And then a noise broke the silence, loud enough to hurt my ears, and I cried out. My hand clapped over my mouth, too late to contain my scream, and I shrank back. My ears rang from the noise. I couldn't hear anything above it.

What had it been? It sounded like a gunshot! Had Rook been discovered?

Oh my god. Had they killed him?

Another shot, and this time I saw a flash of light.

What the hell was that? A flashlight?

I didn't *think* it was. It seemed to have happened at the same time as the gun. *Was that a thing? Was it from the gun?* I knew very little about them, I wasn't sure I was *even* positive if it was gunshots I was hearing.

A third one, followed by a yell. It *had* to be gunfire!

I didn't know what to do.

Should I stay where I was, like Rook had said? Or should I run?

He'd told me if they saw us, I should run.

Did this count as being seen?

I slowly straightened, rubbing my hands over my thighs to ease the ache from being in one position for so long.

And then something broke free from the shadows, coming toward me at speed. My eyes widened and darted around.

"*Run!*" Rook's voice, loud and urgent, and I was moving before the word even registered. But instead of running away, I bolted toward him.

He caught my arm as I reached him and hauled me back around. "Wrong fucking direction!" he snarled and shoved me in front of him. "Now fucking *run!*"

I don't know how long we ran for. It was probably only a couple of minutes, but it seemed longer. The air burned in my lungs as I gulped breath after breath and tried to keep putting one foot in front of the other. My feet stung as they pounded on the uneven floor of the warehouse, and my arm throbbed where Rook's fingers were wrapped around it in an iron grip. When I stumbled, he yanked hard, dragging me back upright. A pain shot up to my shoulder as he hauled me sideways.

"Keep going. There are doors ahead. Straight through them. Don't look back." He snapped the words and then let me go.

"Rook…" I slowed down.

"Don't fucking stop!" he roared at me and spun away.

I couldn't help it. I slowed to look over my shoulder just as he raised his gun and fired. My feet stopped moving, frozen in place, and I watched as the man coming toward us stumbled, faltered and then fell.

And then it struck me… I could see everything around me. The darkness had receded to an almost twilight state … which meant…

I swung my head around and spotted grime-covered windows high on the walls, letting in enough light to break up the darkness and increase visibility. I blinked, then found myself caught up in a tight grip and shook.

"Didn't I fucking tell you to keep running?" Rook snarled, his face inches from mine.

"I—"

"Doesn't matter. Let's get out of here." He set off at a quick walk, dragging me along with him.

A set of double doors appeared ahead of us and his palm hit one, forcing it to swing open. His pace didn't change, and I tripped and stumbled, trying to keep up with him. And then cold air hit me. I gasped, eyes watering at the sudden brightness of sunlight on my face.

"Keep moving." Rook's voice was grim.

"But won't they be able to see us now?"

"He's not chasing us."

"He? But there were two!" I tried to pull free, instinct forcing me to search for evidence of someone following us.

"Not anymore." He gave an impatient tug on my arm. "Keep up. There are gates straight ahead which look like they lead out onto a street. Once we're somewhere public, we can get our bearings."

L. ANN

20

Rook

Magdalena kept glancing over her shoulder the entire way to the gates. I could have told her why no one was going to stop us, but in her heightened sense of panic, I didn't want to risk her deciding *I* was now the enemy and running from me.

I'd catch her—that wasn't the problem—I just didn't want to waste the time it would require to chase her down. If she ran back toward the warehouse, there was a risk the guy I'd chased off would come back and I wouldn't get there in time to protect her. So I left her in her current state of panic and hurried her toward freedom.

The gates swung open with a squeal of rusty hinges, and we slipped through the gap and into a short alleyway. The street beyond it wasn't empty, but it wasn't busy either, with cars driving past at slow speeds and pedestrians gave us suspicious glances when we exited the side road. I pulled Dally to a stop and took out the cell I'd taken from the kidnapper I'd killed in the container.

Flipping it open, I punched in my younger brother's number.

"Who is this?" His voice was clipped when he answered.

"It's me."

"*Rook?* Where the fuck are you? Bishop is tearing the country apart trying to track you down."

"Long story. One I don't have time for right now. Can you ping my location and tell me where we are?"

"We?"

"Remember that *time* thing? Just do it. Then find me a hotel close to where I am and book me a room. Ideally one that won't ask any questions."

"What kind of weekend did you have?" The recognizable tapping of keys sounded down the line. "It must have been pretty good for you not to know where you are."

"Good is a matter of perspective. It was ... *interesting*. Have you got a location yet?"

"Patience, brother. What happened to *your* cell?"

"It was in my car."

"And where's your car?"

"Down an embankment somewhere."

There was a brief silence. "I'm waiting for the punchline, Rook."

"No punchline. Where the fuck am I, Knight?"

"It's narrowing down now ... Baltimore. What the fuck are you doing in *Baltimore?*"

I swore. Baltimore was over one hundred miles east of the town I'd moved to. They must have drugged us to keep us unconscious for the amount of time they needed to bring us here. "Find me a hotel, then wire me some cash. I've lost my wallet."

"Jesus Christ, what the fuck kind of weekend did you have?" More tapping of keys. "Fine. There's a hotel a block away. I've used it before. They are used to … well, our kind of people. I'll text the address to the number you're calling from, as well as directions. I'll book it under your name and pay in advance. Are you going to call Bishop?"

"Once I'm in the hotel, yeah. Can you get a new cell sent to me as well as the cash? Today, preferably."

"No problem. But I want to hear the story as soon as possible."

"You got it."

Magdalena stood shivering beside me. "I gotta go. Text me the details." I cut the call, and seconds later, the cell in my hand beeped to inform me of an incoming message. I tapped it open and read the details, reached for Dally's arm and set off down the street.

"Where are we going *now*?"

"Hotel." I was purposely making her work for any information, knowing if she had time to think about anything other than how annoying I was being, everything that had happened over the last couple of days would catch up with her. If that happened, she was going to break down. It was the normal reaction for someone who hadn't lived the same kind of life *I* had. I wanted to be away from prying eyes and safe behind the doors of a hotel room before *that* happened, where I could bring her out of it without drawing attention to us.

"Who were you talking to? Did he tell you where we are? How are we going to pay for a hotel?"

"Knight is organizing it and having money sent to me on express delivery."

"Who is Knight?"

"My brother."

"Where are we?"

"Baltimore."

"*Baltimore?*" She repeated the word, her voice sharp.

I turned to face her. "Don't lose it on me now, Dal. If you're hysterical when we reach the hotel, I won't be able to explain it. Keep it together for me."

The battle between annoyance at my words and the desperate desire to succumb to the hysteria was clear on her face. I pasted a cocky smile onto *my* face and waited. Sure enough, annoyance won.

"I'm *not* going to *lose it*."

She would. No one who'd been through what she had would continue to behave like it was a normal day in their life. As soon as the fight-or-flight instinct settled, and she knew she was safe, *then* she would react to everything.

"Come on. The hotel isn't far from here. Let's get going."

"Before we go inside, I'm going to need you to do something." I touched her arm to stop her from entering the hotel. "We look a mess. You have no shoes. There's—" I caught myself. I had been about to tell her there was blood on her cheek, but that would keep until we were in the hotel room. "I'm going to tell the concierge that we were attacked on our way here. They'll want to call the police. Just stay quiet and let me do the talking."

"But we *want* to talk to the police, don't we?"

"We will, but not yet." I had no intention of involving the police, but now wasn't the time to tell her that. I stepped closer to her. "Don't freak out, okay?"

"Freak out? What? Why?"

I reached out and swung her up into my arms. She immediately tensed. "Put your arms around me. This way it looks like you're in shock, *and* hides the state of my shirt."

Her eyes held mine, tracked over my face while she chewed on her lip, then she nodded and lifted her arms to loop them around my neck.

"Ready?"

Her head dropped against my shoulder, and I strode toward the entrance to the hotel. The doors slid open at my approach, and the entrance hall was quiet, with only an older man standing at the reception desk. He frowned as I approached.

"You should have a booking for Rook Chambers. My wife and I were robbed on our way here." I injected an element of upper class outrage into my voice. "They took my wallet, cell and even her *shoes!*"

The man's eyes widened. "Do you need me to call the police for you, sir?"

I shook my head. "No. I would like to get my wife up to our

room so she can feel safe and then I'll speak to the authorities.

"Mr. Chambers, you said?" He tapped on the keyboard in front of him. "Ahh yes. Here we are. There's also a note that you're expecting a delivery, sir?"

"That's right. After the incident, I called and arranged for my credit cards to be frozen, as well as cash and a new cell phone to be delivered as soon as possible. If you could have it sent up to my room as soon as it arrives, I would appreciate it."

"Of course, sir." He handed me a swipe card. "Room three forty-seven. If you or your wife need *anything*, please call down and ask for Matthew."

"Thank you." I took the card and turned toward the elevator bay. "Almost there," I said in an undertone to Dally.

I didn't set her back on her feet until the elevator doors had closed on us. She took a step back, her arms moving to wrap around her waist.

"Almost there. You're doing great, darlin'. Keep it together for me for a few minutes more," I murmured, and her eyes flickered up to meet mine. I could see the exhaustion on her face. It was clear in the paleness of her skin, the dark circles beneath her eyes, the way her bottom lip trembled as she fought not to fall into the darkness of panic. Everything was about to crash down onto her. The signs were clear. I just needed her to hold it together a little longer.

The doors slid open, and I caught her arm so I could draw her out and into the hallway beyond. A sign on the wall informed me that rooms three forty to three fifty were to the left, and we moved along the hallway without meeting another person. A single swipe of the card unlocked the door, and I led Dally inside.

Knight had chosen well, going for a small suite instead of a room. We walked into a living room, with two doors set at the opposite end—presumably for the bathroom and bedroom. I didn't stop, resting my hand on the small of Dally's back and guiding her to the bathroom.

"I need to make some calls. Run a bath, have a soak, relax for a while. I'll call down to room service and get something sent up."

She swung to face me. "Where are you going?" Fear was rich in her voice.

"I'll be in the main room. I won't be far away." I assured her while I reached past her, found the plug for the bath and turned on the faucet. "I'm sure there will be complimentary toiletries in here." I waved a hand at the compact unit set against one wall. "There should be bathrobes in the bedroom."

She bit her lip, then nodded. I stood for a second longer, half-expecting her to break down where she stood, but she sucked in a deep breath, squared her shoulders and turned to the bathtub.

L. ANN

21

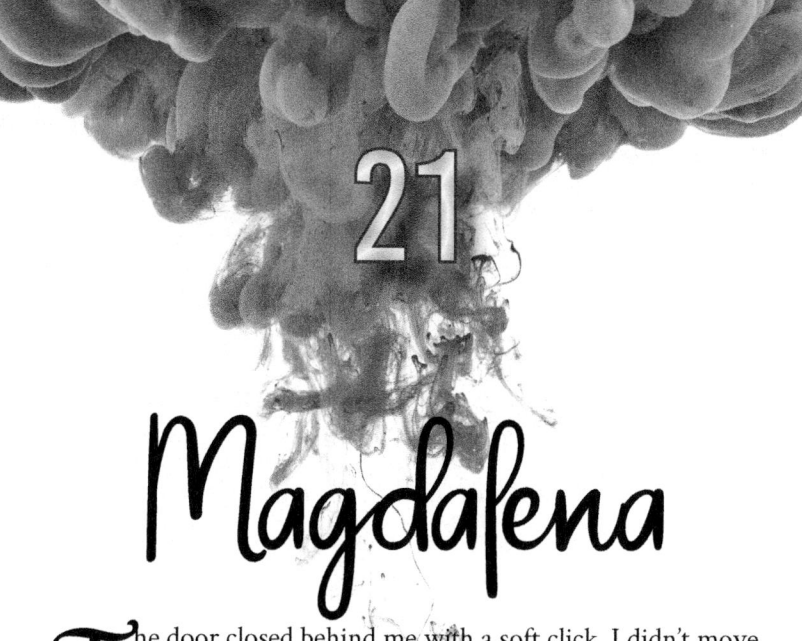

Magdalena

The door closed behind me with a soft click. I didn't move straight away, watching the water as it hit the bottom of the bathtub and slowly filled. My head pounded, my legs ached, but I felt strangely numb. As though I was watching a movie reel or a sequence of events from somewhere else.

I should be hysterical. Someone had kidnapped me. I'd watched Rook *kill* a man. I'd run for my life. I'd heard what I was sure was a shootout.

Yet there was nothing—no panic, no hysteria. Nothing but bone-deep exhaustion. I turned to look at the vanity unit and reached out to pick up a bottle. Twisting off the lid, I sniffed, then poured some of it into the water. When I caught my reflection in the mirror, I turned back. I looked ill—white faced, apart from a dark streak of *something* across one cheek. What was that? I moved closer to the mirror, lifting a hand to touch it. It crumbled and flaked off beneath my fingernails.

Bile rose in my throat.

It was blood. Blood from the man Rook had killed.

My hand pressed to my lips.

Don't think about that!

I spun away and peeled off the filthy skirt and blouse I was wearing. My underwear was next, and I stood, naked, next to the tub, waiting for it to fill.

Had it really only been a couple of days? What day was it? Monday? Tuesday? I wasn't sure. I *should* know, though, shouldn't I? I glanced toward the door. *I should call my parents. Tell them I was safe. Should I do that now? What if they were waiting by the phone for a call from my kidnappers?*

My hand was on the door, and I blinked.

When had I moved?

I turned the handle. Rook's voice flowed through the gap.

"... get here? ... No, bring the information to me ... Okay, great. I'll see you then."

I stepped back, closed the door, and twisted the lock. I wasn't ready to face him. I'd take the bath he suggested, *then* I'd ask to use the phone to call my family. Five minutes while I cleaned up wouldn't make a difference ...

I returned to consciousness with a shriek and surged up out of the now lukewarm bath water.

"Dally?" A bang on the door accompanied my name. "Is everything okay in there?"

I stood, water splashing over the sides, and reached for a towel. Wrapping it around my body, I stepped out. Once again, I caught sight of my reflection in the mirror. That dried blood was *still* on my cheek and I stared at it.

The sound of the man's neck snapping as Rook twisted it echoed through my head. The look in his eyes when Rook pointed the gun at him. The sound it made when he squeezed the trigger. The way the back of the man's head exploded. The pool of blood ... the blood ... *the blood*.

A sound, loud and shrill, reached my ears. A *scream*.

Who was screaming?

I swung toward the door, caught sight of my face in the mirror. My mouth was open. My eyes were wide.

It was me.

I was screaming.

The bathroom door burst open, and I spun to face the man stalking toward me. My hands lifted, warding him away, and I stumbled backwards, that unearthly shriek still spilling from my lips.

"Magdalena!" He barked my name. "Stop it."

But I couldn't. All I could see was the man he'd shot. The blood. His *brains*. The look of terror on his face. The noise of the gun when Rook shot him ... and I *screamed*.

His hands caught mine, pulled them to his chest, and pinned them there. "Magdalena!" He snapped my name again.

"You killed him! You *shot him*!" I shrieked.

"I *had* to."

"He was already down. You didn't need to kill him."

"He was already dead." He secured my hands with one of his and lifted the other to touch my cheek. "Listen to me. He would have killed us ... killed *you*. They had sent him for you. The ransom hadn't been paid. He was taking you out to die."

"You don't know that!" I screamed.

"I *do* know that! My brother checked with the authorities. There was never any report of your kidnap. There was no request for help with a ransom demand."

"No!" I shook my head. "You're lying. They wouldn't do that."

"What reason do I have to lie?"

"You're in this with them. It's part of the plan." I tried to pull free, and his grip tightened.

"There is no *them*. The one who survived ran away before I caught up to him."

"I don't believe you."

"Dally—"

"No! I *don't believe you*!" I wrenched my hands free and darted past him and out of the door.

I didn't make it even halfway across the floor of the main room before he caught up to me. The air left my lungs as I was knocked to the ground, face down, a heavy weight on top of me. A hand gripped my hair, tugged my head back, and I found my hands twisted up behind my back.

"I need you to calm down." His voice was low.

"Get off me." I tried to wriggle free. He tightened his grip.

"You're being hysterical. Calm the fuck down."

"You *kill* people!" I spat the words at him.

"Then why aren't *you* dead?"

The world spun as he flipped me over. I took the opportunity of my hands being free to slam them against his chest and shove. He didn't move, didn't even rock back, but I shot myself backwards across the floor from the force of my shove. I didn't get even half a chance to scramble to my feet before he was on me again, one large hand wrapping around both my wrists and pinning them above my head against the carpet. I bucked and arched, attempting to throw him off, but he didn't move. His legs straddled my hips, the upper half of his body leaning forward so he could keep my hands firmly in place.

"Stop fighting me." His voice was rough.

"No. Let me go!"

"I *said* stop!"

"Or what? You'll *shoot* me, too?"

L. ANN

22

Rook

"I've never been so fucking tempted to shoot a woman in my life!" I muttered the words beneath my breath, but from the way her eyes widened, I guessed she heard me. She doubled her attempt to get free. "I'm *not* going to shoot you, Dal." But my words didn't penetrate her panic.

I bit back a sigh. *This* was why I stayed away from people, why I'd never accepted rescue jobs. I didn't have the patience to deal with panic and trauma.

"For fuck's sake, *stop it*." I tightened my grip on her wrists, and caught her chin with my other hand, forcing her to stillness. "Look at me." I barked the words.

Her eyes were tightly closed, her lips moving, mouthing words silently. A plea to a god, maybe? Her breathing came in short bursts and with every breath she took, I knew that the towel she was wrapped in was the only thing protecting her modesty. The fact it was even still in place was a miracle.

"Dally!" I snapped her name, to no effect. She was too far

gone, too lost to the memory that I'd killed someone in front of her, that I *could* kill her.

And I could. It would be easy enough. I didn't even need a gun to do it. It would certainly make my life easier, for sure.

"Magdalena." I softened my voice. "Dally, I don't want to hurt you. Please stop struggling. If you keep this up, someone is going to come up here to investigate and I'm not going to be able to explain this away. Is that what you want? Do you want attention brought to us right now? Before we find out whether the guy who grabbed us is still around?"

It was a low blow. There *was* a slight risk of him coming after her. It depended on what his employer wanted, and he needed to make contact and receive instructions first. But I hoped that me being with her would act as a deterrent for the moment, at least. He would need to regroup, rethink his play to accommodate for the skills he must now realize I possessed.

Her eyes snapped open and met mine. After a second, she gave a small nod.

"I'm going to let you up now. Are you good?" I released my hold on her wrists and she immediately wriggled free from beneath me. I let her go. She stood, eyes never moving from me.

"You don't really believe he'll find us?"

I gave a half-shrug. "Hard to say. He might, if the payout is worthwhile. He's already lost two men. He might not want to risk his own life."

Her hand lifted to clutch at the towel wrapped around her

body. "But what if he—?" A sharp rap on the door silenced her.

"Room service!"

I frowned and caught her arm as she turned toward the door. "Stay quiet."

"But it's room service."

"Is it?" Maybe I was being overly paranoid, but I wasn't risking it.

She opened her mouth to speak, and I moved quickly, lifting my hand and flattening my palm over her mouth. I shook my head.

"Quiet," I mouthed.

She glared at me. I guided her to the wall beside the door and leaned close. "Don't move and stay quiet."

There was another bang on the door and Dally jumped.

"Room service!"

I stepped back from her, lowering my hand slowly. She swallowed, her tongue sweeping over her lips, but she didn't speak or move. I turned, stripped out of my shirt, then picked up the gun from where I'd dropped it onto the couch, tucked it into the back of my pants and strode to the door. I opened it just enough to look through the gap, keeping my foot pressed firmly against it so it wouldn't swing open. I wrapped my other hand around the grip of the gun at my back.

The man beyond the door smiled when he saw me. "I was about to take this back down to the kitchen. You ordered room service, sir?"

"Yeah, sorry. I was about to take a shower. Leave it there,

and I'll grab it in a few." I started to close the door.

"Sir, wait. A package was delivered for you." He bent, and I tensed, tightening my hold on the gun and easing off the safety, but he straightened with a small parcel balanced between his hands. "Matthew ... at the front desk? He said you wanted it brought straight up."

"Thanks." I made no move to take it. "Put it on the trolley."

"Are you sure, sir?"

"Positive. Thanks. I gotta go. The shower is running."

"Right, yes, sir. Sorry, sir." He placed the parcel down and pushed the trolley closer to the door. "I'll leave it right here."

"Thanks." I closed the door and leaned on it, listening.

"Wha—?" I pressed a finger to my lips and Dally stopped speaking.

"Go into the bedroom," I whispered, "and close the door." If I was wrong, and the guy dressed in the hotel uniform *wasn't* an employee, then I wanted her out of the way before any shots were fired.

Surprising me, she didn't argue. Instead, she crept across the room, slipped through the bedroom door, and let it close behind her. I stayed where I was and counted to thirty. When nothing happened, I reached out and eased the door open. No one was there. The room service trolley was right where he'd left it, the parcel sitting on top. Gun in hand, I leaned out and looked up and down the hallway. It was empty and quiet. Bringing the gun up, I used it to ease the tablecloth draped over the trolley to one side and checked beneath.

I'd seen the extremes a hitman would go to so they could reach their target, and folding themselves up small enough to wedge beneath the serving trolley wasn't outside the realm of possibility. But it was clear. There was nothing beneath it other than plates and silverware. I popped the lid off one of the serving trays to see the exact order I'd placed. Covering it back up, I looked at the parcel. My brother's large bold handwriting was clear, and the tension holding me taut eased a little.

I wrapped a hand around the trolley's bar, and pulled it inside, ensured the door was locked, and wheeled it into the bedroom. Dally sat on the edge of the bed, wrapped in a bathrobe and gnawing on a thumbnail, her eyes on the door. When I walked in, she jumped to her feet.

"Food." I waved at the trolley. "Dig in. I'm going to take a shower." I took the parcel from the top of the trolley and tossed it onto the bed. "Don't open the door to *anyone*. Don't even speak if someone knocks. Come and get me." I paused by the door. "Can I trust you not to run?"

She didn't hesitate. "I won't run. I'm sorry. I panicked. I don't know what came over me."

"I'd have been more concerned if you *didn't* panic. You've been through a lot. Have something to eat. I ordered tea, coffee, and fruit juice as well. We'll talk once I'm cleaned up, okay?"

She nodded and moved toward the trolley. I stayed where I was, watching her for a second longer, then turned away.

"Rook?" Her voice stopped me as I stepped through the door. I glanced back at her. "Thank you."

I inclined my head. "We're not clear yet. But we will be." I closed the door gently behind me and walked into the bathroom.

Stripping off my clothes, I stood under the shower, my head tipped back and eyes closed, letting the water wash over me. Dally was going to want to make a report to the police, and I needed to convince her not to. That was at the forefront of my mind while I washed.

The blood on my skin—caused by the blowback after I put a bullet in the kidnapper's head in the container—turned the water pink as I rinsed it away. And I took a few minutes to scrub my hands, seeing the blood of all my victims in my mind's eye. I thought I'd overcome that, ended the constant battle with my conscience after I quit, but all it took was another death at my hands to bring it all back.

A soft sound brought my head up, and I turned as Dally walked through the door. She froze, catching my eye, and I slowly reached out to cut off the shower and grab the towel from the heated rail. She watched me wrap it around my hips and step out of the shower.

"Everything okay?" I asked, and she bit her lip.

"I... brought you a robe." She lifted a hand, clutching the soft white material.

I took it from her. "Thank you. Go back into the other room. I'll come though in a second."

Dally was curled on the center of the bed, a plate of food in her lap. She'd twisted her hair up into some kind of haphazard knot on the top of her head, and was nibbling on a bread roll. Her eyes darted up to meet mine when I walked in.

"I'm going to call my brother and get an update on a few things. With any luck, we'll be out of here tomorrow and you can go home." While I spoke, I reached past her for the parcel and tore off the packing tape. Inside was a cell phone and a stack of bills in various denominations.

I put the cash to one side, and fired up the cell, then tapped in my older brother's number. Bishop answered as soon as it connected.

"I spoke to Knight. What the fuck happened?" He didn't give me a chance to tell him who was calling.

"That date I told you about? It turned into a kidnap and ransom situation." I glanced at Dally and took the call out into the sitting room.

He sighed. "What the fuck, Rook? What happened to being out of the game?"

"I *am*."

"Only *you* could end up involved in something without even trying. Tell me what happened."

I told him everything—from picking Dally up, the dinner, to everything I knew about the men behind the kidnap. "I think they're probably mercenaries for hire. Not sure if kidnapping is their usual gig. The two I killed were very nervous, but the third... he's professional. I'm not convinced he won't try again. Not if the money was good enough. He didn't seem to care that I took out two of his men. They were cannon fodder. Dally says she thinks they called him Rushka."

"Was he after you or the girl?"

"Definitely her. They had her record a ransom demand."

"Knight said he could find no evidence of a filed police report. We can safely assume they never took it to the authorities. Do you think they sent the recording before you escaped?"

"I'm pretty sure they did. If I had to guess, I'd say her parents refused, and they were about to up the stakes."

"Does she have any idea who could be behind it or why?"

"No, nothing. She's innocent in this."

"What do you know about her family?"

"You mean other than they're fucking awful and she was dealt a bad hand in the parent game?"

Bishop chuckled. "Yes, other than that."

"Her brother is in finance. Mom and dad don't do much of anything these days. Retired, I think, but mom was a lawyer. Her brother followed her dad's career."

"Okay, Knight should be able to see what they've been involved with. Maybe there's something there. Could one of them have caused some underground outfit boss to lose money?"

"I have no idea. I knew nothing about them when I took her job …." I paused, thinking. "Do you remember the guy I pointed out to you in the diner? The one I thought was the one she was supposed to be meeting?"

"Yeah."

"I think he might have been involved. I didn't see him at the location, but I'm pretty sure it was a setup and that the grab was meant to happen *before* she made it to dinner."

"That would make sense. How did she find the ad?"

"Her housemate suggested she hire someone and gave it to her."

"Hmmm. That's a place to start. How well does your girl know her?"

"She's not my girl, and when I asked about her friend, she denied it and said they've been friends since kindergarten."

"Friendships can be bought off."

"I want Knight to dig into her and see what he can find."

"Why? This isn't a job, Rook. You got the girl out. Now take her home and walk away. It's not your business."

"It kinda is, though, isn't it? They grabbed *me* as well. That made it my business."

"You mean it's personal?"

"Something like that."

"Since when did you let feelings get in the way?"

"What feelings? They forced me off the road and wrecked my car. I fucking love that car."

"You can buy another one."

"Not the point."

"No, the point is you should send the girl home and walk away, not involve yourself further. You're retired, remember?"

"Fuck off, Bish."

My brother laughed down the line. "Alright, fine. When will you be home?"

"Tomorrow. I'm going to need a car."

"I'll get one organized for you." He fell silent for a second. "Actually, Knight isn't far from you. I'll get him to swing by and pick you up in the morning. Do you need anything else?"

"Can you go to the crash site and see if anyone has reported it? My gun was jammed in the driver's door. I couldn't get to it when we crashed."

"Licensed?"

"Completely legal. But I happen to *like* that one a lot."

He snorted. "You develop attachments for the strangest things."

"Says *you* ... Okay, I'm going. I'll send you the information on Dally's roommate."

"Dally? That seems rather intimate. Are you *sure* you're not involved, Rook?" The concern in my brother's voice was clear.

"I've been locked up with the girl for two days, and her name is a mouthful, that's all. Haven't even kissed her."

Fucking liar.

That didn't count. The first time was a show for her family, the second was because she was panicking. The rest were to distract her from being trapped and possibly murdered.

Then why do you remember how soft her lips were?

I squashed that thought down. "I'm going. I'll see you tomorrow."

"Alright, brother. Take care. If you need anything, call me."

I cut the connection, then picked up the suite phone and

called down to reception. "Hi. Could you arrange for a dry cleaning service?"

"Certainly, sir. We'll send someone up."

"Thanks." I ended *that* call and walked back into the bedroom. "Where are your clothes? I've arranged for a cleaning service to come and get them." She pointed to the neat pile of clothes in one corner of the room. I gathered them up, added mine to it, and took them out to the main room.

Sure enough, a few minutes later, there was a soft tap at the door. I opened it, found a uniform-clad woman waiting with a linen bag, and tipped the clothes into it. "Thanks, honey." I passed her a folded hundred-dollar bill. "Can you get them back to me as soon as possible?"

"Thank you, and of course, sir!" She took the money, gave me a smile, and walked away.

I locked the door, then returned to the bedroom. "Did you leave me anything?" I asked, heading over to the serving trolley.

Dally laughed quietly into her mug. "Lots."

I piled up a plate of food, then sank onto the edge of the bed. "How do you feel now?"

"I still can't believe what happened. I don't understand why someone would do that."

"There could be a hundred reasons behind it. We need to figure out what we know for sure and see if anything stands out that could give us a reason."

"How do we do that?"

"I'm sure there will be a notepad and pen in the suite somewhere. We'll start with a list of names—your family members, and anyone who you think might hold a grudge."

23

Magdalena

The thought that someone had *paid* to have me grabbed and held for ransom was like a heavy weight in the pit of my stomach. What kind of person would *do* that? More to the point, was it someone we knew? A friend of the family? And why me? My sister would have been a much better target—she had a family, small children, and a husband who I'm sure would have turned the world upside down to find her.

I had no one.

A tiny circle of friends, none of whom had the kind of money they were demanding. I wasn't the most popular of my parents' children and had nothing to do with any of the businesses they'd owned and run over the years. I couldn't even tell Rook who their clients had been.

The list of potential subjects, when we were done, was short.

Me, my sister, my brother, my parents. Beneath those names, Rook had listed my sister's husband and children, as well as my roommate.

"What about girlfriends?"

"I don't know anything about Fraser's love life. I don't think he's ever brought a girl to our parents' home."

"You mentioned someone called Chantelle."

"Oh … he dated her for a couple of months. I only knew about her because he mentioned her name to me."

"What about your sister? Is she committed to her husband? She's never strayed? What about him? Affairs?"

"I don't know… I don't *think* so."

"Your roommate. You said you've known her since you were little."

"Jasmine wouldn't do something like that. She's more of a sister than my *actual* sister. And she wouldn't have the money to arrange it. They said they were paid, didn't they? I doubt it would have been cheap, and where would she have found them?"

Rook shrugged. "The dark web, or taking out an ad in local newspapers using specific words. It would surprise you how easy it is to find someone and how little it can cost. It all depends on what you want."

"Is that how you found your … *clients?*"

"No, I told you. Most of my contracts were through government agencies." His face was an unreadable mask. "I'm not ashamed of what I did, Dal. I'm *good* at it and made a lot of money."

"You killed people, though. People who didn't deserve to die."

"Do you want me to apologize for it? The world isn't black

and white, sweetheart."

"And in the *normal* world, people don't go around killing each other!"

One dark eyebrow rose. "Don't they? Or is it just given a different perspective to make it more ... palatable?" He chewed on a mouthful of food and looked at me.

"You're trying to justify what you've done with your life."

"I don't *need* to justify it, darlin'. Not to you, not to anyone. I did what I did, and I was extremely good at it. If I wasn't, we wouldn't be sitting here having this conversation."

"Do you think I should approve of the fact that you've spent years doing ... what you've done?"

"Well ..." A smirk tilted up his lips. "A thank you wouldn't be unappreciated. I did save your life *and* get you to safety, after all."

The irritating part of that was he was *right* and, from the smile on his face, he knew it. I couldn't understand a world where people *paid* to have other people killed. Maybe something showed on my face, because he sighed and set down his plate.

"In an ideal world, you would *never* have known that people like me exist," he said softly. "People like you shouldn't have darkness like mine touch them." He stood. "Get some sleep. Tomorrow you'll be safely back home and you can go back to your normal life."

"What about the one who escaped? Will he try again?"

"You don't need to worry about that. I have it under control. You won't ever see him again."

And, strangely, I believed him.

I threw myself out of the bed before I even opened my eyes, my heart hammering, and my breathing loud in my ears. In that split second between being awake and asleep, I wasn't sure if what I'd dreamed was real and I needed to know that Rook was beyond the bedroom door. That he was alive. That the kidnapper hadn't tracked us down and killed him.

I threw the door open. It banged off the wall and swung back toward me. "Rook?" My shout was frantic.

A figure rose from the couch, a shadow illuminated only by the moonlight coming in from the window. "Is everything okay?" The words ended with a grunt when I threw myself at him. "What? What's wrong?"

"There was blood. You were dead. He shot you…. There was *blood*. I thought he was here … that he'd found us. *Killed* you."

"Hey." His arm wrapped around me and I clung to him, burying my face against his chest. "No one is here."

"It was so real," I whispered. "I heard the gunshot, saw the blood. I could *smell* it. And then he saw me watching and came for me. I ran … but I couldn't get away. There was nowhere to hide. And I could see you lying there, your eyes staring straight at me… and *blood* … oh god, so much blood." My voice rose.

"You were dreaming. There's no one else here." He tipped my head back with two fingers beneath my chin. "You're safe, Dal. I'm not going to let anyone get to you."

"But you were dead." Tears welled, spilled down my cheeks when the image of him cold and lifeless filled my mind again. "Rook, you were *dead*."

He caught my hand and lifted it to his jaw. "I'm not dead. Feel that? The warmth? It was just a dream. I'm not dead and no one is coming for you."

"But—"

His thumb swept across my cheek, wiping away the tears. "Dally, stop."

I stared up at him, his face blurred through the tears I couldn't stop. He sighed and lowered his head.

"Can a dead man do this?" he whispered, and he kissed me.

L. ANN

24

Rook

I hadn't had any intention of kissing her, of touching her, of having anything other than whatever absolutely necessary interaction I had to until I could hand her off to her family. I was trying to put some distance between us, ignore the attraction she presented. But the absolute terror in her eyes, the way her voice trembled, and the tears spilling down her cheeks reached out to something inside of me. Something I thought I'd killed off a long time ago.

I kissed her because she needed a connection, the way she had back in the container. I kissed her because she needed proof that she wasn't alone, that I wasn't dead. I kissed her to stop her crying. I kissed her to confirm she was awake and not still dreaming.

But her lips parted beneath mine.

And then I kissed her because I couldn't stop.

Her hand on my jaw moved, dropping so she could loop her arms around my neck. I tightened my hold on her waist, pulled her closer, and let my tongue slip between her lips. Her hands lifted to my hair, pulling my head down further, forcing my lips onto hers harder.

I squeezed her waist, let my hand shift to her hip, following the line of the belt holding her robe closed, and I hovered over the knot.

I had to stop. Things were getting out of hand. It was just a kiss. A kiss to calm her ... and yet my fingers loosened the belt, drew it open and my hand slipped inside, finding her warm skin.

She sighed softly against my mouth, but didn't stop me. I didn't break away. I let my palm slide up over her stomach until my fingertips found the curve of her breast, and then I forced myself to lift my head.

"Dally...this has to stop."

She shook her head. "Kiss me again."

"Dal ... darlin'..." I tried again.

She didn't reply. Instead, she leaned up to find my mouth with hers again and I ... stopped ... fighting. Her hands left my hair, ran down my neck, my arms, and found the belt holding my robe closed. She hesitated, pulled her mouth from mine, and looked up at me.

I lifted a hand, ran my finger over her bottom lip. "Go back to bed. It was just a kiss. It doesn't need to turn into more."

Her eyes held mine, her tongue came out to lick at my finger, and the action hardened my dick.

Fuck.

I felt like a fucking teenager, filled with a heady need I hadn't experienced in forever, but the older, *wiser*, part of me warned me to slow down. I wanted to push her limits, make her beg me to stop. I wanted her to tell me we shouldn't. I wanted her to beg me to fuck her ... I wanted to bury myself inside her pussy ... I wanted to hear her come.

My fingers stroked over her lips, along her jaw, slid around the back of her head and tangled into her hair. I pulled her head back. "Tell me to stop." My demand was rough.

"I don't want you to stop."

Fuck.

"You don't know what you're saying."

In response, she dropped one hand and covered mine, where it rested below her breast. "I know what I'm saying. I want you to kiss me." Her fingers curled around my wrist, lifted it, and placed my palm over her breast. Her nipple beaded beneath my touch. "*Please*, Rook."

That whispered plea was my undoing, and I lowered my head and took her mouth again, backing her toward the couch. When her legs hit it and she tumbled back, I followed her down. I pulled my mouth from hers, kissed a path down her throat, nudging the material of her robe away from her body as I went until my lips found her nipple. She clutched my shoulder when I licked a circle around the stiffened peak before sucking it into my mouth.

I shouldn't be doing this. Shouldn't be touching her. She was in shock. Still processing the events of the last couple of days.

She knows what she's doing, the other part of my brain argued. *She can call a halt at any time. You told her to say stop, and she refused.*

Doesn't matter. She shouldn't—

Fuck.

Her fingers pushed between our bodies, inside the opening of my robe, and curled around my dick, splintering any final resistance I had. I lifted my head, sought out her mouth, and kissed her again. Her lips opened beneath mine, and I stroked my tongue along hers.

Our kiss became heated, teeth nipping at lips, tongues dueling, and her body moved below mine, legs parting, so I could settle between her thighs. Her hand on my dick stroked up and down, and I groaned into her mouth.

"Dally, we can't do this." I made one last half-hearted attempt to make her see reason. To convince *myself* I should call a halt to what was happening.

Her response was to give my dick a squeeze and lift one leg to hook around my hips so she could pull me closer until I could feel her wetness, her heat, her *arousal* against my thigh. I was all set to bury myself inside her, to take what she was clearly offering, when I caught myself, and pulled away.

"I don't have a condom."

She reached for me again, and I eased back.

"Dally ... Darlin', no."

"But—"

"Neither of us have any protection." I couldn't stop myself from kissing my way down her body, over her breasts, down her ribs, her stomach. My tongue circled her navel and then I was between her legs. "But it doesn't mean we can't do other things," I whispered, lowered my head and licked along the seam of her pussy.

A soft gasp escaped her. A gasp that turned into a moan when my lips closed over her clit and sucked. Her hands landed in my hair, curled against my scalp, while her legs lifted, opened wider as she writhed beneath my tongue.

I ran my fingers along her inner thigh, wrapped my hand around her leg and lifted it until it rested over my shoulder, opening her up further for my mouth to tease at her wet, willing flesh.

"Rook." My name was a broken whimper, spilling from her lips as her body jerked beneath me.

I rose up a little, so I could look at her, admire the way she was splayed out—legs as wide as they could get on the narrow couch. I ran the tip of my tongue around, then over her clit and the fingers in my hair clenched.

"Like that? How about this?" I shifted position and used the fingers of one hand to spread her open, then blew gently on the sensitive flesh I'd revealed. Her hips jerked.

I smiled and dipped my head, ran my tongue over the outer lips of her pussy, sucked first one, then the other into my mouth. I traced a circle around her clit with one finger, drawing close but not quite touching it. My tongue joined my finger, stroking, rubbing, sucking at her until she was sobbing and arching up in an attempt to bring my attention to her clit.

I ignored her, licked down until I could thrust my tongue inside her. My hands slipped beneath her ass and tipped her hips up so I could bury my face against her pussy, driving my tongue in and out. Tasting her on my tongue as she bucked and whimpered and begged.

"I'm close ... so close .." The words were a plea mixed with moans and pants as she chased my tongue. "Please, Rook. *Please.*"

Hearing her pleas made me harder, and I had a brief image of her on my bed back home, begging for my dick while she played with herself for me.

I reached up and caught her hand, pulling it out of my hair. "Touch yourself."

She didn't need me to repeat the demand, her fingers finding her clit and rubbing around it almost before I finished speaking. I watched her for a moment, noting the pattern and speed she used, filing it away for later, then bent my head, added my tongue to her play and slowly pushed one ... then two fingers inside her. She was wet, *ready*, her body almost vibrating from the stimulation of her clit, and it took no more than three or four pumps with my fingers for her to fall over the edge.

She tried to push me away, stop me from licking at her while she bucked and jerked, and I pressed one hand down on her stomach to hold her still so I could lick away the evidence of her orgasm.

I turned my head and pressed a kiss to her thigh. "Get comfortable, darlin'. We're not done yet."

Dally was fast asleep when I carried her into the bedroom, placed her on the bed and pulled the covers over her. I waited for a second to make sure she didn't wake, then slipped back through the door and into the main sitting room. It was six am, and I'd received a text to say the hotel would leave our dry-cleaning outside the door. Sure enough, it was there, in a clear wrapped package, waiting for me. I picked it up, took it inside, and opened it.

I took a quick shower, ordered coffee via room service, and was dressed before it arrived. At six thirty, my cell vibrated with an incoming call. I connected it.

"Rook." My younger brother, Knight, greeted me. "I'm down in the lobby. Are you ready to go?"

"Change of plan. Come up." I gave him the floor and room number and disconnected the call.

He was at the door a few minutes later. I pressed a finger to my lips and waved him inside. "She's still asleep. Keep your voice down. I don't want to wake her."

"Wear her out, did you?" Knight's voice was rich with amusement as he sauntered past me and flopped down onto the couch.

"Don't know what you're talking about." I picked up my coffee from the table and took a sip.

"Might want to tell her not to use your throat as a chew toy next time, then ... *if* your intention is to keep the fact you fucked her a secret." He tapped the side of his own throat and smirked at me. "Aren't you a little on the old side for hickeys?"

I rubbed the back of my neck, resisting the urge to touch the side of my throat. "It doesn't matter. I need you to take her home."

"Me? I'm here to collect *you*, aren't I?"

"I'll get a rental. Take her back to her parents' place, *not* her apartment."

"Why aren't you taking her?"

"I want to go back and do some digging into where we were kept. I also need to make sure everything is cleaned up."

Knight sighed. "Rook, *why?* You being there was a mistake. They weren't after you."

"My DNA is all over the place. I'm getting Bishop to meet me and we'll dispose of the bodies ... *if* the kidnapper hasn't been back there already. I can't see that happening, though."

"Rook—"

"Don't even try to talk me out of it. If the authorities find the location and the bodies, and link it to me, I'm fucked before it even goes to trial. I can't afford for that to happen."

My brother gave a slow nod. "I understand that, but maybe you should let Bishop organize it instead of going there yourself."

"I want to make sure it's done properly."

"You're such a fucking control freak."

I shrugged. "What's your point?"

"No point. Is there any more coffee?"

"I ordered a pot from room service. It's on the table. Help yourself. Leave some for Dall—" I cut myself off, but Knight sliced a look at me.

"Already at the nickname stage, brother?"

I shook my head. "Of course not." Setting my now empty mug down, I picked up my jacket. "Did you bring me a gun?"

Knight rolled his eyes at me and reached inside his jacket. A Sig Sauer P320 was in his hand when he pulled it back out. "I know it's not your favorite, but it's good enough until you get back home."

I took it from him and checked the mag. "Do I have to tuck it down my pants, gangster style, or did you bring me a holster?"

He sighed, rose to his feet, and shrugged out of his jacket. "Fine, take mine. *I'll* be the gangster in this story." He took off his shoulder holster, removed his gun, placing it beside him on the couch, and handed it to me.

I adjusted the size, and drew it on, tucked the gun into place, then pulled my jacket over the top. "I'm sure you have spares in the car."

He gave me a tight smile. "Of course I do. What's the plan?"

"Take her home. Make sure she's safe. Find out everything you can about her family, friends and anyone who might flag up as the potential employer."

"You're really not going to let this go?"

"Fuck, no."

25
Magdalena

I burrowed further under the covers, wanting to hang onto sleep for a little while longer. I was warm, comfortable and … my eyes popped open.

Oh … my … god!

I'd fooled around with Rook for half the night. Or, more accurately, he had spent hours with his mouth attached to my clit, until I lost count of the orgasms he'd given me.

I rolled onto my stomach and buried my face into the pillow.

I'd thrown myself at him. He tried to say no, and I wouldn't accept it. How long had he waited after I fell asleep before carrying me to the bedroom and vacating the scene of the crime?

I groaned, the sound muffled by the pillow.

How was I going to face him?

Maybe I should stay in the bedroom until it was time to leave? Could I get away with that?

I flopped onto my back and stared at the ceiling.

That wouldn't work. I had to get up and see if our clothes had been returned.

Sitting up, I looked at the door.

Go out there. Act like last night was nothing special ... unless he mentions it. Don't behave like it was the first time you'd had someone feast on you like your orgasms were the key to eternal life.

He did make you see god, though.

Don't think things like that!

I swung my legs off the bed and stood. My legs wobbled, throwing me back to the night before. My cheeks heated, and I took a breath.

Get control of yourself.

I looked around for the robe I'd worn after showering, and my eyes fell on the neat pile of clothes sitting on a chair in one corner of the room.

I guess that answered the clothes question.

Rook must have brought them into the room while I was still sleeping. The top and skirt I'd worn for dinner with my parents had been cleaned and pressed, as well as my underwear and I dressed.

Had it only been four days ago? How was I supposed to go back to normal after what had happened?

My throat tightened, and I pressed a hand against my chest, my heart rate picking up.

Don't think about it. It's over. It could have been much worse.

If Rook *hadn't* been there. If he'd been more insistent that I was talking to the wrong man, I could be dead now.

A pulse throbbed behind my eyes, an ache that hurt my head. *Stop thinking about it. He was there. You didn't die ... or worse.*
Idiot, what was worse than death?
There were three men. You know what could have been worse.

I took in another shaky breath, straightened and turned to the door.

You've just survived being held for ransom. You can survive facing a man after a one-night stand.

I stiffened my spine, walked across the room, and opened the door. My eyes fell on the jacket-clad back of the man on the opposite side of the room, pouring coffee into a mug.

My first thought was that it *wasn't* Rook, followed closely by the desire to run. I stepped back into the bedroom, wondering if I could close the door before he spotted me. I must have made a noise because he swung to face me. He looked similar to Rook.

"It's okay. Don't panic." He didn't move from his position across the room. "My name is Knight. I'm Rook's brother. I'm here to take you home."

"Where's Rook?" I didn't want to look away and check for him in case this stranger came toward me.

"He left earlier."

"Left?" *Had he left because of what happened?*

"That's right. He asked me to make sure you got home safely."

"Where did he go?"

The man—Knight—glanced away.

"Don't lie to me. Please tell me where he went."

"He's gone back to where you were both held."

That hadn't been the answer I expected, and my lips parted. *"Why?"*

Knight rubbed a hand over his jaw. "You're going to have to ask him for the answer to that."

"He's coming back before we leave?"

"Well ... no, but I'm sure you'll see him again."

I shook my head. He didn't even *sound* convincing. The fact of it was Rook had left before I woke up—and no matter what his brother claimed, I was sure it was because of what we'd done the night before.

"I need to go to the police and report what happened."

Knight shook his head. "That's not a good idea."

"Of course it is! Someone ran us off the road, then kidnapped us, and *then* forced me to record a ransom video! I need to report it so whoever was behind it can be found."

He looked at me for a long moment, then sighed, placing his mug down. "Listen, Magdalena ... that's your name, right?" He didn't wait for me to confirm. "Rook has gone back to make sure there's nothing that can be traced back to him. There are *two* bodies there. Two men that *he* killed. If you report it, they'll want to talk to him and ... that's not a good idea."

"But my parents will have been worried. They'll have already been to the police." A little voice in my head reminded me of what Rook had told me yesterday, but I ignored it. For all the problems I had with my family, they wouldn't have left me to die.

"They didn't report it. The authorities don't know anything about it."

"That's a lie."

"I'm sorry, sweetheart. I can't give you a reason, but they never contacted the police about it."

"All the more reason for *me* to talk to them."

"If you do that, they'll arrest Rook."

"What? Why?"

"He killed two men."

"To *save* me!"

"That's not how they'll see it."

I gave him a helpless look. "But one got away. What if he comes back?"

"He won't. From what Rook told me, it sounds like the intention was to grab you while you were away from your family home. Trying to take you while you were would be so much harder. They're not going to try that. And now that they're down by two men, there's a high probability that the plan will have been scrapped, anyway." He checked the watch on his wrist. "Do you need to do anything before we head out? Your home is over two hours drive from here, so we should think about leaving."

L. ANN

26

Rook

"You didn't have to come."

My brother didn't even bother gracing that with a response. He pushed away from where he leaned against his car and crossed to meet me as I slipped between the broken metal gates I'd escaped through with Dally the day before.

"How did you get in here?" I looked around.

"Wasn't difficult. Once Knight pinpointed your location from the call yesterday, I matched that to the description you gave of where you came from and figured it out." One broad shoulder lifted in a shrug. "Wasn't rocket science." He pointed behind him. "The entrance is back that way. The entire area is derelict. I can see why they chose it."

"Have you been inside?" I unholstered my gun and tapped it against my thigh.

"No, I waited for you. I sent one of my men to check the crash site last night. Nothing had been touched. Whoever this outfit is, they're not fucking professional."

"One of them is ... or *more* professional than the other two, anyway. That's why he's still alive."

"But not used to this kind of job, otherwise they'd have covered their tracks."

I walked toward the door leading into the warehouse where the container they had kept us in was located and eased it open.

"Do you think he'd have come back?"

I considered the question. "Not sure. He ran out of here yesterday with his tail between his legs. He'd just seen me shoot his remaining partner in the face, and I'm sure he was aware I'd already killed the other one. He was more interested in staying alive."

"Did you get a good look at him?"

"Enough of one so that when I catch up to him, I can rearrange his fucking features for him."

Bishop chuckled. "You're taking this very personally."

"Fucking right, I am. Have you got a flashlight?" There was a quiet click, and then the area ahead of me lit up. "That's a yes, then. Let's go." I set off, my brother on my heels, and retraced my steps from the day before.

We passed the place where I'd told Dally to wait for me in silence. Nothing appeared to have been touched or changed, and a few minutes later, we stood next to the body of the second man I'd killed.

Bishop crouched and rolled him onto his back. His fingers scratched along his jaw as he studied the body. "You made quite a mess of his face." He was referring to the fact I'd had to hit him a few times before I shot him. His nose was broken, and one of his eyes was a bloodied mess where I'd pushed one thumb into the socket.

"He went for my gun. It took a few minutes to clarify that wasn't going to happen."

My brother nodded and set to work, pulling open the dead man's shirt. "No tattoos, no scars. We don't have a lot to work with." He stood, pulled out his cell, and snapped a couple of photographs of the body. "I'll see what the team can do, though. Where's the other one?"

"In the container." I led the way, pausing at the small area where they'd had Dally record her ransom video. The video recorder and lights were missing, but the chair and table remained. I turned in a circle. "I don't know if everything had been removed before we escaped or whether he's been back since."

"We have to assume they removed it beforehand, otherwise he'd have taken care of the bodies as well."

"True."

"I'll get someone in here to try and lift prints, though. It might give us something."

I nodded. "Everything about this setup makes no sense. On the one hand, they were prepared—the container had been set up to keep her alive for at least a week with no kind of interaction, yet once they'd had her record the ransom demand, they seemed to be in more of a hurry."

"That could be because they knew who you were by then.

Killing you both makes sense at that point. They must have known there was no way you were going to quietly sit there. Maybe they thought taking action quickly would preempt anything you could have put into place."

"Maybe. But by that argument, it would have made more sense to take me out first."

"Unless they thought they could implicate you."

I swung to face my brother. "You think they were going to kill her and set me up to take the fall?"

"If they'd worked out who you are, it's the only plausible explanation. Having you found here by authorities, after your very public mistrial result last year? Come on, Rook. They wouldn't even bother trying to find out if you were innocent. They'd be all over that. It would be an immediate win for them. Taking down Rook Chambers and redeeming their original conviction, even though they wouldn't be able to repin that on you, in one fell swoop. No one would believe that the mistrial was correct after that."

I had no answer for that. He was right. The media frenzy alone would have ensured a guilty verdict before it even went to trial. I gave myself a mental shake. "The container is over here."

The body of the first guy I'd killed was right where I'd left him.

"Fuck. Did you kill this one with the girl watching?"

"Didn't have much choice."

"That's years of therapy bills in the making."

"She's still alive, isn't she?"

Bishop frowned at me. "That's cold, even for you."

"It's not cold, it's logical. If I hadn't killed him, she'd be dead. It was my only option." And I was going to kill the last man—partially because he'd fucking annoyed me, but mostly because I wanted the terror in Dally's eyes to end. I didn't want her to live the rest of her life waiting for someone to appear and grab her. To do that, I needed to find the one who'd escaped. I didn't look too closely at *why* that was the most important reason.

"This one has a tattoo. We might be able to track that and hopefully get a name." Bishop's voice intruded on my thoughts.

I nodded. "Great. It's a starting point. It might even link to the one who got away."

"If they've worked together before, it will. We'll see what my team comes up with. Let's get out of here, then I can get the cleaners in." He punched a number on his cell. "It's me. Send a team to the address I'm about to text. Make it fast. I want the entire place swept for prints and then cleaned." He cut the call, pocketed his cell and turned to me. "What now?"

"Now? Now I go home and sleep."

His eyebrow hiked. "That's it?"

"What else is there?"

"The girl...you're going to walk away from her? Just like that?"

"You know we were only pretending I was her boyfriend, right?"

"The bites on your throat suggest otherwise. Did you think I didn't notice them?"

My hand had lifted to touch the marks before I could stop

myself. "It means nothing. She was in shock and needed some way of grounding herself. I was the only available body."

Bishop snorted. "Sure … are you telling me that you fucked her out of kindness?"

"Didn't fuck her. Just made her come a few times." And, holy fuck, she'd been responsive to my touch. I'd been avoiding thinking about that, but now Bishop had put the image of her body back in my head. Of the way she held my head against her pussy and took her pleasure from my mouth and tongue. Of how her body had arched, how she'd moaned my name. How greedily she'd taken everything I gave her and demanded more.

I shook my head, dispelling the image, and spun away to regard the state we'd left the container in. My eyes fell on the flat pumps I'd told her to leave behind. Crossing to them, I stooped and picked them up.

"Get these sent back to her. She has no shoes at the hotel."

"I'm sure Knight will have left by now."

"Send them to her home."

I tossed them at him. He caught them and laughed. "Not boyfriend material at all, no sir."

"Fuck off."

27

Magdalena

"We're here." The quiet voice jolted me out of the half-doze I'd been in for most of the two-hour journey back home.

I blinked and straightened in my seat, looking at the house growing larger as we drove toward it.

"I'd rather be back in my apartment." We'd had this argument when we first got in the car.

"You know that's not wise. Stay here, with your family, until you feel safe again."

"So, forever?" I muttered the word beneath my breath.

"You *will* feel safe again, I promise. I know you don't think so right now, but you will. Give yourself some time."

"You say that, while still claiming I shouldn't report it to the police."

Knight twisted in his seat to look at me. "Look, Magdalena. I can't *stop* you from filing a report. But you need to understand that there will be repercussions from doing it. For you, *and* for Rook. The first thing they'll ask is why you didn't report it the second you escaped. How are you going to answer that?"

"Rook said—"

Knight made a noise like an buzzer going off. "Wrong. The second you say he convinced you not to do that, but to go to a hotel with him instead will make the police believe he's involved in your kidnap *or* you're lying."

"But I *wanted* to go straight to the police!"

"And if you had, Rook would have been arrested. He killed two people to get you out of there."

"I *know!* I was there!"

"Then you have to trust me when I tell you the police wouldn't have seen it as him protecting you. He's already on their radar."

"I know about him being imprisoned and then set free."

Knight's eyes widened. "He told you about that?"

"He told me a lot of things ... like what he did for a living prior to being in prison."

He stared at me.

"What?"

"Rook doesn't ... I mean ... he ..." He rubbed a hand over his jaw. "What exactly did he tell you?"

"He showed me the tattoo on his arm where he keeps his death tally."

He hadn't described it that way, but that's what it was.

Knight blinked. "He showed you his ..." He closed his mouth

with a snap of teeth and shook his head. "Do you want me to walk you inside?"

I shook my head. The last thing I needed was a witness when I confronted my parents and asked them if what I'd been told was right and they *hadn't* even tried to find me.

"Rook said I wasn't to leave until I was certain you were safely inside. I'll wait for fifteen minutes ... if you need to come back out, we'll find you somewhere else to go."

"Thank you." I looked toward the house. The main door was closed. I licked my lips, unclipped my seatbelt and opened the door.

"Hey, Magdalena?" Knight's voice stopped me as I went to climb out. I turned my head to look at him. "Rook bought the old manor house in Glenville .... If you need to reach him."

"The one on the edge of town? That's been empty for years. I'd heard someone bought it a few months ago. That was Rook?"

He nodded. "That's right. But ... if you decide to visit him, be careful, okay?"

"What do you mean?"

He sighed. "Look, I saw his neck this morning. It's clear something went on between the two of you." He held up one hand. "I'm not asking. I don't want to know. If something *happened*, and it wasn't because you thought you were going to die ... and you wanted to see if something more could come of it ... well, I'm just saying ..." He shrugged. "Take a sledgehammer with you to work on the walls, that's all."

I could feel my cheeks heating up. "He didn't even give me

a cell number to reach him on. I don't think he's interested in exploring anything further."

"Rook is ... he's used to being alone. His business required it. Maybe it's time that changed."

I frowned, but didn't reply to that. Was he suggesting I should *date* his brother? The man who had killed someone in front of me, and god knew how many others? Actually, I knew how many others. He'd *told* me.

My mind shied away from that. If I thought about it, I'd think about what I'd just survived ... and I wasn't ready to do that. I wanted to walk inside my parents' home, act normal, pretend nothing was wrong. If I started thinking about everything now, I'd curl up into a ball and cry. I had to be strong. Now wasn't the time to break down.

"Thank you for bringing me home," I said instead.

"You're very welcome." His hand landed on my arm before I stepped out of the car. "I meant what I said. I'll wait for fifteen minutes. If you need to leave, come back outside.

I nodded, climbed out, and walked toward the front door without a backward glance. My heart was hammering inside my chest, banging against my ribs, making it hard to breathe. Chills broke out across my body the closer I got to the house.

I was about to find out whether Rook had lied.

Did I want to know?

You don't believe him. He was lying.

Was he?

Your parents wouldn't leave you to die.

Wouldn't they?

My hand was shaking when I reached out to open the door. It opened on silent hinges and I stepped inside the cool hallway.

"Mom? Dad?" I called out. "Are you home?"

I don't know what I was expecting—maybe for them both to appear in front of me, expressing relief at my appearance—but silence greeted my words.

"Mom?" I raised my voice. "Dad? Are you home?"

It wasn't unusual for them not to be home—they both had a very active social life—but for there to be *nobody* in the house was... odd. I moved along the hallway and down the three steps which led to the kitchen. Pushing open the door, I let out a relieved breath when Katy turned.

"Miss McCarthy!"

"Hi, Katy. Have you seen my parents?"

"No, miss. They're away. Didn't they tell you?"

"No, I've been ... umm..." I bit my lip. I couldn't exactly tell her what I'd been doing for the past four days, not without then having to explain why I hadn't gone to the police. "I've been out of reach. Do you know when they're due home?"

"Saturday, I think. They've gone to their annual retreat in New York."

As soon as she said it, the details came back to me. My parents went away every year the day after my birthday, to a mental health retreat in New York. That explained why they hadn't responded to the ransom demand. I tried to ignore the relief I felt over the confirmation they hadn't dismissed it out of hand because they didn't care.

"Okay. I'm going to stay here until they're back. Can I use my old bedroom?"

"Yes, miss. Why don't I prepare it while you relax in the Summer Room? I'll let you know when it's ready."

28

Rook

"For fuck's sake!" I tossed the laptop onto the couch and stood.

Bishop quirked an eyebrow, but said nothing.

"How the fuck can he completely disappear?"

"You're asking *me* that?"

I nailed my brother with a glare. "Are *you* responsible?"

Bishop Chambers was well known in the underworld for being *the* person to go to if you needed to disappear. *My* talent was killing people. Knight's was finding people.

"Why the fuck would I hide him from you?" His words were mild, but I was aware I was treading on dangerous ground. You didn't accuse Bishop Chambers of betrayal unless you had cold, hard evidence, and you certainly didn't do it when he was your older brother.

Blood was stronger than money. I *knew* he wouldn't betray me, but this man had been wiped from existence so well, it would take someone with Bishop's skills to achieve it.

"You didn't get that good a look at him. You have a partial name. All we have are the two men you killed, and they barely had anything searchable. We haven't been able to find a link yet. If we had a photograph, or footage of him, Knight could do a facial recognition scan. But we have nothing like that. All we have is your vague description and a tattoo." He stood and stretched. "Maybe it's time to call it a day and move on. He's not after you, anyway."

I forced myself not to react to that. Bishop wasn't wrong. This wasn't my business, not really. My presence had been accidental, a coincidence due to Dally's mistake in coming to my table instead of someone else's. If she hadn't, I'd have been none the wiser and she ... *she'd be dead*.

I ignored the way my skin went cold at the thought. I'd spent less than a week with the girl, and it had been in a highly volatile situation. There wasn't a connection there, merely a period of forced proximity which turned into a moment of heat.

Then why do you dream about her?

"Rook?" My attention snapped back to my brother.

"What?"

"You're growling. What really happened between you and this girl?"

"*Nothing!*" That was the truth. Nothing had happened between us ... unless you counted her coming on my tongue four times. I shook my head. I *wasn't* thinking about that.

"Don't bullshit me."

I blew out a breath. "She's different."

"Different how?" He frowned. "Well, other than being the target of a ransom demand and having the best hitman in the business on the hunt for the person behind it."

"*Retired* hitman."

"Sure."

I snatched up my bottle of beer from the coffee table and took a long swallow. "I don't know, Bish. She's ... *different*."

"You like her, you mean. She's not just another warm body to spend the night with."

"She's strong. Anyone else in the situation we were in would have been a mess on the floor. And she *wanted* to break down. I could see it in her eyes. She refused to let it overwhelm her. She kept it together, held on. She was fucking terrified, but she just ... I told her what I do ... what I *did* ... and ..." I shook my head. "I don't know. She's different from the women I know."

"You *told* her you killed people for money?" The shock in my brother's voice didn't surprise me. It wasn't something I ran around sharing.

"She needed to know why she could trust me to get her out of there alive."

"And she accepted it?"

I chuckled, thinking about her reaction. "Not at first, no. But she rallied, and dealt with it. I'm telling you, Brother, *nothing* broke her. Every blow ... every single thing that happened ... it made her stronger." I couldn't hide the admiration from my voice.

"You've got it bad."

"What are you talking about?"

"I won't go so far as to use the word *love*, but you've definitely caught feelings."

"Bullshit. I just respect how well she dealt with everything." I did *not* have feelings for her. That wasn't who I was.

Bishop tipped his bottle toward me. "Whatever you need to tell yourself to sleep at night. But, I'm putting it out there. You wouldn't put this much effort into a job you're not getting paid for if you didn't have feelings for her."

"I'm putting this much *effort* in because the fucker took *me* as well."

"It's a matter of pride?"

"I can't have him running around claiming he caught me and escaped."

"Nothing to do with the fact he's running around and might come back for your girl?"

I stiffened. Bishop laughed. "You don't even need to answer that. Your body language gives you away."

"Fuck you."

My brother grinned and placed his empty bottle down. "Well, as fun as this has been, I have to get back. My empire won't run itself."

"Who are you hiding now?"

His smile turned hard. "Some mafia princess whose father pissed off the wrong man. He wants her kept well away from his business, so she's about to 'die', and her family and friends will mourn the death of their loved one. In a day or two, a kindergarten school teacher will arrive in Nowheresville, Missouri, far away from New York and her father's new enemies."

"I'm sure she'll love that lifestyle change."

"I doubt it. From my experience, these women are pampered princesses who are waited on hand and foot, and ruled over by their devoted father." His lip curled, disdain dripping from his voice. "If she's like any of the others, she'll get a taste of freedom and become a fucking nightmare to contain." He slipped on his jacket. "But that won't be my problem. That'll be her handler's."

"And you wonder why I didn't follow you into that business. A bullet to the head is much more effective ... and quicker."

"Sadly, blood and brain matter are a bitch to get out of Armani." He smoothed a hand over his jacket.

I snorted. "Like you don't know a dry cleaner who could do it with no questions asked."

"Not really the point, though." He checked the Rolex on his wrist. "Okay, I have to go or I'll be late." I walked out with him, propped my shoulder against the doorframe, and watched as he climbed into his car. "If you think of anything that'll help your search, call Knight. I'm going to be out of touch for the next forty-eight hours," he called, lifted a hand to wave, and then reversed down my drive.

I went back inside, locking the door behind me. A week had passed since walking out of the hotel room and leaving Dally with

Knight. I'd reached a dead end in my search for the remaining man behind the kidnapping/ransom. Knight didn't have enough information to be able to make use of his usual sources, and I couldn't find anyone who looked even remotely like the guy in the database of potentials my brother had sent to me.

I dropped onto the couch, reached forward for my beer, and took a mouthful. I had to be missing something, some connection that would lead from Dally to the kidnapper in some way.

Maybe I was looking at it wrong. I rubbed a hand over the back of my neck. We'd been focusing on her parents being the primary targets, but what if they weren't? What if the true target was her sister or brother or even Dally herself?

I pulled the file Knight had sent to me closer and flipped it open, focusing on the photograph of the girl who'd hired me to be her boyfriend two weeks ago.

"Come on, Dal, what am I missing?" I tapped the image with one finger, then flicked through the pages stapled to it, detailing her life from birth to twenty-four. There was *nothing*, no reason for her to be targeted other than her parents having money … which took me back to her parents or siblings.

I went to grab another beer from the kitchen, taking the file with me, and settled at the table, spreading the pages out. I was pouring over the information when I heard a noise. My head lifted, and I frowned, listening.

There it was again. The scrape of a shoe against stone. I stood, reached for my pistol where I'd left it on the countertop, flicked off the safety and moved through the house so I could exit out of the front door.

On silent feet, I made my way around the building. A figure stood in front of the door, which led to my kitchen, fingers curling around the handle as I watched. I moved closer and placed my gun against their temple.

"Talk fast. Who are you and what do you want?"

L. ANN

29

Magdalena

I think maybe a part of me knew that once everything was quiet, and I stopped finding things to do, a delayed reaction to what had happened would finally hit, so I kept myself busy. I tidied up the bookcases in the Summer Room, organizing the books by author, color and height. I watered the plants in the dining room, plumped the cushions on the couch in the sitting room, and straightened the chess board, resetting the game that had resulted in black winning.

The staff at my parents' house didn't live there, and by the time I ran out of things to do, they had left me alone. It was a little before midnight when I finally walked around the house, making sure the doors and windows were locked, and made my way upstairs to the bedroom I'd grown up in.

The room hadn't changed since I moved out on my twentieth birthday, and I had stayed in it a total of three times since then. I pulled open the drawers on the dresser, found an old pair of pajamas, clean underwear, and then walked into the adjoining bathroom. There were bottles of bubble bath on one shelf. I opened and sniffed at each one before picking the raspberry scented one. I started the bath running, poured some of the bubble bath into it, then stripped out of my clothes while I waited for the water to fill the bath.

Sinking into the scented water a short time later, I let my head rest against the back of the tub and closed my eyes, only to surge up seconds later when a noise broke the silence—a gunshot. Heart racing, I grabbed the towel and almost threw myself out of the bath.

Had he come back? The man who'd grabbed us? Was he here to finish the job?

Wrapping the towel around my body, I crossed the room and reached for the door, only to freeze.

What if he was waiting in the bedroom?

My heartbeat was loud in my ears, my mouth dry, as I slowly turned the handle. No one jumped out at me when the door swung open, and the room beyond was empty.

I let out a shaky breath and stepped into the bedroom. My eyes fell on the digital alarm clock on my nightstand, and I frowned. Half an hour had passed since I went into the bathroom.

Wait ...

Had I fallen asleep?

Had I dreamed the noise?

I walked over to the bedroom door and opened it to look out.

The hallway beyond was in darkness and silent.

I must have imagined it.

Closing the door, I turned the lock and turned to look around. I'd go to bed, sleep, and things would look better in the morning.

Things *didn't* look better in the morning, or the next, or the one after that. For the three nights following the day Knight dropped me at their house, I barely slept.

During the day, it was easier. The staff were in the house and I spent most of my time in the kitchen with Katy and the cook. My parents still hadn't returned home and, once I realized where they'd gone, I knew they would have given up their cell phones or any means of outside contact for another week. I cursed the timing. They went to this retreat every year, but with everything that had happened, I had forgotten all about it.

At night, after the staff had left, I would go to my bedroom, lock the door and sit in the center of my bed, fighting against sleep and praying that when I lost the battle, it would not be full of nightmares. Every time my eyes closed, I heard gunfire, shouts, and found myself back in the container. Only this time Rook wasn't there to save me, and I'd wake up screaming less than thirty minutes after falling asleep.

By day six, I could barely keep my eyes open, and I knew I couldn't carry on like that. I couldn't stay in the house alone at night. I was sure I was going crazy. And then Knight's words came back to me…

I was sitting on the stairs when Katy and the cook walked toward the main doors. I jumped to my feet.

"Could you drop me off in town?"

Katy glanced at the cook, who nodded, and I followed them out to her car and slipped into the back seat. They dropped me near the train station, and I bought a ticket back to Glenville. Knight had said Rook bought the old manor house at the edge of town. That was a ten-minute walk from the station, and I drew the hood up on my jacket, shoved my hands into my pockets and set off.

It was dark by the time I reached it, and I checked over my shoulder during the entire walk, half-expecting someone to jump out and grab me at any moment. The long, curving drive was overgrown and my nerves were unraveling by the time I reached the house itself. I knocked on the front door and waited.

No one answered. I knocked again. Still nothing. A light shone through one of the windows. Maybe he couldn't hear me, so I set off to find the back door. I stumbled on a loose stone and flung out a hand to stop myself from falling. I caught the door handle and froze.

Cold metal touched my temple. "Talk fast. Who are you and what do you want?"

"Please don't shoot me." The words tumbled from my lips.

"*Magdalena?*" The gun didn't move from my head. "What are you doing here? No, don't answer that. Open the door and go inside."

"Will you...?" I cleared my throat. "Could you move the gun?"

"No." His voice was sharp, angry. "Open the door... slowly."

My hand shook as I curled my fingers around the handle and pushed it down. The door swung open, and I took a step forward, into a brightly lit kitchen. I stopped, and the gun tapped against my temple. "Keep going. Over to the table and sit down."

I swallowed. "Are you going to shoot me?"

"I haven't decided yet. Move."

The chill in his voice scared me. I hadn't expected hugs and kisses when I turned up, but I hadn't thought, for a second, he'd hold a gun to my head.

Why was he acting like I was here to kill him?

"Rook..."

"Pull out a seat and sit down. Place your hands on the table where I can see them."

I did as he said, sitting on the nearest chair and flattened my palms onto the tabletop. "Could you please move the gun?" I whispered.

"How did you find me?" The relief when the gun left my temple was short-lived when he rounded the table and faced me. He kept the gun leveled at me, his aim steady.

"Your brother told me you'd bought the manor house."

"Why are you here?"

"Because I didn't know where else to go! My parents aren't home. The house is empty at night."

"Where are your parents?"

"At a retreat. They go to one every year after my birthday. So my mother can ...." I shrugged. "I *don't know!* Get over my birth?"

He frowned, but said nothing. He didn't lower the gun, either.

"I can't stand it." I whispered.

"Stand what?"

I ignored the question. "I have money. I want to hire you to find him. To do ... whatever it is you do. I need to know he's not coming back."

"You want to hire me to hunt him down and kill him?" There was no inflection at all in his voice. He could have been asking me what the time was.

"You don't understand. Every time I hear a noise I think *he* has come back, that I'm going to wake up back in that container. I can't *sleep!* I close my eyes, and I'm back there ... but this time you're not there and I can't get out. I can't leave. And they keep coming back and making me beg for money, for my *life. I can't sleep!*"

I was shrieking, my fingers curling into fists on the tabletop. I took in a shuddering breath and lowered my voice. "Rook, I can't sleep. It's been six days and I think I'm going crazy. I need this to be over."

He stared at me, his dark eyes giving nothing away, but that damned gun didn't move from where it was pointing at me.

"Stand up."

I shoved to my feet, fear and exhaustion overwhelming me. "Are you going to kill me now?"

"Head through the door on the left. I'll be right behind you."

ROOK

30

Rook

I followed her out of the kitchen and into the hallway, lowering the gun and tucking it into my belt. I wasn't really going to shoot her. She wasn't a threat to me. I'd been surprised to see her and gone on autopilot. The desperation in her voice had finally got through, though, but by that point I was committed to the path I'd chosen and saw no reason to alter it. Not yet, anyway.

"Up the stairs." I didn't tell her the gun was no longer aiming at her, and she didn't look back to check. "First door on the left. Go inside."

"Rook—"

"Keep moving. We'll talk when I say we'll talk." I threw that out solely to see how she'd react. Her spine stiffened. I smiled. She wasn't as scared of me as she thought she was. I wondered how long it would take for her to realize I wasn't going to shoot her.

We reached the door I'd mentioned, and she lifted a shaking hand to open it. I followed her in and watched as she looked around.

"Turn around."

She slowly turned to face me. I kept one hand on the gun's grip, ready to draw it if I needed to. I had no intention of pulling the gun on her again, but she didn't know that.

"Where did your parents go?"

Her eyes were on the gun, but she lifted them at the sound of my voice. "They usually go to a place in New York for two weeks."

"You said they always go away after your birthday. You never mentioned it while we were kidnapped."

"I ..." she swallowed. "I didn't think about it. I thought we were going to die. The last thing on my mind was whether my parents had gone away."

"Didn't you call them?"

"The place they go to has a no cell phone/no outside contact for the duration of the retreat policy."

I nodded. It put an interesting slant on the whole kidnap. Whoever was behind it must not have known they would be out of contact. Maybe they hadn't refused to pay the ransom, after all. Maybe they simply hadn't been aware of it.

"Tell me about the house. You said there are staff there during the day?"

She nodded. "A cook and maid. You ... you saw Katy at dinner."

I thought about that night. Dally had held a brief conversation with the girl who had served us. I'd gotten the impression they were hiding a friendship from her mother.

"And they don't live in the house?"

"No. They come in daily."

"Even when your parents aren't home?" I thought that was peculiar.

"My parents like them to be there in case my sister or brother go home."

"Do they often do that?"

"My brother does. My sister doesn't do it as often now she's married."

"Did your brother come home at all this week?"

"No."

"Hmm." I waved a hand toward her. "Take your clothes off."

She blinked. "Excuse me?"

"Clothes. Remove them."

"I don't ... *why?*"

I raised the gun slightly and tapped it against my thigh. "Because I'm armed and you're not?"

"You'll shoot me if I don't?"

I shrugged. "Jury's out. I haven't decided yet. You're stalling. Remove the clothes."

"*Why?*"

"Because if you don't, I will. You don't want me to take that step."

She glared at me, and I wondered if she'd fight me on it. I half-hoped she would, but after a second or two, she pulled the hoodie over her head and dropped it to the floor. The plain black t-shirt followed.

"Leave the bra." I stopped her when her hands reached around to unhook the bra. "Take off the jeans."

Her hands shook when she popped the button and pushed the denim down her legs. I knew what she was thinking. Right now, it suited me for her to believe I was going to take advantage of her.

"No, don't take off your panties." I pushed away from the doorframe and stepped deeper into the room. She shuffled backward. "Get on the bed."

"I don't—"

"Don't forget I have a gun." That was a low blow, and she flinched. "Bed, Dal."

She glanced behind her and then sat on the edge of the mattress. I rolled my eyes. "Get *on* the bed properly, beneath the covers."

"Why are you doing this? I thought you'd help me." Tears spilled down her cheeks as she followed my instructions, drawing her legs up and wrapping her arms around them.

"Lie down." She shuffled down the bed and dragged the sheets up to her chin. "Great. Good girl. Now close your eyes and go to fucking sleep. We'll talk about your insane idea to hire me tomorrow." I turned, flicked off the light, and walked out, closing the door behind me.

Could I have simply told her to get some sleep before regaling me with her madcap scheme to hire a retired hitman to take out a kidnapper? Sure, I could. But that wouldn't have been as effective in showing her how fucked up people could be.

I headed back down to the kitchen, opened a fresh bottle of beer, and returned to where I'd left the file full of everything I knew about her and her family. Pulling the sheet with her parents' details toward me, I scowled down at it.

Why hadn't Knight picked up on the fact they were out of contact? There was no record of these retreats Magdalena said they went on.

I reached for my cell and hit my brother's number. "Can you do a deep dive on Dally's parents?"

"You think they have something to do with it?"

"I'm not sure. Apparently, they go on a retreat the day after her birthday to a place in New York for a two week stay."

"Shouldn't whoever was behind the kidnapping have known that?"

"If they'd done their homework, you would think so. Something is off with this, Knight."

"I'll see what I can dig up."

"Thanks." I cut the call and tossed my cell onto the table. "What am I missing?" I muttered.

I was *still* trying to find the answer when a scream echoed through the house. I grabbed my gun and was running toward the bedroom I'd left Dally in before it fell silent. Throwing the bedroom door open, I scanned the room and found her sitting up in the bed, hands covering her mouth, eyes wide.

I tossed the gun onto the chair and crouched beside the bed. "Talk to me."

"I heard ... oh god ... he grabbed me ... he grabbed me and ..."

"Take a breath. No one is here. Just me and you."

Her fingers fisted into her hair, and her head bowed. "I can't ...

I can't... I need you to find him. *Find him*, Rook."

Her belief that I could fix this, that I could find and take out the man who had kidnapped her, took me aback. I straightened, turned, and sat on the edge of the mattress beside her.

"Is this how it's been since you went home?"

She nodded.

I sighed. "Dal, listen to me. The chances of him coming to get you again are low. You need some time to process what happened. Sleep will help."

"When I sleep, I dream. I *can't* sleep without seeing his face, without everything playing out differently in my head. You said you killed people for money. I want to hire you to do this."

"No, you don't."

"Why won't you do it? I *have* money. I can pay you."

"It's not about the money, darlin'." I reached out and touched her cheek. "Look at me." I waited until she lifted her head. "As much as he deserves to die, you don't want the weight of that responsibility. You're not thinking clearly. You're tired and you're scared, and you're looking for a way to combat that. To take back control. But trust me, darlin', this isn't the way." While I spoke, I eased her legs down and pushed her back until she lay against the pillows. She stared up at me.

I rubbed a hand over my jaw. "Okay. Look, if you try to get some sleep, we'll talk about this in the morning." She said nothing. I sighed. "Fine. Scoot over."

"Why?"

"Do I need to get my gun again?"

Her eyes narrowed, but she shifted to the center of the bed.

"Roll onto your side." I gestured to the wall, and she moved until her back was to me. I toed off my boots and swung my legs up onto the mattress. "No one is getting in here, you know that, right? I have this place locked down tight." I slipped an arm around her waist and pulled her back against me. "Go to sleep, Dal. You can trust me to keep you safe, the same way I did in the container. No one is going to get you while I'm here." I slid my other arm beneath her head and wrapped her in an embrace. "Close your eyes, darlin'. Time to sleep, now."

L. ANN

31

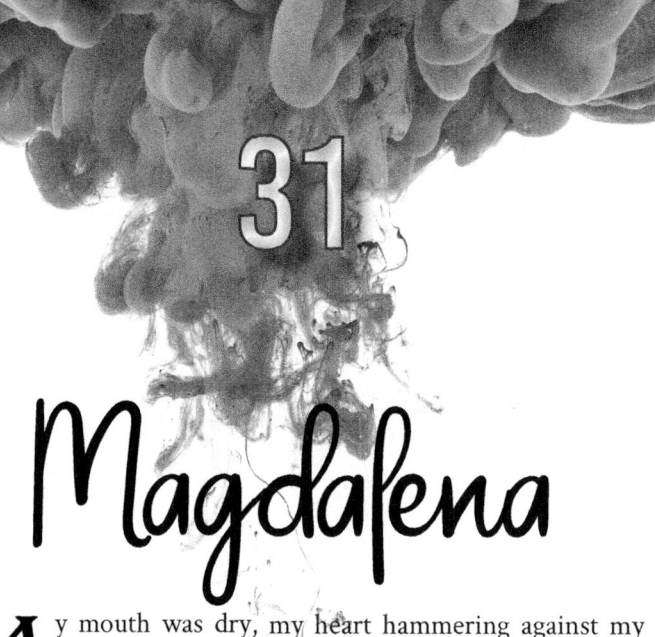

Magdalena

My mouth was dry, my heart hammering against my ribs, and the scream tore from me seconds before my eyes snapped open. A heavy weight held me in place, and I struggled against it, bucking and writhing in a bid to escape.

"Stop it." The snapped words hit me like a bucket of ice-cold water and I froze, memories of the last couple of hours coming back.

I was in Rook's home. In Rook's *bed*, and not in the container, trapped and alone.

"Back with me?" A shadowy form leaned over me, and I blinked up at it, trying to see through the darkness of the room. I recognised his voice, though, and knew it was Rook.

I licked my lips. "I think so."

"Are your dreams always that bad? You've only been asleep for twenty minutes."

"I told you I couldn't sleep, that I keep dreaming I'm back there." My voice sounded thick, raspy to my own ears.

"There? In the container?"

"Yes." The mattress moved, and I found myself tugged into the warmth of his body, his arm sliding beneath me to wrap around my waist again.

"Tell me about it. How does it start? Do you relive being taken, or are you already there when the dream starts?"

"Already there. I wake up on the cot like ... like I did that first day. I'm alone. You're not there. I expect you to be. I *look* for you. But the more I search, the darker it gets and I hear footsteps. They get louder and louder until they're echoing around my head." My heart rate was increasing and my words almost fell over each other as I hurried to explain it.

Rook's palm pressed against my stomach. "Take a breath. Slow down. You're not there, you're here. Ground yourself."

I could feel my pulse hammering in my throat. "How?"

"Close your eyes. Take a deep breath. What happens when you hear the footsteps?"

I squeezed my eyes closed. "The door opens. There's light coming in from outside. It lights up the area in front of the door."

"Is someone there? Do you see them?" His thumb stroked a small circle on my stomach, and that, combined with his calm, quiet voice, soothed my nerves.

"N-no. When the door opens, the footsteps stop. I know he's out there, but he's waiting for me to leave the container."

"Do you leave?"

I clutched the sheets in front of me. Rook ran his hand down my arm, interlaced his fingers with mine, and squeezed. "Take another breath, Dal." His other hand was still pressed against my stomach. "Deep breaths."

I did as he said, taking a deep breath in through my nose and then out through my mouth.

"I have no choice but to leave. Once the door opens, the room starts to shrink. The walls close in and I can't stay there. I run outside. I know he's there, in the shadows, waiting. I can hear his breathing, so I run as fast as I can." I licked my lips. "There's barely enough light for me to see a door and I run toward it. But I'm not fast enough. I'm *never* fast enough. And he grabs me just before I reach it."

"Relax." His voice was close to my ear, and the word drew my attention to the way my body had tensed. "Is that when you wake up?" The hand on my stomach moved again, his fingers tracing a pattern around my navel. "Keep breathing. What happens next?"

"He pulls me away from the door. I fight him, screaming at him, and then he pulls out a gun." I pause and let loose a shaky breath. "He points it at me, and as he pulls the trigger, I wake up."

"Do you see his face?"

"I see his face every time I close my eyes." I admitted in a whisper.

"You know that might not change even if I kill him."

"But I'll *feel* safer. I won't be watching every shadow waiting for him to step out of them."

"You know the nightmare is your mind's way of trying to reconcile what you went through. Killing him won't stop them."

"Then what should I do?"

"Find a way to live with what you experienced. Become stronger from it."

It sounded easy when he said it, and the conviction in his voice almost made me believe it was possible. But I knew it was temporary. As soon as I closed my eyes, the nightmares would begin again. I didn't say anything, and we lay together, with only the sound of our breathing breaking the silence. His fingers continued stroking light patterns across my stomach, and my eyes drifted closed, my body relaxing back against his.

"Why did you leave the hotel without saying goodbye?"

His breath was warm against my shoulder as he sighed. "I didn't want to make things awkward for you. What happened... I shouldn't have taken advantage of you like that. I thought you would be more comfortable if I wasn't there when you woke up."

"I knew what I was doing!"

"It was a natural reaction. You've been through an experience where you almost died. You needed a connection, something to prove that you were still alive."

"So you were... what? *Grounding* me?"

The hand on my stomach stilled, and he chuckled. "To begin with, maybe.

I stiffened. "I'm sorry for being such a chore for you."

"Oh, you've been many things since you burst into my life, but I wouldn't call you a chore." His voice was a husky whisper.

"What would you call me, then?" My heart rate had increased

again, only this time not in fear.

He moved behind me, his fingers unlinking from mine to run up my arm to my shoulder. "Annoying … Irritating … Distracting …" One finger hooked beneath my bra strap and slowly drew it down. "Brave … Strong … Infuriating …" His lips kissed my shoulder. "Fascinating … Tempting … Intoxicating …"

L. ANN

32

Rook

She was everything I avoided in a woman—too sweet, too *normal*, too fucking young. The women I usually bedded were cynical, older, and understood that any time spent between the sheets was scratching a mutual itch and nothing more.

But with Magdalena ... *Dally* ... She wasn't a fuck 'em and flush 'em kind of girl. Even without everything that had gone on, she wouldn't be a one-night-stand dance-between-the-sheets temporary distraction. This girl was a white picket fence, two-point-four kids, and a dog, full-on relationship, and even as I lowered my head, I knew I was playing with fire. And yet...

My fingers toyed with her bra strap while I kissed my way over her shoulder, up her throat until my lips were against her ear. "Are you sure?"

In response, her face turned toward me, and her hand reached back to curve over my jaw so she could pull me closer. She pressed a soft kiss against my lips, then another, before parting her mouth from mine. "You smell good," she whispered.

I lifted a hand to cup her jaw, turned her face away from me and closed my teeth over the lobe of her ear, nipping gently. My other hand, still flattened against her stomach, stopped her from twisting to face me, but her back arched.

My hips shifted against her, bringing her into closer contact with my erection, and her breathing turned shallow. She closed her eyes, lips parting so her tongue could lick along them.

"I want more."

"I know." I let my hand smooth over her stomach, down toward the lacy edge of her panties, sank the fingers of my other hand into her hair to tug her head back around to mine, and crushed my mouth to hers.

And, just like that, it spiraled out of my control. Dally clung to my neck and kissed me back, her tongue stroking against mine. Her ass pressed against my erection and I bit back a groan. Her answering moan shot through my veins like wildfire. Our kiss turned fierce, no teasing touches or hesitant kisses. It was all heat and hunger. I couldn't deny that I wanted her. All of her. Not just the sample I'd had back at the hotel.

I slid my palm down over the silk covering her pussy, squeezed her through the panties and moved my mouth to her throat, pressing quick, biting kisses over her flushed skin.

"You know nothing good can come of this," I warned her, lifting my head to meet her eyes, "but I want you." My fingers pressed against her through the silk, feeling the wetness of her arousal.

She gasped and pressed her mouth to mine, her tongue

plunging between my lips. I pulled my mouth away from hers again, pushed her panties to one side and thrust a finger inside her. She pressed against me, a moan falling from her lips.

"More!"

I added a second finger, thrusting them into her body, and dragged down the cup of her bra with my other hand. Her breasts were full, nipples hard and jutting out, begging for attention. I curved my hand over one, my thumb sweeping across her nipple, and she arched into the caress.

"Oh, God, Rook... this is... I need you... please" She twisted, dislodging my fingers from her body, until she faced me and grabbed a fistful of my shirt in her fingers. "Please..."

I leaned back, pulled the shirt over my head and threw it to one side without breaking eye-contact. Our lips met again, and her hand dropped to fumble with the button on my pants, dragging them open. Before she could thrust a hand inside, I caught her hips and rolled, pinning her beneath me.

She clutched at me, lifting her legs and linking her ankles behind my back, her hands sinking into my hair. I rocked my hips against her, and she groaned against my mouth.

"Now," she pleaded. "Now." Her hand dropped, pushed between our bodies and down until her fingers could curl around my erection. "Please, Rook."

I let my eyes close, savoring the way she gripped me, the way her fingers wrapped around my dick and slid up and down in a steady rhythm, until I could stand it no longer. I rolled away, shoved my pants down my legs, and returned to her. My fingers stroked over her breasts, around her nipples, and I watched the way her body responded, how her breath hitched, while her skin pebbled and tightened under my caresses.

The way she'd responded to my tongue at the hotel was imprinted on my brain, the way she'd moaned and writhed, begged and pleaded. I'd fought not to think about it, but now she was here, in my bed again, and I was too enamored with her to walk away.

I caught a nipple between my teeth, nipped at it, enjoying her sharp intake of breath, and then her hand landed in my hair, fingers curling against my scalp, and her back bowed again.

"Again," she demanded.

I did as she asked, caging her nipple with my teeth and flicking my tongue over it, tugging it out and away from her body until it pulled free. I curved my hands over her breasts, squeezed them, pressed them together, *plumped* them up while I lapped, licked, and sucked at them. Until she was writhing and whimpering beneath me.

She dragged my head back up to hers, her ass lifting, hands clutching to pull me closer, so she could rub against me. I pushed my thigh between her legs, and she ground her pussy against it.

"Rook." My name was a moan falling from her lips. *"Please!"*

Any thought of refusing her was a distant memory, and I reached for the drawer on my nightstand to pull it open and take out a condom. I placed it on the bed. Leaning forward, I hooked my fingers into her panties, drew them down her legs, and tossed them to one side. I came down over her, arms braced either side of her body, and settled between her legs. My dick slid along her pussy, and she bit her lip. I lowered my head, replaced her teeth with mine, and bit into her bottom lip gently, then slid down her body so I could press a kiss to her pussy.

Using my thumbs, I spread her open and gave her pussy one long lick. Her body jerked. I did it again. Her hands came down to push at my shoulders. I ignored her, flicking my tongue over her clit. She gasped, bucked, forgot she was trying to stop me and let me feast on her until she was whispering my name like a prayer. I pushed a finger inside… two… a third… pumping them in and out in time with the rhythm of my tongue, and felt her tighten around them.

"Oh god… oh… " Her words turned into intelligible moans, and then into breathless sobs as my fingers and tongue drove her toward orgasm and as she fell over the edge, I rose up and reached for the condom.

Her body was still jerking and pulsing when I pressed my dick against her and pushed inside. Her legs lifted, wrapped around my hips, and she moved in time to my thrusts. Her lips found my throat, pressed biting kisses along it, and I *knew* I'd have the evidence on display tomorrow.

She was a biter. I'd learned that at the hotel when she'd latched onto me with her mouth and nipped and sucked at my skin while I made her come with my fingers. And I was more than okay with that. I *liked* the small stings of pain she dealt.

Her fingers slid down my back, nails scraping along my spine, and she begged me to take her harder, faster, *deeper*. I hooked my hands under her ass, tilted her up at a better angle and complied, driving us both up the bed. My fingers stroked over her clit, teasing until she threw her head back, her eyes squeezed shut, and tumbled over into another orgasm.

The way her body clenched and pulsed around me broke the last of my control, my nerves stretched and tightened, and I hurtled over the cliff after her.

33

Magdalena

I was still catching my breath when Rook eased off me. His lips brushed over my shoulder, and then he was moving, rising to his feet.

"Where are you going?" I couldn't stop myself from blurting the words. *Was he going to disappear like he did in the hotel?*

He stopped in the doorway, turned, and studied me, his eyes tracking over my body. I *felt* that look like a physical touch. "Bathroom to clean up. Don't move." And with that, he disappeared through the door.

I rolled onto my side, and reached behind me to unhook my bra and pull it off, laughing to myself at the way it had twisted and tangled. I threw it to the floor and tugged the sheets up over me. Now I'd lost the heat of his body, I could feel the chill in the air. My eyes were drifting closed when the bed dipped, and I blinked them open to find Rook sliding beneath the covers beside me.

Before I could say anything, his arm wrapped around my

waist and tugged me across the bed until he could tuck me into his side.

"This wasn't meant to happen." He kissed the top of my head.

I digested the words. It didn't *sound* like he was regretting it, but I couldn't be sure. I raised my head to look at him.

"Don't look at me like that," he muttered, letting his own head drop back against the pillows. "I'm old enough to be your father."

"I doubt that."

"Fine. Maybe not *quite* that old, but still. There's at least fourteen years' difference between us, and you don't belong in my world."

I curled against him, tracing around the tattoo covering his chest. "Are you saying this is a one-night stand?"

He made a noise... I was sure it was a growl. "I should say yes to that question."

"But you're not going to?" I tried to keep my voice light, but butterflies danced around my stomach.

His sigh was heavy. "No, I'm not going to."

The butterflies in my stomach settled. "Does that mean you're accepting my job offer?"

I found myself on my back with him poised above me. "No, it fucking doesn't."

I blinked up at him. "But—"

"Oh, don't get me wrong, darlin'." He didn't give me the chance to finish my protest. "I'm going to find that bastard and kill him, but I'm *not* taking your money for it."

"You're not? But I thought this is what people hired you for."

"They *did*. I'm retired." He rolled away and onto his back, then pulled me into his body again. "But you're not hiring me for this." His hand squeezed my hip. "We'll talk about it tomorrow. This isn't an after-sex conversation, darlin'."

I laughed and dropped my head against his chest. "What *is* an after-sex conversation... in your world?"

His chuckle vibrated against my cheek. "I have no fucking idea. I rarely stick around long enough to have them. This is unfamiliar territory for me."

I smiled, liking the way those words warmed me. "Why, Mr. Chambers," I affected a 'southern belle' accent. "Am I popping your after-sex conversation cherry?"

"Yes, ma'am."

My fingers returned to the tattoo covering his chest, stroking over the bold black lines and following the pattern as it swirled around his nipple and down over his ribs. His stomach muscles tightened as my fingertips stroked over them.

"Are you ticklish?"

"No." He reached up and captured my fingers. "Bruised ribs from the beating they tried to give me when they drove us off the road."

"Oh!" I rose up on one elbow to look down and, sure enough, I could see yellow and purple bruising beneath the tattoos. "Are you sure they're not broken?"

"I'm fine, Dal. I've had broken ribs before. This isn't it." He placed my hand back on his chest and rested his own on top of it. "You should get some sleep if you want me to listen to all the reasons why I should let you be involved in finding out who is behind your kidnapping."

"How did you know I was—?"

His laugh was low and rich. "Did you *really* think I believed you would want to hire me, and then sit at home and wait for my report? What you went through would have broken anyone else, but you ... you haven't let it overcome you."

"That's not true. I'm *scared*, Rook. Scared he'll come back for me again. *That's* why I need to be involved."

"Fear isn't a bad thing, darlin'. Listening to your fear can keep you alive." His hand stroked down my spine. "We'll talk about it tomorrow, *after* we've slept."

"But—"

"No, Dal." He stretched out an arm and hit a button on the wall beside the bed. The room went dark.

"The light switch is next to your bed?"

"It always seemed stupid to have only the one light switch *and* it be on the opposite side of the room. I like to see where I'm going, so I added a second one close to the bed." He shifted on the bed, drawing the covers up and over us both. "Get some sleep, now."

We lay in the darkness, my head resting against his shoulder, his fingers skimming up and down my back lightly, and the gentle caress combined with the steady beat of his heart in my ear relaxed me, until my eyes drifted closed.

The sun was streaming through a gap in the curtains when I woke up. I was lying on my stomach, one hand tucked beneath the pillow, head turned toward the window and the light shone directly onto my face. I blinked, buried my face into the pillow, and took a deep breath. My lungs immediately filled with the scent of Rook's cologne, and my body came to life.

There was an ache between my legs, my nipples were sensitive against the cotton sheets, and images from the night before flooded my mind. Of Rook's hands on my body, his mouth, the way he felt inside me. Heat warmed my skin, and I burrowed deeper under the sheets.

"I know you're awake." Rook's rich, deep voice broke the silence and I couldn't contain a gasp of surprise. "Coffee's brewing. Throw some clothes on and come down to the kitchen."

I rolled onto my back and pushed up on one elbow to look at him. He stood in the doorway, one shoulder propped against the frame, dressed in black pants and a crisp white shirt.

"Where are you going?"

His brow pleated. "Nowhere. Why?"

I waved a hand at him, covering my mouth with the other as I yawned. "You're overdressed for just hanging around the house."

His eyebrows rose. "Maybe I'm making up for you being *underdressed.*"

"Whose fault is that?" My voice was tart. Apparently, having sex with him had made me brave. "You held me at gunpoint and forced me to strip."

"And now I'm telling you to get dressed." He pushed away from the wall, stepped into the room, stooped to pick up his shirt from the floor, and tossed it at me. "Put that on and come downstairs."

"Will you point your gun at me again if I don't?"

He scratched his jaw, looking at me. "Will it make you do what I want?"

I pursed my lips, considering it, then nodded. "Probably."

"Then, yes, I will. Do I have to go get my gun?" His tone suggested he was prepared to do just that.

I sighed. "No."

A smile flickered across his face. "Good girl. Get dressed. We need to talk."

At any other time, those words would have filled me with dread. But right here, coming from Rook, they made me sit up straighter and grab the shirt he'd thrown at me. I pulled it on, threw back the sheets, and stood. Rook's eyes tracked up my legs, followed the path of my fingers as I buttoned the shirt closed, then lifted to my face.

"Come here." HIs voice was soft.

I crossed the carpet and stopped in front of him.

"In a perfect world, we would never have met, yet I can't help but wonder what would have happened to you if you *hadn't* messed up the table numbers. Do you believe in fate, Dally?" He lifted a hand and tugged a lock of my hair. "I've been in too many situations where everything needs to be ... just so ... for everything to work out ... and this feels like one of those times."

"You think some higher power sent me to you?" I tipped my head back to meet his eyes.

"Nothing like that." He laughed. "Come on." He turned away, leaving me staring at his back, and walked out.

I followed him along the hallway and down the stairs. The floors on the lower level were dark wood, warm underfoot, and I wondered if he had installed underfloor heating. I'd heard that when the manor house had been bought, a lot of work had been done on it and, looking around, I could definitely see where things had been updated.

"Take a seat." Rook nodded toward the large table, which took up the center of the kitchen, when we entered the room.

I pulled out a chair and sat down, glancing at the papers spread out across the tabletop. One in particular caught my eye, and I dragged it toward me.

"This is *me*!" I flicked through the pages that had been stapled together. My name jumped out at me, my photograph, and the name of my doctor. "My entire life. My *medical* records. How did you get all this?"

"You met my brother, Knight. He's a computer genius. Nothing is hidden from him."

"But *why*? Why do you have it?"

"Coffee first. How do you take it?"

"You mean that isn't in your report?"

His eyebrow arched. I huffed. "White, with sweetener." I stared down at the photograph of myself stapled to the front sheet. I remembered when it had been taken. I'd been to a party with Jasmine only a couple of months earlier. In the photograph, I was walking down the steps, out of a house, laughing at something someone out of the shot had been saying.

I should be angry at the clear invasion of my privacy, maybe disturbed by how much information Rook had in front of him. But I wasn't. Instead, I felt ... *safe*.

34

Rook

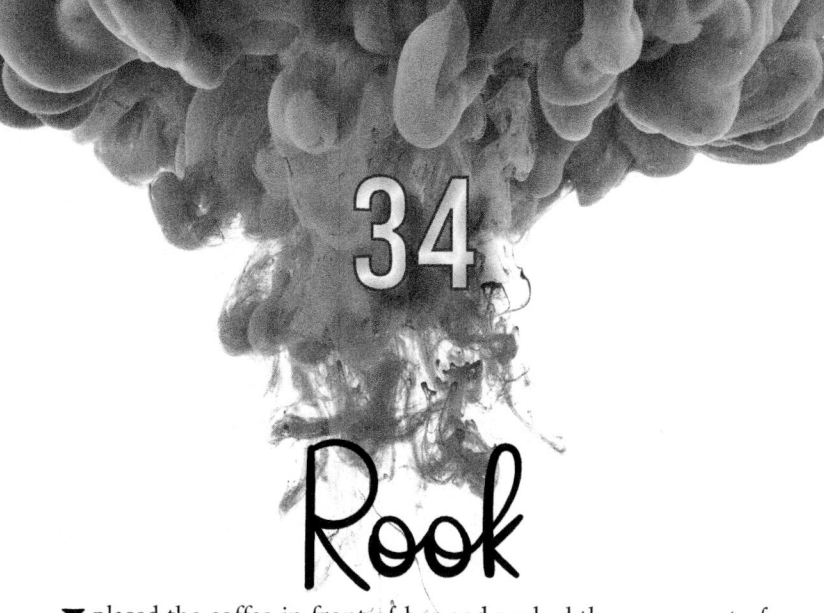

I placed the coffee in front of her and pushed the papers out of the way. I couldn't say for certain whether seeing all the details I had worried her, but if she really wanted to be a part of finding her kidnapper, then she had to understand how I worked.

I couldn't believe that I was even considering letting her be involved. I worked alone, *always*. I laughed to myself. *Considering it?* Try already working out how to make it happen. *Why the fuck was I doing that?*

"Rook?"

I turned back from where I was pouring my coffee and crossed to the kitchen table. Pulling out a chair, I sat opposite her.

"I was already investigating who was behind your kidnapping before you tried to break in."

She visibly bristled at that. "I wasn't trying to break in!"

"You were creeping around my property and about to let yourself in through the back door. What would *you* call it?"

"I *knocked*, and no one answered."

"You didn't think that meant I didn't want visitors?"

"No, I thought it meant you hadn't heard me!"

I hid a smile behind my mug. She was much feistier than initial impressions suggested. "I know I asked you before, but can you think of *anyone* who could be behind it?" I gathered up the papers and put them into a neat pile. "This is everything my brother could find out about your entire family." I placed the pile in front of her. "Go through it. Flag anything that is wrong, missing, or stands out as odd to you."

"You mean in case they took me because of something one of them did?"

I avoided replying by taking a mouthful of coffee. I wasn't ready to tell her I thought it was more likely that one of her family was behind the kidnapping. I hoped that when she read through all the information I had, she would come to that conclusion herself. But I also knew from experience that it wouldn't be something she would accept without a fight. She would want proof ... and she would not like my method of acquiring it.

I had my theories on who was behind it. The problem was I wasn't sure *why*. I hoped, by getting her to go through everything I had, she might see something which gave me the answer.

"At the bottom of the pile, you'll find some photographs of known mercs who would take on a kidnapping job like this. We couldn't find the guy who got away. The one who seemed to be in charge of the operation. Without any identifying marks or a photograph, we had to use guesswork. The men I killed aren't in any of the systems Knight could access, so either the tattoo one of them had was recent, or they've never been caught before."

She didn't speak for a minute or two, flicking through the pages and sipping her coffee. I waited for her to tell me she was struggling with the text, but she stayed quiet. When she reached the photographs, she lowered her mug to the table and stared at them.

"The thing your brother uses to search faces ... does it need photographs or could it work from a sketch?"

"If the sketch was detailed enough, I guess so." My answer was cautious. The information Knight had pulled for her said she'd studied art, but he had supplied no evidence of her talent. I knew she worked part time in an art gallery, but had taken two weeks' vacation for her birthday.

"I could sketch him," she offered.

"You could ... if you think you can put enough detail for the computer to recognise it."

"His face is imprinted into my mind. I see it every time I close my eyes."

The tone in her voice caused me to reach across the table and grasp her hand.

"I *will* find him, Dal. I promise you that." And I'd fucking kill him for the fear he'd put into her eyes. I kept that part to myself.

She gave me a slow nod. "If you have a pencil, I could do a sketch for you now."

I stood and moved to the cabinets set against one wall. Pulling open a drawer, I took out a couple of pencils and some paper. She was frowning at me when I turned back.

"Something wrong?"

"I ... no, not really. I just didn't think you'd have everything in your kitchen."

I smiled. "I find having something to write on within reach wherever I am is useful. You never know what you might need to write down."

She took them from me, nodding again. "That makes sense, given your line of work. I would imagine you have to make notes?"

"Notes?" I chuckled. "That's not how it works. Most contracts are sent to an encrypted device—" I broke off when my cell rang.

Scooping it up from the countertop, I connected the call and lifted it to my ear.

"I found the tattooed guy." Knight didn't bother waiting for me to speak. "Jeremy Rankin—he was released from prison eight months ago for the rape and murder of a schoolteacher."

"Nice guy. Give me a minute .... Dal?" She looked up. "I need to take this call. Help yourself to food, if you're hungry. I'll be back soon. *Don't* leave the house."

"I won't."

I walked out of the kitchen, closing the door behind me.

"Dal? Did the lovely Magdalena come to visit you?"

"Don't act surprised. *You* gave her my address."

"Because you like her. I was just helping you out."

"You were interfering."

Knight laughed. "What's your point?"

I ignored him. "What connections did Rankin have? Should I be watching my back?"

"You're not going to like this." His voice turned grim.

"I'm pretty sure you're going to confirm something I already know."

"So, this guy isn't someone who flies above the radar, usually, which is why it took me so long to track him down. He got the tattoo on his chest a month ago at... wait for it... Inkspirations in Glenville. The tattoo parlor put a photograph of the work on their social media yesterday, and that's when it pinged my system. A quick call gave me the details. The receptionist was *very* talkative. According to her, the owner threatened to throw Rankin out because he was creeping out the girls who worked there."

"Creeping them out, how?"

"Kept asking them if they were tattooed all over, whether they like to be tied up, if they had any kidnap fantasies."

"You said he kidnapped the school teacher... How long was she missing?"

"A week. He admitted to having her for four days before killing her, claimed he didn't mean to, but she fought him and he strangled her."

"Fuck's sake."

"But there was talk that he had a partner. One who wasn't caught."

"Oh?"

"Once I had Rankin's identity, things started coming together.

The other one you killed was called Matthias Theroux. Another ex-con. He was cell mates with Rankin. Imprisoned for bank robbery, murdered a security guard. He was inside for six years, then released for good behavior a few weeks before Rankin."

"Who approached who first?"

"I still haven't found Rushka—*that* appears to be a false name. There's *nothing* in my databases under it."

"Dally is doing a sketch of him now. Maybe it will help."

"You don't sound sure."

I glanced toward the kitchen door and lowered my voice. "She's the receptionist in an art gallery..."

Knight laughed. "And you think if she was talented, she wouldn't be doing that?"

"No, but—"

"A lot of art students take jobs like that, Rook. It puts them close to the artwork and can help get them contacts inside the art world. Don't dismiss her before you see what she can do. Even if it's little more than something the cops would put together, I can use it. It's better than a verbal description. Send it over to me when it's done." He paused. "When I went through Rankin's life history, I found something else."

"This is the thing you think I won't like."

""It's ... well, it could mean a few different things. I found his senior class yearbook. You'll never guess who he was at school with."

"I bet I can."

35

Magdalena

The face of the man who'd kidnapped me, forced me to record a ransom video, and threatened to kill me, stared up at me from the piece of paper. I added darker shading to his jaw, a scar above his left eyebrow, and an earring in his right ear.

Straightening on the chair, I reached around to rub the ache in my back, and found Rook watching me.

"When did you come back?"

"About an hour ago. I spoke to you, but you didn't reply. You seemed very focused, so I didn't disturb you." He stood and moved around the table to stand beside me. "Are you done?"

"I think so." I dropped the pencil to the table, leaned back, and stretched.

"It's good." He reached past me and picked up the sketch. "Lots of little details."

"I hope it helps."

"It should. Let me send a copy to Knight." He pulled out his cell, placed the sketch back on the table, and took a photograph. A couple of taps on the screen and he smiled, pocketing his cell. "Done."

"Are you hungry? It's almost lunchtime. How about we go into town for something to eat?"

I hadn't been hungry until he mentioned it, at which point my stomach gave an embarrassing gurgle. I nodded.

"We should also talk about what you want to do from here."

I frowned. "What do you mean?"

"When I told Knight to take you to your parents, I assumed they'd be there and you wouldn't be alone. Had I known that, I would have made other arrangements."

"I don't expect you to invite me to stay with you." I blurted the words. "Just because we ... well ..."

One eyebrow shot up. My cheeks heated.

"We'll go to your apartment and you can pick up some clothes. I have a spare room you can use, if you'd rather not sleep with me."

I let out a quiet sigh, relieved he wasn't about to make things awkward.

"Even if we hadn't had sex," he continued, and I closed my eyes, groaning internally. "I'd suggest you stay here. We're about to pull the dragon's tail, and he's going to bite back."

My eyes snapped open. "Dragon? What dragon?"

He waved toward the door. "Go and get dressed. We'll go for lunch first, and then head to your apartment."

I took a quick shower, stole a clean shirt from Rook's dresser, paired it with my jeans and headed back downstairs.

Rook didn't say a word about my theft of his shirt, but his eyes lingered on my chest for a moment longer than was appropriate. I folded my arms, covering my breasts, and his lips quirked up into a smile.

"I didn't bring any clean underwear with me." My tone was defensive.

His eyes dropped lower, and I resisted the urge to flatten my palm over the front of my jeans.

"I'm not complaining, but now I'm wondering whether we should stay *in* to eat."

My cheeks heated. Rook laughed.

"Come on, darlin'. Food first …" His tongue swept over his lips. "Dessert later."

I gaped at him. "Did you *really* just …? You didn't mean to …"

He didn't reply, strolling past me and out of the kitchen. I trailed along behind him until we reached the front door.

"Wait. What happened to your car?"

"Bishop had it recovered. It's in the shop. I'm hoping it's repairable."

"Are we walking to my apartment?" It was across town and, if that was the plan, then I couldn't pack more than a couple of day's worth of clothes.

"No, I have another car." He pointed at the Jeep I hadn't noticed the night before. "I guess you didn't see it when you were creeping around last night."

"For the last time, I *wasn't* creeping!"

"If you opened a dictionary to the definition of the word *'creeping'*, there would be a photograph of you."

I gaped at him.

He grinned at me, and my breath caught. The genuine humor in his smile transformed his face from handsome in a dark, brooding way to boyishly charming. Either way, it struck me how gorgeous he actually was.

His smile faded as I stared at him, and his head tilted. "Problem?"

I blinked and shook my head. "No." I wasn't about to admit I'd been admiring his looks. "I just remembered I left my purse inside."

"You won't need it. Lunch is on me."

36

Rook

We drove to the same diner she'd first met me at, and we sat at the same table. The server greeted me with a smile and called to say she'd bring coffee over.

"Guess you're a regular here," Dally said, settling onto the seat.

I smiled. "I prefer not to cook, if I can help it. I often have lunch here." I handed her the laminated menu. "What would you like?"

She glanced down at it, and I could see her eyes scanning over the words, a small crease between her brows as she frowned.

"I recommend the grilled cheese, and cherry pie. Not together, obviously."

She nodded. "That sounds good."

I waved the server over and placed the order.

Knight dropped me a text as lunch was being served. I read the message telling me he had sent the sketch Dally had supplied to a mutual friend. I replied with a thumbs up and pocketed my cell. I still hadn't told Dally what my brother had discovered. I needed to, but first I wanted to go to her apartment and look around. I had a few questions, and I hoped her place would hold the answers.

Dally turning up at my home, while unexpected, could actually turn out to be a good thing. I avoided thinking about what we'd done, how responsive she was ... how she tasted ... how she sounded when she came.

My fork clattered to my plate, and she jumped.

"Is everything okay?"

I rubbed a hand over my jaw and eyed her across the table.

In the time directly after our escape, I could put the attraction down to the adrenalin and highly emotional situation, but what about last night? I didn't have that excuse. There had been no danger, no distress. So *why* did I find myself drawn toward her?

"Rook?"

Her voice reminded me I hadn't answered her question. "Sorry. No, everything is fine." I glanced at her empty plate. "Ready to go?"

She nodded, and I tossed a handful of bills onto the table. I ate at the diner often enough for the staff to be accustomed to me getting up and leaving before they brought the check and I *always* overpaid.

We walked out to where I'd parked my jeep and I unlocked it so she could climb in. As I walked to the driver's side, my cell rang.

"Rook." My voice was clipped, and I waited for whoever was calling to speak.

"It's Deacon. Knight asked me to check out a person for you."

"Did you find anything?"

"Wouldn't be calling if I hadn't. Asher did whatever it is he does and came up with a name for the sketch Knight sent."

I stopped, one hand on the door. "What is it?"

"A guy called Rushka Zane. He is Shestyorka ... a known errand boy for one of the Bratvas working out of Florida." He paused. "Are you going up against the Russian Mafia, Rook?" He sounded amused. "I thought you'd retired."

"I'm not and I *have*."

"Doesn't sound that way."

"It's a long story. Thanks for the intel."

"No problem, Brother." The line went silent.

I scrubbed a hand down my face and blew out a breath. This fucking thing was getting more and more complicated. I looked down at my cell, then called Knight.

"Have you spoken to Deacon?"

"Yeah. I told him to call you."

"This Zane guy..."

"Already on it. Things are making more sense now. He works for Sergei Alexeyov. . My guess is that someone owes Sergei money, and the kidnap was a way to get it."

"That still leaves the questions of *who* owes the money and *why* take Dally."

"I'm working on that. My gut says it's going to be the simplest reason."

"It makes no sense. I'm heading to Dally's apartment now. Hopefully, her roommate will be there and I can feel her out."

Knight chuckled. "As long as you don't feel her *up.*"

"That's not even funny."

"It was kinda funny."

"No. It really wasn't. Let me know if you find anything else." I cut the call before he could reply and opened the door to climb into the jeep.

"When do you need to go back to work?" I put the key into the ignition and turned it.

"Monday, but—"

"Do you have any more vacation time available? Until we find this guy and you're safe, I don't think you should go back there."

She paled. "You think they might try again? I thought you said—"

"I was trying to keep you calm. There's always a chance they'll try again. It depends on why they wanted you in the first place."

I reversed out of the parking space and joined the traffic. Dally was silent beside me. I glanced over at her. She stared out of the window, chewing her lip. I stretched out an arm and took her hand.

"I'm not going to let anything happen to you."

"You can't make that promise."

I squeezed her fingers. "I got you away in one piece the first time, didn't I?"

She didn't reply. I held onto her hand until we arrived at her apartment building, then let her go so I could park.

"Dal, look at me." I waited for her head to turn toward me. "You're doing an amazing job of holding it together. I *can* keep you safe, and I will find out who's behind it." I was certain I already knew, but now wasn't the time to tell her. "What I need you to do now is smile, pack some clothes, and convince your roommate that everything is okay. Can you do that?"

She swallowed and licked her lips. "What if … what do I tell her?"

"That we discovered we had chemistry at dinner, hooked up afterward, and you're staying with me to explore where things go."

"I…" She took a deep breath and nodded. "Okay, I can do that."

"Good girl." I swung out of the car, strode around, and opened the door. Reaching in, I took her hand again and helped her out. "You have to sell this, Dal, you understand? If she thinks there's *anything* wrong, this could all go sideways."

L. ANN

37

Magdalena

The door to the apartment I shared with Jasmine wasn't locked, and it slowly swung open when I turned the handle. Music spilled out—a nineties boy band—and that told me Jasmine was home. She had a love for all things nineties, much to my disgust.

"Jas?"

My blonde roommate came out of the kitchen. "Oh! What are you—?" Her eyes moved past me and widened. "Isn't that—?" Her brows pulled together. "Did you hire him again?"

"No, I—"

Rook's arm wrapped around my waist and pulled me into his side. "Dal and I wanted to explore this *thing* between us. We felt it at dinner with her parents, and afterwards we took off to explore it." His hand squeezed my hip. "She needs clean clothes and then she's coming back home with me, so we can investigate things further." His voice was rich with innuendo and I blushed.

"Oh, that's..." Her eyes darted between us. "Look, no offense to you, but..." She focused on me. "Are you sure this is wise, Mags? You barely *know* him."

"Wasn't it *your* idea for her to hire someone in the first place?" He dropped his arm. "Go and pack your things, darlin'." His hand patted my ass.

I threw him a look but walked across the living room to the hallway, which led to the two bedrooms. Closing the door behind me, I pulled a suitcase down from the top of my closet and placed it on the bed. Rook had said to pack for a few days, and I wasn't staying that far from the apartment. It wouldn't be impossible for me to come back if I desperately needed something. I unzipped the suitcase, then turned to look at the clothes hanging in the closet.

What should I take? Would it be best to keep it simple? Jeans, a couple of t-shirts, underwear. So far I'd only ever seen Rook in dress pants and a shirt, but surely he wore casual clothes sometimes? I nodded to myself, grabbed my favorite tees, tossed them into the case, and then picked out three pairs of jeans. Underwear was next and socks so I could wear my sneakers.

I took another look around, found my make-up bag, and dropped that on top of the clothes, then headed into the bathroom for toiletries.

It took no more than ten minutes before I was back in the living room, dragging the suitcase behind me. Rook stood near the door, back against the wall and arms folded. Jasmine was on the opposite side, seated on the coach. I slowed as I crossed the room, the tension in the air raising the fine hairs on the back of my neck.

"Is everything okay?" I looked between them.

"Your new *boyfriend* accused me of trying to—"

"I didn't accuse you of anything." Rook's voice was mild. "I simply asked why you suggested to Dally that she should hire someone to pose as her boyfriend. And then you got all defensive, which made me question whether you had an ulterior motive for it, after all."

"I don't think you should go with him, Mags. Only a *psychopath* would leap from me suggesting you take someone with you to your birthday dinner and turn it into me having some nefarious agenda!"

"You have to admit it was an odd thing to suggest *and* there just happened to be an ad in the newspaper you grabbed. How often does that happen?" Rook asked before I could speak.

"*You're* the one who posted the ad!"

"No, I wasn't." His smile was cold. "But you already know that. Why didn't you tell her I wasn't the man you hired when I came to pick her up? Were you having second thoughts about the plan?"

"*Plan?* What plan?" Jasmine shot to her feet. "I have no idea what you're talking about."

Rook's laugh was derisive. "Oh, come on. Don't even try to bullshit a bullshitter."

I knew what he was talking about. He was accusing Jasmine

of being involved in the kidnapping.

"Jas," I began slowly. "How did you know there are guys who hire themselves out as pretend boyfriends?"

Her eyes jerked toward me, and then she sighed. "Okay, fine! It wasn't my idea. But I knew if I told you that, you would dismiss it, and you *needed* someone there with you, Mags! As soon as he suggested it, I knew it was a good idea. That it would make the dinner go easier for you."

"He? Who?"

"Fraser."

"*Fraser* suggested it? When?"

"I ran into him at lunch a couple of months ago, and we got talking about your birthday. He said he didn't like how your parents invited some random guy last year and was certain they were going to do it again. We got talking, and he said you should tell your mom that you were dating. Do you remember when I suggested it to you?"

I nodded, but didn't speak.

"When that worked so well, I told Fraser, and he said that maybe you could hire a guy for your dinner party. He showed me the classifieds in a newspaper and pointed to an ad for a guy offering to be a fake boyfriend. It seemed like the perfect idea, so I called him up and arranged everything, then came home and talked to you about it."

I thought back to the conversation we'd had. I'd wondered at the time how she arranged it all so quickly, but didn't really question her. Now I knew. They had arranged it before she even presented the idea to me.

"I can't believe you and Fraser arranged it behind my back." I glanced at Rook, who was looking at me. I couldn't read his expression, but I could see the muscle clenching in his jaw. "That explains why Fraser was so casual about you being there. He *knew* you weren't really my boyfriend."

"Yeah, *that's* the reason." He pushed away from the wall. "Are you ready to go?"

L. ANN

38

Rook

The missing piece of the jigsaw fell into place with Jasmine's confirmation that Fraser had been involved in planting the idea of hiring a boyfriend. I moved past Dally and picked up her suitcase.

"Let's go." I was on edge and had been since we walked into the apartment. The surprise on Jasmine's face, quickly hidden, at our appearance raised red flags, and I wanted Dally out of the building as quickly as possible.

Something wasn't right. I couldn't pinpoint what that was, but my trigger finger was twitching and I had to fight to stop myself from reaching for the gun hidden at the base of my spine. The girl who shared Dally's apartment seemed genuinely confused when I threw out the accusation that she had an ulterior motive for convincing the other woman to hire a boyfriend, but still... I'd learned never to ignore my instincts.

Dally followed me to the door, then stopped and turned. "I lost my cell over the weekend." Her voice wobbled, and she stopped talking to take in a steadying breath. "I ordered a replacement while I was at my parents, but it hasn't arrived yet. Once it does, I'll text you."

Jasmine nodded and stood in the doorway while we walked down the hall to the elevators. I glanced back while we waited for it and found her staring after us, her face troubled.

The doors slid open, and I placed my palm against Dally's back and guided her inside.

"I'll get a new cell delivered to the house for you."

"I've already spoken to my provider, and told them it was lost and needs replacing."

"That's no good. You need to cancel your existing contract."

"What? Why?"

"New number, new provider." I ignored her question. "In fact, I'll speak to Knight and get him to arrange one. First, though, we need to stop at the art gallery so you can tell them you won't be back for a while."

She rubbed a hand across her forehead. "Can't we go to the police? If we explain everything, surely they'll believe us."

I shook my head.

"But—"

"No. We are going back to my place, and then we'll go through everything we know."

"What do we know?" Her tone was angry. "The way you spoke to Jasmine ... you think she knew what was going to happen? Why was that? I told you she wouldn't do something like that to me."

"You don't always know people as well as you think you do."

"In *your* world, maybe! But not for normal people. We don't go around kidnapping or hiring hitmen to murder people we don't like!"

"It happens more often than you think."

The elevator stopped with a soft bump, and the doors opened onto the entrance hall of the building. A familiar figure came toward us, dressed in a silver-gray suit, and his lips stretched into a smile, which faltered when I stepped out behind Dally.

"Mags!" Fraser opened his arms. "I was coming up to see if you wanted to join me for lunch."

"Fraser!" Dally shot past me before I could stop her and into her brother's waiting arms. He smiled at me above her head. "Rook, right?"

"That's right." My hand moved toward the gun at my back.

His smile broadened. "You don't mind if I steal my sister away for an hour, do you? We barely had the chance to catch up at the parents' place."

"Actually, I—"

"I'd love that. We've already had lunch, but coffee would be great." She twisted to look at me. "I'll get Fraser to drop me back at your house. That's okay, isn't it?" She didn't give me a chance to finish speaking.

"It's not a good idea."

She frowned at me. "It's just coffee with my brother. Why

don't you come with us?"

"I'd rather we had some time to ourselves, Mags. We need to talk about mom." Her brother draped his arm over her shoulders, steering her toward the exit. I moved up behind them, and he looked back at me. "No offense, but this is a family thing. You're not the jealous type, are you? Surely, you can handle her being out of your sight for an hour without thinking the worst?" His eyes dropped to where my hand was inching closer to my concealed carry. One side of his mouth lifted. "Here, Rook? Now?"

He was goading me, but Dally couldn't see it, didn't *hear* it, and I had to stand there and watch as he guided her out and into the car parked at the base of the steps. The second the car drove away, I ran to my car and dialed Knight's number.

"Take down this registration and trace where the fuck it's going." I snarled the words, then added the registration number of the car I was following.

"Who is it?"

"Fraser fucking McCarthy. He's taken Dally for *coffee*."

"Is *coffee* code for something else?"

"Pretty sure it is, yeah. I'm in the jeep behind them. I'm pretty sure he's going to break off at some point and try to lose me. I need to hang back, because if they are really going for coffee, and she spots me following them, she'll never fucking trust me again."

"And if they're not?"

I ground my teeth. That was the problem. I still didn't have conclusive evidence Fraser had any involvement in Dally's kidnap. I had to either follow my gut and believe he did, or trust Dally and let her go for coffee with her brother.

I wasn't used to being indecisive. It was because I'd allowed myself to become emotionally involved with her. It was clouding my judgment. Had it been anyone else, I'd have thrown out my suspicions right there. But because it was Dally... because I didn't want to hurt her... I'd stayed quiet and now I might have put her fucking life at risk.

"Just track the fucking thing, Knight."

L. ANN

39

Magdalena

"Your boyfriend seems a little on edge." Fraser kept his eyes on the road while he spoke.

"It's been a strange couple of weeks." I wanted to tell him what had happened, but Rook's warning about the police not being helpful was still in my head, and I knew Fraser would want to contact them.

"Oh? Anything I should know? He's not mistreating you, is he?" His hands tightened on the steering wheel.

"What? No! He's been the perfect gentleman." *Most of the time.* When he wasn't growling at me, making demands, or … I shied away from thinking about the sex. "Where are we going for coffee?"

He'd driven past at least three cafes.

"There's a place I know a couple of miles outside of town. It's quiet, and the view is worth the drive. Have you spoken to mom or dad lately?"

"They're away on their annual retreat." It was hard to keep the bitterness out of my tone, but I managed it.

"Oh fuck. I forgot about that. When are they due back?"

"Sunday, I think." I fell silent. Fraser's fingers drummed on the steering wheel. "Is everything okay with you?"

"What? Me? Yeah, fine."

"Work's okay?" I pressed.

His jaw clenched. "Work's ... work, I guess. Nothing different there."

Silence fell, and I gazed out of the window, watching as the town flashed by until we were leaving the outskirts.

"Where did you say we were going?" I asked when another ten minutes passed.

"Not far now." He turned off and drove down a narrow lane as he spoke.

"There's a cafe down here?" I pushed the button to slide down the window, but nothing happened. "Fraser?" I twisted around to face him. He stared straight ahead, his hands gripping the steering wheel so hard his knuckles had turned white. "Fraser?" Uneasiness settled in the pit of my stomach.

He glanced at me. "I'm sorry, Mags. I ran out of options."

I didn't want to wake up, but I was cold. I tried to roll over. Something was wrong. There was a pressure on my arms, a pull that I could feel through my shoulders. I needed to wake up ... I didn't *want* to! There was an odd taste in my mouth. I tried to lick my lips, but my tongue wouldn't cooperate. My head felt thick, fuzzy, and opening my eyes was an effort which exhausted me.

When I finally got my lids to lift, *that's* when I realized I couldn't move my arms. And once that awareness washed over me, I could *feel* something digging into my wrists. I twisted my wrists and hands, to no avail. My arms were stretched high above my head, I was standing upright, my feet barely touching the cold floor, only my toes keeping the weight from my wrists.

My heart picked up speed, causing my eyesight to dim and swim. I frowned, trying to remember what had happened.

"Fraser?" My voice sounded thick, raspy, and it echoed around wherever I was. He'd apologized and then … my breath hitched. A shadow had fallen over me and I turned my head just in time to see someone rise from the back seat of his car. He'd been holding a needle, and I hadn't been fast enough to avoid it going into my neck.

I couldn't remember anything after that. What had been in it? Something that had knocked me out.

"*Fraser?*" I called my brother's name again. Silence greeted me.

I tugged at my arms harder, ignoring the bite of pain as whatever was wrapped around my wrists dug into my skin.

"Good, you're awake. " The rough voice startled me, and I flinched. "Don't hurt your pretty arms." A shadow detached itself from the darkness and came toward me. "Relax, *knyachna*, the drugs should wear off soon. Do you understand?"

I stared at him. His hand came up and wrapped around my

jaw. "I *said*, do you understand?"

"I ... y-yes."

"Good. You'll feel better in a moment or two." His voice was calm, cool, and I recognised it as that of the man who'd been waiting by the car when I'd fled after the crash. The same man who had forced me to record a ransom demand for my parents. The one I'd been having nightmares about for the past six days.

He moved out of my line of sight and I tried to twist around, to keep him where I could see him. Hands landed on my hips, forcing me to stillness. "Stop struggling. I'm not going to hurt you."

"Then why—?"

"Because you are paying off a debt." He guessed my question and spoke over me. "Your brother owes money to a very powerful man, and since he has failed to pay, it was decided that *you* would suffice."

40

Rook

I lost them when we reached an intersection and Dally's brother shot across as the lights turned red. I put my foot down, but a school bus sailed across and I slammed on my brakes. By the time it had passed and I'd navigated across the junction, they were out of sight. My fist hit the steering wheel.

Fuck.

I pulled over and called Knight.

"Do you have anything?"

"The registration you gave me is fake."

"Fuck's sake!"

"Talk me through what happened."

"There's nothing to talk through. Her brother showed up. I hadn't told her I thought he was involved, and she went with him. This is my fucking fault."

"Rook, less than two weeks ago you didn't even know the girl existed. It was pure chance that she walked up to your table."

"If you're about to tell me to walk away—"

"No, but this isn't your area of expertise. You can't blame yourself for handling the situation the way you have. Your job rarely involves this much interaction. You're more the get in, blow someone's head off, get out kinda guy. You don't even see your clients face to face. Your contracts tell you when and where. You only have to supply the how."

"What the fuck am I supposed to do?"

"You let *me* do *my* job. Instead of tracking the car, I'll trace the brother. Then, once we know where he is, *you* can do *your* job. Go home and wait for my call."

"But—"

"Rook, there's *nothing* you can do right now. Seriously, go the fuck home. The longer you keep me on this call, the longer it'll take to find her."

He was right, which didn't help my temper. *"Fine!"* I cut the call and tossed my cell onto the passenger seat.

It went against every instinct I possessed not to drive around the town and search out the car Dally had been in. When I parked outside my house, I stayed where I was, fingers drumming against the steering wheel while I replayed the meeting with Fraser McCarthy and his expression when he'd walked away with his sister. He'd been relieved.

Why the fuck was he relieved?

I was missing something. Something important. My gut screamed at me—there was something I'd overlooked.

What the fuck was it?

I closed my eyes, visualizing him in my mind and then compared him with how he'd looked during dinner on the previous weekend. At the dinner, he'd been surprised to see me. He'd hid it well—a slight widening of his eyes and quick snatched glances throughout the meal. I'd thought nothing of it. I had no reason to. But if he'd been behind the date for hire, it changed *everything*. He hadn't expected to see me there.

Had he known before we arrived? Was that why he'd been late? Had he been rearranging the grab? Was he who Rushka Zane had been referencing when Dally overheard them talking about waiting for instructions?

I threw open the car door and stepped out. Silence greeted me. No birds were singing. The hairs rose on the back of my neck and I slowly reached back for the gun hidden in its holster.

"Easy, Brother."

I handed the mug of coffee to the man sprawled on a chair beside my kitchen table. I met Deacon Jacobs eight years ago, when he interfered in a hit I'd been hired for. He'd been searching for his brother, who he believed had been taken by an illegal underground fighting ring. The man he had tracked was someone I'd been hired to kill.

He somehow got in my way—more than once—and asked me to give him twenty-four hours to get the information he needed before I killed my mark. I'd agreed, and we had struck up a wary friendship, which had branched out to include my brothers, and we had helped each other out over the years.

"What are you doing here?"

His brown eyes gleamed as he lifted the mug to his lips. "I was passing through."

"You were passing through," I repeated, and he smirked.

"Don't believe me?"

"No, I fucking don't. Did Knight send you?"

"Nobody *sends* me anywhere."

I sighed. I'd forgotten how annoying he could be. If you didn't word things very specifically with Deacon, he could *and* would use that against you.

"Then why?"

He placed the mug on the table and leaned forward. "I have a very particular set of skills. I could quote that actor. What's his name?" He squinted at me, then snapped his fingers. "Liam Neeson from those Taken films. But I'll just say I wasn't lying when I said I was passing through. I was a hundred miles away, doing a job for some big tech company." He waved a hand. "Not important. When Knight called and asked for Asher's help, the whole situation caught my…" His teeth flashed when he smiled. "It caught my interest."

"Why?"

"Come on, Rook. Don't play coy. The coldhearted hitman we all know and love has gone and caught feelings for a girl. And not just any girl, one that has absolutely no links to the life you lead."

"I barely know her." I denied his claim, and ignored the little voice whispering in my head, telling me I was a liar.

Deacon snorted. "Because *that* matters.

"What has Knight told you?"

"You took her to dinner because you didn't like the guy she was supposed to meet. You know, that really doesn't sound like a you thing. Do you remember that club in Berlin with the girl hitting on you? You turned your back on her. Because, apparently, normals have no place in your life. Yet here you are—"

"She was grabbed while I was with her."

"So? You got her free. That's your part in this over."

"You sound like Knight. I'm not fucking walking away from this."

"Because you've caught feelings." He picked up his mug again. "It's okay, man. You can admit it. We all fall, eventually."

"It's fuck all to do with feelings. I *know* they have snatched her. I *know* there's a high chance they'll fucking kill her if I don't find her. I'm not having that on my conscience."

Deacon's lip curled. "And you haven't touched her at all in the past week, have you? Didn't fuck her at least once?"

I couldn't answer that without lying, so I stayed silent.

"Once Knight finds out where the brother is, we'll pay him a visit."

"We?"

Deacon grinned. "Didn't think I was gonna come all this way and not invite myself to the party, did you?"

L. ANN

41

Magdalena

I couldn't feel my hands or arms. The blood had left them long ago, deferring to the call of gravity, leaving them numb. My shoulders were on fire from bearing my weight for so long.

How long had it been?

I had no clue. Long enough to wish I had listened to Rook.

Rook.

What was he doing? Had he realized something was wrong? Was he looking for me? Or did he think I'd stayed with my brother?

My brother...

Why had he done this? Did he hate me so much that he wanted to get rid of me? I'd seen no signs of it. Out of both my siblings, he was the one who had always been nice to me, never treated me like an unwanted child.

So *why?*

I had no answer to that. And I worried at it in my head until I fell into a fitful sleep. Light flaring and the sound of a door slamming jerked my head up.

"Wake up, knyachna." Pain radiated outward from my cheek when he slapped me. I blinked away the tears that sprung to my eyes. "Open your mouth." He didn't wait for me to comply, wrapping a hand around my jaw and prising my lips apart. "Drink!"

I considered refusing, but was sure he'd find another, more painful, way to force me to do it. Relief washed over me when water hit my tongue.

He patted the cheek he'd slapped. "Good girl." He set the plastic cup on the floor. "Now then ... your new owner will be here soon and—"

"Owner?" I couldn't stop myself from blurting the word. My head snapped sideways, the coppery taste of blood filling my mouth, when he slapped me again.

"Do not interrupt me." He moved behind me and used my hair to pull my head back. "I have to search you. The man you were with ... *Rook* ... may have put some kind of tracker on you." His breath was warm against my ear. "Who knows *where* he might have hidden something like that?"

I shivered. There was a note in his voice that scared me.

"There isn't ... he hasn't ..." I stammered, and gasped when the grip on my hair tightened.

"I didn't give you permission to speak, knyachna. Now hold still. I'd hate to cut your pretty skin." He released my hair and moved back in front of me. My eyes widened when he lifted a knife, long, curved and wicked looking.

"Please—" I cut myself off when he frowned.

"That's better. You *can* learn. Good. Stay still."

My heart hammered in my chest, battered against my ribs like a caged bird, as the knife came toward me.

Instinct drove me to scramble backwards, my feet losing purchase on the floor and wrenching my shoulders. He grabbed the front of my shirt and slid the knife through the material. I froze, not even breathing as he sliced through the thread holding the buttons in place. They fell, one by one, and I watched as they hit the floor, bounced and rolled away. The tip of the knife slid down over my stomach and I stopped breathing, terrified he would cut me.

I closed my eyes, not wanting to watch as the last buttons detached and fell, then cool air touched my skin as he pulled my shirt open.

"Ah, very pretty. Tomek will be pleased." A finger stroked along the waistband of my jeans, popped open the button and drew down the zip. "Don't worry, kynachna. I know it's cold in here, but I'll keep you warm for when Tomek arrives."

L. ANN

42

Rook

Dally had been missing for almost twenty-four hours. Knight couldn't find any sign of her brother, and I was losing what little patience I had left. If he cautioned me to wait one more time, it was extremely possible that I would kill *him*. When my cell finally rang and his number flashed up, my initial response wasn't pleasant.

"If you are calling to tell me there's no news, I'm going to fucking kill you."

"I love you, too, Rook." He didn't give me a chance to respond. "I'm sending you an address where I think the brother is hiding out."

"Why did it take so long?" I was already up and moving across the room, unlocking a cabinet, and studying the array of weapons inside.

"It didn't, not really. I needed to verify some information first. That's what caused the delay."

"What information?"

Knight sighed. "You're not going to like this."

"I already don't like this. Just like you're not going to like the feel of the bullet I shoot you with if you don't get to the fucking point. Dally could be fucking dead while you fuck around."

"Deacon was right. You *have* caught feelings."

"Knight." My voice was a growled warning.

"Stop threatening me, Rook. Fraser McCarthy owes money to Tomek Alexeyov."

"*Tomek?*"

"That's right."

My eyes swept over the handguns, and I picked two out. "Send me McCarthy's location."

"Rook, you don't understand. Tomek is—"

"I know exactly who he is," I cut in. "Send me the details." I ended the call. The address came through a couple of seconds later—a place out in the forest a couple of miles outside of town.

Perfect.

I climbed the stairs and rapped on the door to the guest bedroom ."Deacon? We have a location. Are you coming or staying?"

The door swung open to reveal the other man pulling on his boots. He flashed me a grin. "Let's go."

We traveled separately. Deacon on his motorcycle, me in my jeep. He was already parked and standing beside the road when I pulled up.

"I had a quick look around," he said when I climbed out.

"The cabin isn't far away. He certainly didn't pick it to get back to nature."

"Did he see you?"

"Don't be ridiculous."

I opened the trunk and unzipped the bag I'd placed there to take out two handguns and a knife. I checked the ammunition in both guns, slipped the knife into the sheath on my leg, then turned to face Deacon, who cocked an eyebrow.

"Isn't this dude her brother?"

"Yeah."

"And you're going to kill him?"

"Probably."

"That's one way to win the girl's heart."

"It's better than getting her kidnapped because you owe money to the son of a Bratva Pakhan." I holstered both handguns. "Ready?"

Deacon grinned, eyes gleaming. "Let's go."

He led the way to the cabin which, like he'd said, was only a couple of minutes walk through the trees.

The lodge came into view and the car I'd last seen Dally climbing into was parked, at an angle, outside the front door.

"There's another door around the back." Deacon's voice was low. "If we stick to the trees, we can get there without being seen."

I nodded, and we set off. Deacon pointed out the door, which blended into the wooden exterior wall.

"Did you see him at all?"

He shook his head. "Heard him, though. He was on a call,

shouting at someone. I think he's panicking over *someone* coming for him." Deacon's tone of voice told me exactly who he thought that someone was. "Whoever he was talking to wasn't telling him what he wanted to hear."

"What a shame." I unholstered one of my handguns. "Let's go say hi."

He laughed, and we moved cautiously toward the door, keeping to the shadows of the trees and watching for any sign of movement from behind the windows. Deacon reached for the door handle and glanced over at me. I nodded, and he eased the door open slowly and slipped through the gap. I followed close behind. The low noise of voices reached us as he stepped into the kitchen, and we both stopped, listening.

"Television," Deacon mouthed. He indicated he was going to go ahead and set off across the tiled floor.

I locked the back door and drew the blinds. If he *had* called for help, I didn't want anyone turning up and discovering what we were doing before we were ready. Deacon had reappeared by the time I was done.

"The room he's in is along the hallway. The guy has no spatial awareness. He didn't even notice me. What's the plan?"

I tapped one finger along the barrel of the gun I held and reached into my pocket to bring out a roll of duct tape. "I want him in the kitchen. Easier to clean up blood from tiles instead of carpet."

Deacon nodded. "Want me to bring him through?"

I glanced around the room, crossed to where the kitchen

table was located, and pulled out a chair.

"His throne awaits."

Deacon's smile was tight, and then he disappeared through the doorway again.

There was a shout, the sounds of a quick struggle, and then ... silence.

I waited.

One minute passed, then two ... and then the door swung open and Fraser McCarthy appeared, white-faced and eyes darting wildly around. Deacon was close behind him. Fraser's gaze landed on me, and his eyes widened.

"You!"

"Me," I agreed, and waved my gun toward the chair. "Take a seat."

"Why?"

A low rumble, almost a growl, sounded behind him. Fraser turned even whiter and bolted across the room and dropped onto the chair. I looked at Deacon, who smirked at me. "He thinks I'm a monster."

"And we haven't even got started yet." I shook my head and moved to stand in front of Dally's brother. "Where is she?"

L. ANN

43

Magdalena

He stood behind me, hands running over my breasts, down my stomach, over my thighs. I couldn't evade his touch, his invasion. I *tried* ... I twisted and arched away, dislodging his grip more than once, until he struck me repeatedly—raining blows over my face until I was dazed and disoriented.

I squeezed my eyes closed, ignored the fingers which stroked over my body, didn't react to the sting of pain when he pinched me, biting back any sound I might have made by pressing my lips together.

"Your bravery won't help you." His voice was close to my ear. "Tomek *will* break you. You are nothing more than a piece of property now. A body to be put to work to pay off your brother's debt." His teeth closed over my ear and bit down. "You'll learn to react in the right way, knyachna. To scream for those that want your screams, to beg for those who enjoy hearing pleas, and to *bleed* for those who wish to hurt you." He squeezed my breast.

"You will learn to please your new owners."

"Rushka." An unfamiliar voice, harder and deeper than the man pressed against my back. "Let go of the woman."

Fingers touched my cheek, stroked along my jaw, and then pressed against my chin and lifted my head. "Open your eyes, kotenok."

I shook my head.

"You won't like it if I have to force you to look at me." His grip on my chin tightened. "Three ... two ..."

I opened my eyes.

"Much better. Do you know why you're here?"

"My brother."

"That's right. Your brother owes me a lot of money. I gave him a chance to pay it back, and he chose to arrange a mock kidnap hoping to part your parents from the considerable sum of money he has to give me. Turns out your brother is as bad a kidnapper as he is a gambler." He patted my cheek gently.

"But Rushka here ... he told me you were pretty ... and he was right. So, unfortunately for you, you are going to pay off your brother's debt and then maybe ... *maybe* when you're done, I will let you go ... and maybe you won't want to leave. *Maybe* by then you'll enjoy your new life."

His eyes were cold, as emotionless as his voice, and I knew ... *knew* I wouldn't get out of this alive. He would never free me.

"Open your mouth for me, kotenok. I have something that will help ease you into your new life."

When I resisted, his grip tightened, exerting pressure on my jaw until he prised my lips apart. His finger forced its way into my mouth and he pressed something against my tongue.

"Swallow it like a good girl."

I glared at him, my only means of defiance. He smiled, pinched my nose closed, and held his free hand over my mouth. I fought against him as best I could, thrashing my head back and forth.

"Hold her." He instructed the other man, and I found myself wrapped in his arms and pinned in place.

The tablet on my tongue dissolved, fizzed, and, unable to stop myself, I swallowed. The man in front of me patted my cheek. "Good girl." He took a step back. "Bring her to my room. It should have sufficiently worked its way through her system by the time you've unchained her. Do not touch her." His smile broadened. "I want the pleasure of being the first one to introduce her to her new position in life."

The walls were melting, a spiral of colors that slid down to the floor, and turned my stomach. A part of me whispered it was the tablet he had forced me to swallow, that they had drugged me. The rest of me watched as the colors brightened, sharpened, swirled, and danced.

Someone spoke to me, but their voice was slow and slurred and I couldn't understand them. Something touched my face, and then laughter sounded, echoed around the room, warped into something darker, something dangerous.

My vision swam in and out, my concentration wavered, and I thought someone had released my arms because I was on my knees, pain shooting up from my hands to my shoulders. And then the world spun and my face was pressed against dark material that smelled of gunpowder and blood. I didn't struggle, didn't fight against the hands stroking up my legs to probe between my thighs, as my stomach bounced up and down on someone's shoulder.

I guessed we were walking somewhere, but I couldn't form the words to ask, and instead focused on the dark material close to my eyes and battled not to throw up from the nausea caused by the swaying gait.

I should be scared. I *was* scared. But somewhere between the knowledge of that and the place where my brain should be sending me into panic, I lost the emotion, the ability to react, taken over by a numbness instead.

The world spun again, and I bounced when I landed on something soft. My fingers curled into the soft silky material beneath me and I fought to focus on the room I was in. The colors still danced and swirled, but a darker shape detached from it and moved toward me, slowly forming into the shape of a man.

I frowned. I should recognise him. I should be scared … especially when he smiled.

"One tablet and you're completely out of it. That makes things much easier, kotenok."

My skin heated, and I looked down to find a hand covering my breast. I blinked at it, trying to make sense of what was happening, but the thoughts splintered before they took shape. Pressure forced me backwards, until I was laying down, looking up at the ceiling.

"You're making this too easy for me. I like a bit of fight in my toys, kotenok. At least try." A sharp sting and my face twisted sideways, fire spreading out from my cheek.

All it did was make me moan.

"Make sure she only gets half a tablet next time. She's barely even conscious. That's no good to me." Whoever it was, he sounded irritated.

"Put her under a cold shower. That should bring her out of it a little. It's hard to gauge the dosage sometimes." Another voice, one I should recognise.

The first man grunted, and the world spun again as he threw me across his shoulder. I fell limply, like a rag-doll, my arms hanging. I stared at them, willing them to move, but they didn't even twitch.

Ice cold water hit my back, and I gasped, throwing up my head, clarity of thought returning for a brief second—long enough for my mind to scream at me to fight, to escape what was coming, but gone before I could take action.

44

Rook

Deacon leaned against the doorframe, tapping out a message on his cell. He glanced up as I straightened from securing Fraser McCarthy to the chair, and a smile tipped up one corner of his mouth when our eyes met.

"Ready to begin?" He pushed away from the wall and strode toward the man slumped on the chair in the center of the room. Wrapping one hand into his hair, Deacon pulled his head back. "Where is she?"

Fraser spat in his face.

I crouched in front of him, bringing me down to eye level. "She's your sister. You gave your *sister* up to pay off your debt. Do you know what they'll do to her? You've handed her to Tomek Alexeyov, a man who is well-known for running a prostitution ring. He'll addict her to drugs and then put her to work. He'll *whore* her out until your debt is paid. *You* have sold your sister into slavery. She'll be dead within a year."

My voice was soft, calm—a far cry from the rage boiling

beneath my skin. "How big was the debt they wrote off in return for her? The ransom was for five million. You didn't owe that much, though, did you? There's no way they would have let you run up a debt that large." Something occurred to me. "Unless ... were you dealing for them, McCarthy?

The way his eyes jerked away answered that question without him needing to say a word.

"Doesn't matter. You don't have to say anything." I picked up the knife from the table and pressed the tip beneath his chin. "Now then ... where was I?" I cast my eyes over him and slid the blade up to his ear.

"If you remove the ear, he'll use that as an excuse to stay quiet longer," Deacon offered. "I think we should move down to his feet. Remove each toe, then do the same for his fingers."

"I was thinking about removing his tongue. He's not going to talk, anyway, so it's not like he needs it."

"Hmmm, good point. I'm sure I spotted an open fire in the other room, which means there will be a poker. We could stoke the fire and use that to cauterize the wound." He rubbed a hand over his jaw. "Tongue, then eyes. Removing those won't kill him."

I nodded. "Go check the fire and get it started if you need to." I propped my hip against the table and folded my arms, tapping the blade of my knife against my cheek.

"You won't do it." McCarthy sounded defiant, sure of himself.

I smiled, but didn't reply.

"If you hurt me, my sister will never forgive you."

His words drove my anger to the fore, and I backhanded him, splitting his lip and sending blood spraying across the room. "*You sold your sister into slavery*, I don't think she's going to care what I do to you."

"I *haven't*." He spat out a mouthful of blood. "They're holding her as collateral … until I get the money to them."

"Are you really that fucking stupid? Tell me who you handed her off to."

"I can't!"

"Bullshit." I pressed my knife to his throat. "Fucking tell me."

"Hold his head still." Deacon appeared beside me, poker in hand. "We'll take his right eye first."

"What? *No!*" McCarthy tried to shrink back into the chair.

I moved behind him and wrapped my arm around his neck, anchoring his head into place with one hand in his hair. Deacon stepped closer, lifting the long thin poker, the end glowing red.

"Don't! No! *Don't!!*"

"Last chance." I nodded at Deacon, and he dragged the tip of the poker along McCarthy's cheek. His shriek of pain was high pitched. The smell of burning flesh hit my nostrils. His skin blistered and split. McCarthy wrenched his head to the side and Deacon tutted.

"Now look at what you made me do. The line is uneven. I better match it on the other side." He stepped sideways and repeated the action down McCarthy's other cheek.

His scream broke midway through and he panted, eyes streaming.

"Ready to talk yet?" Deacon asked.

"I *can't!*"

Deacon didn't even wait for my nod, he pressed the poker to McCarthy's face. "Wrong answer."

Another scream rang out, echoing around the room, but he still refused to talk.

"Hold out his hand." I rolled up the sleeves on my shirt, and dragged the kitchen table closer. "Put it palm down on there and hold him still."

Deacon followed my instructions, leaning his weight on McCarthy's arm to keep his hand in place on the table. I looked at him.

"Last chance. Where did they take her?"

He stared at me, expression sullen. I brought my knife down, and severed his little finger. "Nine more to go," I said once his screams died down. "Cauterize the wound. I don't want him bleeding to death before I get the information I need."

Deacon pressed the poker against the nub I'd left.

He passed out after he lost the third finger. I moved to the sink, filled a bowl with cold water and threw it over his head. McCarthy came around with a start.

"Don't think fainting is going to help you. I want to know what you've fucking done with her and you're not going to sleep through what I'll do to you to find out."

"You'll have to kill me," he panted between whimpers of pain.

Deacon stooped and leaned close to him. A sound, very much

like a wolf's growl, sounded. I was sure it was the way the light fell on the other man, but for a brief second it looked very much like his teeth had lengthed into fangs.

He caught my eye and winked, and the strange impression was gone, but whatever he whispered into McCarthy's ear drained the man's features of his last remaining colour and he started to babble.

―○―

The water turned from dark red to pink and then to clear as I rinsed the blood from my hands. There was a white towel folded beside the sink and I reached for it, dried my hands, and turned back to face the room.

McCarthy's unconscious body slumped forwards on the chair, the duct tape the only thing holding him in place.

"Are you sure you want to do this? We could finish him off and get rid of the body"

I glanced over at Deacon. "No, I need to take him and hand him over. They won't let her go without something in return."

Deacon shrugged. "We could kill them."

"I don't really feel like being on the run for the rest of my life. Let's try it my way, first. If that doesn't work, *then* we'll consider wholesale murder."

"Okay. Then let's get this asshole into the car."

First, I needed to get the Jeep from where I'd parked it on the outskirts of the small forest. Thankfully, there was a narrow dirt road leading back to the cabin, and I was back before McCarthy regained consciousness—not that I was concerned. If he had woken up, Deacon would have put him back to sleep.

I used my knife to cut through the tape, and we manhandled him through the house and into the back of my Jeep. I retaped his hands behind his back, wrapped another piece around his face, covering his mouth, and secured him in place, stepped back, and slammed the door.

"Are you coming with me or following?"

"I'll follow. Don't want to leave my motorcycle here."

I opened the driver's door and climbed in. "Don't go in without me."

Deacon grinned. "Don't listen to what my brother says. I really *don't* have a death wish." He set off at a brisk pace back toward the main road.

I was still laughing when I pulled off the dirt road and caught sight of him astride his motorcycle. He lifted a hand in acknowledgement and followed me.

The drive to Baltimore took almost two hours and by the time we arrived at the address McCarthy had given up, the man was conscious. I'd given thought to stopping and changing that, but decided against it. The longer I took to get to Dally, the more they could do to her. I pulled up outside the private estate as the sun was setting. Deacon's motorcycle came to a stop beside me, and I wound down the window.

"Are we announcing ourselves?"

"Fuck, no. I need to make a point to get their attention. You stay here with our … gift. I'll call you when I need you to bring him."

Deacon frowned. "Are you sure that's a good idea?"

"I know these people. I've worked for Sergei before. If I want to get Dally out in one piece, I have to show him I'm too dangerous to cross and too important to kill." While I spoke, I checked my weapons, tucked them into their holsters, and swung out of the Jeep. "Stay here."

I strode along the sidewalk, past the gates and round the corner. There was a blind spot there, where the guards wouldn't see me enter. I had worked for Sergei a couple of times and made it my business to ensure I could get to him if things ever went sideways and I needed to remove him. Not that he knew that.

I found the section of wall I was searching for and climbed up. At the top, I paused looking around. I couldn't see any security, but that didn't mean they weren't there. I waited, counting to thirty in my head, and watched for signs of activity. My patience was rewarded when a man, dressed in black combat gear, rounded the corner and walked past me, gun in hand as he patrolled.

I crouched down, hiding behind the overgrown trees and waited until he passed, then hopped down into the garden beyond. I stuck close to the wall and moved in the opposite direction to the guard, until I was in front of the house. Checking left and right, I kept low to the ground and crossed the grass until I could flatten myself against the wall, and waited once again. Almost on cue, the guard appeared. But he wasn't focused on me. He was looking down at his cell phone.

My lip curled—Sergei needed to hire better security guards. If they spent as much time focusing on their surroundings as they did on their cell phones, it wouldn't have been as easy for me to get inside. As soon as he was out of sight, I turned and ran my fingers along the edge of the window frame. Finding a gap in the corner, I wedged my finger beneath it and pushed upwards. The window slid open silently. Checking around me once more, I climbed through.

The room I entered was empty—empty of people *and* empty of furniture. I crossed the floor and paused by the door, listening. I could hear voices beyond. Not loud enough to hear the words, but close enough to know that they would see me if I stepped out. I waited, the voices growing fainter as they moved down the hallway. Once I could no longer hear them, I eased the door open, and stuck my head out. The hallway beyond was devoid of people. I've been in the house enough times to recognise where I was and I set off towards the study where I knew Sergei would be.

There were two guards standing outside the door when I arrived and they straightened, one lifting his weapon to point at me. I held his gaze and strode towards them.

In my line of work, the trick to getting close to your mark, especially when they're surrounded by people, was confidence. Forcing those around your target to believe you had every right to be there. It was a proven method. And one I used to my advantage successfully all the time.

"I'm here to see Sergei."

One of the guards straightened. "Is he expecting you?"

I didn't bother replying, drew my knife and slit his throat. He fell to the floor with a pained gurgle. I had my gun trained on the second guard before he could lift his own weapon. "If you think you're fast enough, take your shot."

He hesitated.

I didn't, and he joined his partner on the ground, a bullet to his head. I stepped forward and pressed my gun against the first guard's head and squeezed the trigger. There was little point in leaving him to die slowly. His only crime was being a guard to a Bratva boss. Unfortunately, that job role came with the risk of death. I stepped over his body and pushed open the door.

Sergei sat at his desk as I walked through and kicked the door closed behind me. He surged to his feet. I pointed my gun at him. "Where is she?"

"Rook" His hand inched towards his desk.

"By the time you've hit the silent alarm, you'll be dead." I told him.

He froze. "Why are you here? What do you want? I haven't hired you for anything."

"No, but your son has something of mine and I want it back."

Sergei frowned. "I have no idea what you're talking about."

"Tomek took a woman. *My* woman. In payment for her brother's debts. I want her back."

Sergei's frown deepened. "I know nothing of this. Who is this woman?"

"Magdalena McCarthy. Sister to Fraser McCarthy. He owes a debt to Tomek and couldn't pay. Tomek decided his sister would make an acceptable alternative."

"Rook." Sergei's voice was calm. "I really don't know what this is about. Tomek has said nothing to me. I have never heard of this name ... *McCarthy*. Please, come and sit down. Let us talk about it."

I kept my gun trained on him. "Stand up, keep your hands where I can see them, and come toward me."

His features hardened, but he rose to his feet, arms outstretched to either side of him. "As you can see, I'm not armed."

"This isn't about you, Sergei. Give me my woman and we'll be done here."

"I don't have her."

"Your son does. Where is he?"

"As far as I know, he's in his quarters. Why would he take a girl in lieu of money owed? Tell me what has happened. I have no interest in crossing you." What he *meant* was that he had no interest in starting a war with me and my brothers. If he tried to kill me, he knew Bishop would get involved and *no one* wanted to find themselves on the wrong side of his temper.

45
Magdalena

If I hadn't vomited, I was certain I wouldn't have been left alone in the bathroom. But fear combined with the shock of ice-cold water had sent my stomach into a spin and I'd thrown up all over the shower's tiled floor. The man holding me cursed and dropped me. I landed on my knees, the pain ricocheting up through my legs, and I vomited again.

"She's no good to anyone like this." His foot swung out, caught me in the ribs and sent me sliding across the wet floor. My head connected with the wall and I lay there, dazed and sick. "Get the bitch cleaned up." He walked away.

I stayed where I was, pushing myself back up onto my knees, teeth chattering as I fought to regain control of my stomach and stay conscious. No matter what, I *could not* succumb to the darkness that wanted to pull me under. That would be worse than being awake for whatever they had planned for me.

The shower cut off, and a set of legs came into my line of

sight. I tensed, waiting for ... *I don't know what* ... nothing good. A hand touched the top of my head and I scrambled backward. A pair of legs clothed in black pants followed me until I was cornered, with nowhere left to go. He stopped and crouched, kneeling in a pool of water.

"Dal."

One word in a voice I'd convinced myself I'd never hear again. A voice that, to my drug--hazy brain, promised safety. Warmth cocooned me and I briefly wondered when I'd moved, and then he was standing, swinging me up into his arms.

"Did he touch you?" When I didn't reply, he frowned. "Dally, talk to me. Did anyone touch you?"

What did he mean?

I was naked, bruised, sick, and drugged. I had done none of that to myself ... and then his meaning hit me and my blood ran cold. I'd avoided thinking about that, about the possibility of it happening. Even now, my mind shied away from the word, from the action, from his meaning.

A whimper sounded, and I realized it was coming from me. He swore softly and lowered me back to my feet. Pulling off his jacket, he placed it over my shoulders, then lifted each of my arms and threaded them into the sleeves. I cried out at the agony the movement sent through my arms.

"Are you able to walk?"

I stared at him.

Was it even him, or did I just wish it was? Maybe the drug they'd forced me to swallow was making me see things that weren't there?

"Dally!" His voice was sharp.

Okay, maybe not. I wouldn't hallucinate that much irritation in his voice.

I licked my lips. "I ... th-think so."

"You think you can walk or that someone touched you?" He reached out and buttoned his jacket, covering my nakedness. "Talk to me." His fingers touched my chin, tipped my head up and his eyes tracked over me, darkening at something only he could see. "Who hit you?"

My tongue touched the split in my lip at his question. "I don't—" My voice sounded hoarse. I cleared my throat. "I don't know his name."

Rook's hand closed over my arm. "Come into the other room with me."

He drew me forward, and I went without argument. If Rook was really here, then everything was going to be okay ... right? I'd seen what he could do. I was safe with him.

We entered the room, and I blinked, taking in the scene in front of me. The man I'd heard called Rushka was on the floor, face a bloodied mess.

"Did he touch you?" Rook swung a kick at him.

"He ... he chained me up and ... and took my clothes. He ... yes, he tried t-to touch me."

Rook nodded. His gun rose and he shot the man on the floor. Blood sprayed out onto the white sheets of the bed behind him.

The other man, sitting on the edge of the bed, flinched. His face drained of colour and he stared up at the another, older man I hadn't noticed when Rook first guided me into the room. That one glanced over at us when Rook lowered his gun, and his features clouded.

"Is this your woman, Rook?"

I turned my head to search Rook out, and he squeezed my arm gently and nodded.

The other man sighed. "I'd hoped you were mistaken."

"I wasn't." His hand dropped from my arm. "Stay there," he whispered and moved to stand beside the older man. "I said I wouldn't kill him if he didn't touch her." His voice was soft.

"Rook—" The man on the bed twisted to look at him.

"Shut the fuck up. You had every intention of taking her. You drugged her. You stripped her, and you hurt her." His head turned to look at the man, standing quietly at his side. "I gave you my word I wouldn't kill him." His attention returned to the man on the bed. "Give me your hand."

"Why?"

"Because I'm going to blow your fucking head off if you don't." He delivered the threat in a cool, calm voice.

"Tomek, do as he says."

The younger man lifted his hand slowly. Rook wrapped his fingers around Tomek's wrist and gripped his middle finger.

"Look at me." Rook's command was impossible to ignore, and my eyes jerked up to his face before I realized he wasn't talking to me.

"The only reason I'm not putting a bullet in your head is because your dick didn't go near her. But if you think that absolves you from any guilt for what you *did* do, think again." He gave a sharp jerk, and a sickening snap reached my ears.

Tomek howled.

"That's for stripping her." Rook's voice was cool.

He moved to another finger and a second snap sounded. "That's for drugging her."

He did it again ... and again ... until only Tomek's thumb was left. "Those are for the bruises you left her with." He looked around. "Dal, come here." He reached back and tugged me forward. "Tomek, look at her."

When the man whimpering on the bed didn't move fast enough, Rook grabbed the top of his head and wrenched it back. "Stop fucking snivelling and look at her."

Tomek's eyes jumped to me and then away.

"Imprint her image into your head because if you even *breathe* in her fucking direction once we leave here, I'll come back for you. You will watch while I destroy every part of your body. You will beg me to end your life. I will fucking rip you apart and stitch you back together. I will peel the skin from your bones and let you bleed. I will break every bone in your body and leave you to heal and then I'll do it all again. I will feed your fingers and toes to fucking rats. And when I finally let you die, it will be with her face in front of you so you know *why* I've done it."

L. ANN

46

Rook

I shoved Tomek backwards, and he toppled onto the mattress, clutching at his broken fingers. I turned to Sergei.

"He's still alive, as promised. Are we clear?" I didn't need to clarify my words. He knew exactly what I meant without me spelling it out.

He held my gaze for a second, then looked at his son. His features changed, darkened, and he shook his head. "My son has learned a valuable lesson today and still kept his life. Nothing more will come from this." He bent over the bed and caught Tomek's wrist. "You have made mistakes, son. You should never have agreed to take this girl … *any* girl … as payment without speaking to me first. What were you thinking?"

Tomek glanced up at his father. "He owed us money!"

"And you thought *kidnapping* someone connected to the Chambers family was the answer? You allowed a man who owed a debt to kidnap his sister to pay it off? You gave him one of our men to help in his scheme and then made our *family* responsible for kidnapping *Rook Chambers*. How did you think that was going to end?"

"I didn't know he was involved with her." Tomek's voice was sullen.

"And red flags didn't fly when he killed two of the men the idiot hired and disappeared with the girl?" Sergei roared. "This ... this *mudak* ..." He swung a kick at the body of Rushka. "He knew who he had taken. Rook is within his rights to demand your life to clear our family's honor with him! I ask you again, *what were you thinking?*"

I missed Tomek's whined response when Dally clutched my arm and whispered my name.

"Rook ... I don't feel right." She swayed, and I caught her as she tumbled forward.

"As fascinating as this is," I said, lifting her up into my arms. "I need to get Dally out of here and flush the drugs your *son* forced into her out of her system."

Sergei nodded. "Go in peace, my friend."

"I brought her brother to pay his debt. I'll leave him with your men."

Tomek straightened from where he slumped on the bed. "You brought Fraser here?"

"It's what *you* should have done, but you were too busy thinking with your dick." My eyes dropped to his waist. "Maybe I should break *that*."

Tomek's unbroken hand covered himself. "No! No!"

"Remember that fear, Tomek." I adjusted my grip on Dally, who had dropped her head against my shoulder, and turned toward the door.

"Rook ... this doesn't change our relationship. I still—"

"I'm retired." I cut in before Sergei could offer me a job. "I'm out of the game." I opened the door and walked out before he could reply.

I didn't have to creep through the house the way I had when I'd entered, and I strode along the hallways until I found the front door. I'd been here so many times, I could traverse the place with my eyes closed. The guards on either side of the door straightened when I approached them, then relaxed when they recognised me.

"Rook," one greeted me with a nod. "I didn't see you arrive."

I didn't slow my pace. "No, you didn't. I have a gift for Sergei waiting outside the main gates. Can you come and collect it?"

"Does he know?"

I nodded. "He's expecting it. One of Tomek's errors in judgment."

"Ahh." He walked with me down the long curved driveway to the electric gates. I pointed to the left.

"We parked further down there. Sergei should think about checking the blind spots along the road."

"Most people don't spend that much time analyzing the security set up of someone like Sergei."

I laughed. The tone in his voice suggested I was not like most people. It wasn't something I could argue with.

When the car came into view, a figure peeled away from

beside it and moved toward us.

"Is she okay?" Deacon's eyes were on the woman in my arms when he reached us.

"She will be. Give the asshole to Dmitri." I jerked my head at the man beside me. "He'll take him back to Sergei."

Deacon nodded and pulled open the back door of my Jeep, reached in and dragged Fraser McCarthy out by the back of his shirt. The other man struggled, ineffectively swatting at Deacon. Dmitri's eyebrow rose at the bloodied mess we'd made of his face.

"Did he annoy you?"

"He sold his sister to pay for his own fuck up." I couldn't keep the bite of anger out of my voice.

"So ... yes, then?"

"Get him away from me!" McCarthy screamed and attempted to break out of Deacon's grip. "He's not what you think he is!"

Deacon snorted. ""He still thinks I'm a monster."

"Well, it *does* look like you both tortured him, so it's kind of understandable."

Deacon's grin was all teeth. "That's not why."

"He's not human!" McCarthy tried to escape him again.

Deacon ignored his outburst and shoved him toward Dmitri. "He's your problem now."

"Why does he think you're not human?"

"I growled at him."

"You ... growled?" Dmitri sounded confused.

Deacon shrugged. "I'm *really* good at it."

Sergei's security guard took hold of McCarthy's shirt, frowning at Deacon. "Okay... Well, I've got it from here. Thanks, Rook." He dragged the still-whimpering man away.

"Open the passenger door," I said to Deacon once Dmitri was out of sight.

He did as I asked, and I lowered Dally into the seat. She stirred, eyelashes fluttering, and then she looked up at me. Her eyes were dull, unfocused. I touched her cheek, and her lips parted on a soft sigh.

"We'll be home soon. Try to sleep until then, okay?" I reached in, clipped her seatbelt into place, then straightened and looked at Deacon.

"Are you coming back to the house?"

Deacon looked up at the sky and pursed his lips. "No, I think I should get back home. I've been away for too long." He slanted a look at me. "Unless you need me?"

I shook my head. "No, I'm good." I held out a hand and Deacon looked at it. I rolled my eyes. "You're supposed to shake it."

"Oh." He gripped my hand. "Stupid tradition."

I laughed. Deacon had always been a little odd. "Thanks for everything."

He shrugged. "Anytime. You know where I am if you need anything." He turned and strode over to his motorcycle, swung one leg across it and threw me a grin. "Catch you soon, Rook." The engine roared to life, and a few seconds later, he was gone.

L. ANN

47

Magdalena

The faint rumble of the engine, the low sound of soft music and the repetitiveness of street lights flashing by the window lulled me. It all combined to send my mind into an almost hypnotic state, where nothing touched me. I was vaguely aware of the man beside me, hands gripping the steering wheel, shirt sleeves rolled up to his elbows, tattoos on display.

Occasionally, he'd reach across and touch my arm, my leg, and ask if I needed to stop. My response was the same each time. I shook my head. If we stopped, the numbness would end, and I'd have to think about everything and... I wasn't ready for that.

When the engine did finally fall silent and he switched off the music, I knew I'd run out of time and avoidance was no longer an option. Rook didn't speak, throwing open the door and climbing out. I watched through the window as he strode around the car to my side. Cool air hit my legs when he opened the door and crouched down.

"Dal?"

My head turned toward him, pulled by the sound of his voice.

"Do you want to walk?"

Did I?

"Dally?" He took one of my hands in his. "If you don't think you can walk, that's okay. I can carry you inside."

His fingers were warm, heating my chilled skin, breaking through the numbness. I stared down at them. There was blood on those hands, invisible to the eye but there, staining him. He'd killed people. *Lots* of people. He'd killed in front of me ... *for me*. And yet he held my hands with a tenderness at odds with the man he claimed to be. Tears filled my eyes, and I blinked them away.

"Hey ..." His other hand lifted, and he brushed a thumb over my cheek, catching the stray tear which had escaped. "Let's get you indoors." He unclipped my seatbelt and lifted me out of the car. "You can take a soak in the tub, have some food. Are you hungry? Thirsty?" He carried me to the front door. "It's not too late to order something. Or I can take a drive into town. Is there anything you'd like?"

I clutched at his shoulder at the suggestion of him leaving me alone, fear rising. "No. Don't leave." I hated the neediness in my voice, but he didn't mention it.

"Do you like pizza? I'm sure I have a menu for the local pizzeria." He unlocked the front door, and we went inside. He moved through the hallway, into the living room, and lowered me onto the couch. "How about I run you a bath, and you can decide what you want to eat?" When I nodded, he patted my hand. "I'm going to get you a bottle of water. I need you to drink it all, understand?"

"Okay."

He'd reached the door before I spoke again. "Rook?" I twisted on the couch to look at him. He stopped in the doorway and turned back to face me. "Thank you."

He didn't speak, a look I couldn't decipher flickering over his face, then he nodded. "Stay there."

"I can walk." After drinking an entire bottle of water, my head felt a little less fuzzy. I was sure I could manage the stairs, but Rook ignored my protests and scooped me up into his arms.

I clung to his shoulders as he navigated the stairs and strode along the hallway and into the bathroom.

"I had to improvise. I rarely use the tub," he explained, lowering me to my feet.

"Improvise?" I twisted around to look at the bath filled with water.

"I don't have any of those bath fragrances you women like, but I *do* have honey. I'm told by Google that it's good for your skin and makes for a nice addition to bath water ... and ... well, you smell like honey," he finished softly, then cleared his throat and continued in a brisker tone.

"Anyway, take your time. The suitcase you packed is on the bed. I'll wait downstairs. Did you think about what you would like to eat?"

"Pizza is fine." I was moving toward the tub, then a thought occurred to me and I swung to face him. "Rook?"

"Hmm?" He looked back at me.

"You ran me a bath and fed me that night in the hotel."

"I find it helps to ground you after a highly emotional situation."

"Are you …?" I licked my lips, then rushed out the rest of my question. "Are you planning on repeating *everything* you did that night?" There was a long silence while he stared at me, and my cheeks heated up. I spun away, presenting him with my back. "Ignore that."

Warm hands curved over my shoulders. "I would never assume." His voice was low, his breath warm against my ear. "But I have to admit, finding you naked in Tomek's bathroom. I was ready to kill him, and to hell with the promise I made to his father. I *would* have killed him, had you shown any signs of wanting me to."

I found myself turned around, and his hands left my shoulders. He touched my cheek, avoiding the bruises.

"Make no mistake, darlin'. We may have started out accidentally, but *this* is real. You are *mine* now." He lowered his head, so slow that I could have taken a step backwards and avoided his mouth connecting with mine. I didn't even consider it.

My hands lifted, curled around his neck, and I stepped closer so I could meet him halfway. Our mouths touched, his hands falling away from my face, so he could slide one into my hair and cup the back of my head. His teeth nipped at my bottom lip, dragging a gasp from me. When my lips parted, his tongue delved inside, found mine and stroked along it.

His fingers flexed against my head, while his other hand lifted to curve over my jaw, tilting my head so he could deepen the kiss. My heart pounded, my pulse a rapid beat in my throat, and I pressed even closer against him. The hand in my hair dropped, sliding leisurely down my spine, over the jacket of his I was still wearing, and lower, until his fingers found my skin and reversed direction up my thigh.

His palm was warm when he cupped my ass and squeezed gently … and then he stepped away. I blinked up at him. Dark eyes raked over me, and he frowned.

"Take your bath, Dal." His voice was rough, and he spun away, leaving me alone in the bathroom.

I stripped out of the jacket slowly, and let it drop to the floor, then stepped into the tub and sank down into the water. I took my time, enjoying the way the heat relieved the tension in my body. Taking a deep breath, I slipped beneath the water, letting it cover me completely. I lay there, my eyes closed … floated until my lungs burned with the desire to breathe. Even then, I waited, held off until it became unbearable and rose from the water, gasping and spluttering. Eyes closed, I groped around for a towel, stood and dried my face before wrapping it around my body.

Rook had said there were clothes in the bedroom, so I made my way there. My suitcase was open on the bed, and I pulled out underwear and pajamas. I dried and braided my hair, and twenty minutes later, I headed back downstairs in search of Rook.

I found him at the kitchen table, a gun in pieces in front of him. I think he was cleaning it, as there was the scent of metal and oil in the air, and he was using a rag of some sort to rub one of the gun's pieces. He looked up when I entered and smiled.

"Pizza is on the way. Would you like something to drink?" He stood and moved around the table. "How about tea?"

"Tea?"

He nodded, and I watched as he pulled out a mug and tea bags. "I'd offer you something alcoholic, but you don't drink it…" He tapped the side of the mug. "Tea is the next best thing."

"Is it?"

He didn't respond straight away, focusing on making the drink. When it was ready, he handed it to me. "Let's go through to the other room."

48

Rook

I didn't like how calm she was, how *normal* she was acting. I'd expected her to freak out, to melt down worse than she had at the hotel. Yet she was calm, relaxed, behaving as though she hadn't been almost raped by the man her brother had sold her to. And that was another thing—why hadn't she asked about *him*?

I was certain her behavior was because she was still in shock, and her mind hadn't finished processing everything, so like I had after we escaped the kidnapping, I watched and waited for a reaction to set in.

The pizza arrived as she sat down, and I left her in the living room and walked down the hallway to the front door. I had a gun tucked into a hidden holster at my back and I kept one hand on the grip as I opened the door. The teen beyond grinned at me, his mouth full of braces and a face covered in acne.

"Pizza delivery!" he bleated, voice breaking mid-sentence, and I nodded.

He handed over three boxes and a bottle of Coke, took the

money I held out, and scurried away. I kicked the door closed, turned the key to lock it, and returned to the room I'd left Dally in. She was curled up on one corner of the couch when I entered, sipping her tea.

"I went with basic options on the pizza," I told her as I placed the boxes down. "Cheese on one, pepperoni on the other, and a large garlic bread with cheese."

She nodded.

"Feeling okay?"

Another nod.

I busied myself opening the boxes, returning briefly to the kitchen for plates, and then took a seat on the opposite end of the couch. She was watching me when I glanced over at her, worrying at her bottom lip with her teeth. I leaned forward and placed two slices of pizza—one of each type—and a slice of garlic bread onto one plate and handed it to her. She didn't take it.

"You must be hungry. When did you last eat?"

Her eyes lifted to find mine. "When we had lunch." Her voice was soft. "When was that? Was it yesterday? I don't know how much time passed. Rook, what day is it?" Her voice rose, grew shrill.

I slid closer, put the plate on the table, and covered her hands with mine. "Deep breaths. It's okay. You're okay. You've done so fucking well keeping it together. Can you take a breath for me?"

She did, sucking in a shaky breath.

"Good girl. In through the nose ... out through the mouth. Fill your lungs with air. That's it, darlin'. One more time."

"Did you ...? Did you kill him?" She asked between breaths.

"Who?"

"The one who took me. He was on the floor ... You shot him. Did you kill him? Is he dead?"

"Rushka? Yeah, I killed him." I studied her. How would she react to me telling her what I did? Only one way to find out. I explained how I broke into the house and got into Sergei's office.

"I made him a promise not to kill his son, Tomek, but only if he hadn't touched you. If he had ... Well, all promises would have been void at that point. But Rushka ... there was no way I was leaving him alive. Sergei knocked on the door to the room and he answered. I put a gun to his head and walked him back into the room. Told Tomek that what I was going to do to Rushka, I would be repeating with him if I found you harmed. Do you remember telling me what he did?" She nodded. "He hurt you, so I put a bullet in the fucker's head."

"What about my brother." Her teeth caught her lip again. I waited. "They'll kill him, won't they?"

"Probably." I didn't tell her that Sergei had already told me that Fraser McCarthy would be dead before we made it back to my house.

"How did you find me?"

I eyed her. She was still relatively calm. I wasn't sure whether telling her what I'd done to her brother would send her over the edge. But I also didn't want to lie to her. If I was reading things right, what I was ... what I *had* been ... hadn't made her fear me.

But would the lengths I went to so I could find her change that?

"Rook?" The way she said my name warmed my skin, did something to that muscle pumping the blood around my body—the heart I'd always claimed never to have.

"I hunted your brother down and tortured him until he broke down and told me where you were." I couldn't hide the anger in my voice.

Her eyes widened, jaw falling open. I waited for her to demand to leave, to want to get away from me. It would be the natural response, the *normal* one. I'd tortured her brother—it didn't matter that he'd sold her to pay off his debts. She wasn't built in a way to separate her love for the brother she'd grown up with from the man who had seen her as a means to an end.

"Good. How did you make him talk?"

"I—" I frowned. *That* hadn't been the question I'd expected to hear. "You don't want to know that."

"I do." She leaned forward, rising up on her knees and clutching my hand. "My brother handed me to someone who he knew had no intention of just letting me sit in a room somewhere until he'd found the money to pay back. I want to know how long it took before he broke." Her voice was fierce.

"Dal, darlin', I don't think—"

"You kill people. You told me that. Yet he was alive when you handed him over. You didn't kill *him*."

"Because he's your brother."

"He *sold* me ... like an unwanted possession!"

"But he's still your brother." I squeezed her fingers. "Don't mistake me, darlin'. I *wanted* to kill him, but I didn't think coming to you with his death on my hands would have been right."

She pulled her hand free and flicked the front of my shirt. "His blood is on your clothes."

I looked down, noting the blood spatters clear against the white of my shirt. I'd been in such a rush to get to her, I hadn't given any thought to changing clothes first. "Yes, that's his blood."

"How long, Rook? How long did he stay silent?"

I sighed. I could see from the stubborn set of her jaw that she wasn't going to let this go. "Four hours."

"How long since he took me?"

I glanced at the wall clock. "Forty-two hours. They had you for just over thirty hours."

"And you looked for me." It wasn't a question, but I nodded anyway.

"It took over twenty-four hours to track your brother—"

"Don't call him that. After what he did, he is no brother of mine."

"To track *McCarthy* down, then another four to get your location out of him. It took me far longer than I wanted for me to find you."

"But you *did* find me." She swallowed, blinked away the tears shining in her eyes, and took in a deep breath. "My parents will be back from their retreat. I need to tell them about my—about Fraser."

"I don't think that's a good idea, darlin'. It'll be best to let them believe he's gone missing. They'll report it to the police once he doesn't check in, and the investigation they will do should lead them to his gambling and the family he owed money to. The Alexeyov's won't break rank and let their leader's son be taken away. In a week or two McCarthy's body will turn up somewhere unrelated and the police will get an anonymous call about it."

I lifted my hand and used my thumb to brush away the stray tear escaping down her cheek. "It's okay to be upset."

"I'm *angry*," she whispered.

"That's good. Be angry, Dal. Wrap yourself in it. He doesn't deserve your tears."

49
Magdalena

I stared at the man beside me. Had it only been two weeks since my birthday? Since the day he came to my apartment and drove me to my parents' home? It felt like a lifetime ago. I felt like a different person. Rook was quiet beside me, his eyes on my face. A smile tilted my lips.

"When I first saw you, back in the diner, I wondered if Jasmine had hired a hitman to take out my mother and was hiding it by telling me it was a fake date."

He chuckled. "Your instincts were talking to you that day."

"Why did you go along with it?"

"Eat the pizza before it goes cold." He reached out for the plate on the table and handed it to me.

"Don't avoid my question." I took a bite from the slice of cheese pizza, and my stomach gurgled in anticipation of the food.

Rook's shoulders moved as he laughed quietly. "Let a girl get kidnapped a couple of times and she becomes a hardened pro."

I narrowed my eyes. "What does *that* mean?"

"It *means* ..." He stretched out an arm and selected a slice of pizza, raised it to his lips and stared at it for a second before taking a bite and chewing. The way his throat moved as he swallowed had me licking my lips. He caught me looking and one side of his mouth kicked up into a smile, but he didn't comment on it.

"It *means*, darlin', that most women would be curled up in a fetal position crying after what you've just dealt with. But you ... you're behaving like it's another bump in the road. Your survival instinct is strong. You were kidnapped, saw someone killed, ran for your life and spent a week coming to terms with it. Then you were betrayed by your brother, taken again and yet ..." He paused and waved a hand at me. "Here you are, holding it together perfectly well and eating pizza."

"Fake it until you make it, right?" My voice wobbled.

"Is that what you're doing?"

"No ... yes ... maybe a little."

"You don't have to, you know. If you want to scream and shout, do it. Cry if you need to."

"I don't *want* to cry!" But now he'd put the thought into my head and I could feel tears burning the back of my eyes. "I don't want to cry." I repeated in a whisper. "I want to *hit* something, hit *him*!" My voice rose.

He stared at me in silence for a long moment, then rose to his feet. He leaned forward, and I found myself lifted off the couch and set down in front of him. One powerful hand wrapped around my wrist and placed my palm against his chest. "Embrace the anger. Visualize him. What would you do if he was in front of you right now?"

"I'd ask him *why*? Why does he hate me so much? Am I so unworthy of the family that he didn't even think using me to pay off his debt would matter? Does *no one* in my family care?" The words ended on a shriek of demand. The hand resting against his chest clenched into a fist.

"If I hadn't been available, would he have done the same to Charlie? To our *mother*? Or was I the only option?" I raised my fist, slammed it against his chest. Rook didn't move, didn't even rock backwards under the blow. "I'm weak, *useless*. I couldn't even protect myself. If you hadn't been there, I'd be *dead* now or worse!"

My fist hit his chest again, tears blurring my vision. "I wish he was here so I could hurt him the way he's hurt me. Why didn't you kill him? *Why* wouldn't you do that?" My voice rose. "I want him dead, Rook. *Dead*. He deserves it. What kind of person sells their sister? Fakes a kidnapping to get money from their parents? *Who does that?*"

I was pummeling his chest, both hands raised, raining down blows over and over, while I ranted and screamed and cried. It was as though a door had opened and everything I'd dealt with, been through, *felt* over the past two weeks flooded out. All the *pain* of discovering that the one person I was related to who I'd thought cared for me ... *didn't!*

"Bring him back! Show me how to kill him. I want him to

bleed. I want to see him beg for mercy. I want to see him scared ... the way I was!"

"No, you don't." He caught my wrists and tightened his grip when I tried to wrench free.

"Yes, I do. Why didn't you kill him?" I screamed the words at him.

"Because no matter what he did, he's still your brother. That's going to take time to separate yourself from." Rook's calm voice stoked the anger bubbling inside me.

"How can you stand there and talk about what happened as though you were telling me what you had for lunch? Why is it so *easy* for you? Don't you *feel* anything?"

"Of course I do."

"Then why don't you *show* it?" I pulled a hand free, dashing away the tears dripping down my cheeks. "Why is it so easy for you?"

"Because this is *who* I am, darlin'. This is what I do. I wouldn't be much of a killer if I cried over every person I took out, would I?"

"How many people have you killed this week because of *me?*"

"Does it matter?"

"If you hadn't come with me ... you said you'd retired from your *business*. I dragged you back in. How long has it been since you last killed someone?" *Was I really standing here calmly ... okay, not calmly exactly ... discussing when he'd last taken someone's life?*

He shook his head. "It isn't relevant."

"Tell me! How long has it been?"

A soft sigh escaped him. "Over a year. After they released me from prison, I packed away my guns ... metaphorically speaking. I put out word confirming that my retirement before I was imprisoned was still in effect. That I was *done*. I was out of the game and not coming back. I was no longer available to hire."

"Until you met me."

"Dal—"

"No! I dragged you back into it. I covered your hands in blood!"

"That's not what happened."

"You wouldn't have killed anyone if you hadn't been with me."

"But I *was* with you." His hand lifted, caught my chin, and forced my head back. "Dally, listen to me. Falling apart over what happened is understandable, looking for answers is understandable. Trying to take the blame for it ... that's not acceptable. What I did ... the lives I took ... they are *not* your fault. The blame for that lies firmly on your brother, Tomek, and their stupidity. I *chose* to kill those men. I could have just as easily incapacitated them and left them alive, but that wasn't practical. The blood is on *their* hands, not yours. You need to understand that."

"But—" I couldn't explain why I felt responsible, only that I did. Rook had his reasons for retiring, for no longer taking contracts to kill, and I'd put him in an impossible situation where he'd had no choice. That was *my* fault.

"Stop it." His thumb brushed over my lip, swept away the tears dampening my cheeks, and then he lifted me again, and turned to lower us both to the couch. He settled me across his legs and wrapped an arm around my waist, anchoring me in place. "Listen to me, now."

50

Rook

"I was seven when I first killed someone. He was a drunk, violent, and unpredictable. He lived in a house on the same street we … my brothers and I … lived on. I was on the front lawn, fooling around with my brothers, when we heard screaming. Bishop was nine and had developed the unshakeable belief that he was old enough to take on anything life threw at us, so he set off to investigate. Knight and I followed him, because where one went, we all went."

I paused to look at her. Her face was turned away from me, but her breathing was quiet and her tears had stopped flowing, so I carried on. "He … the drunk … had picked up a woman, a local prostitute, and was beating her, screaming abuse with every punch he landed. We didn't even discuss it. Knight went to the left and yelled at him. The second his head lifted to see who had shouted, Bishop took the right and did the same. He stopped hitting the woman and pushed her away. She stumbled and fell, hitting her head against the coffee table." I stopped, building up a memory in my head that I hadn't thought about in years.

"I didn't move from where I stood in the doorway. It had only taken me a quick glance around the room to realize that where I stood was a blind spot and he couldn't see me from where he was. While my brothers kept him distracted long enough for the woman to scramble to her feet, I checked the room for something I could use. "

"Use?" Dally sniffed and twisted to look at me.

My smile was a tiny twitch of my lips. "Even back then, I didn't think like most people. I assessed every situation for danger, for how I could turn it into something that benefited me best. But this situation wasn't about me, it was about the woman and my brothers. They were visible targets for a man who had thought nothing about beating up a woman. Giving two young boys the same treatment wasn't going to worry him."

"What did you do?" she whispered.

"What I eventually learned to do well. There was a gun on a small card table beneath the window. I allowed my brothers to distract him and crept around the room to where it was. He'd obviously tossed it to one side when he brought the woman to his house. I'd seen my dad use handguns, and he'd taught all three of us about gun safety." I gave a quiet laugh.

"The gun was large, too large and heavy for me really, but it had no safety mechanism, so it really was a case of point and press. It took three rounds to hit him. I almost shot Bishop, but I winged the drunk on my third attempt. I worked out my balance before I shot him the fourth time and hit him in the chest, the heart. He dropped to the floor, and we all stood and stared while he bled out."

"You shot him in the heart?"

"It was a fluke, pure luck. There was absolutely no skill involved, only anger at what I'd witnessed and a need to ensure he didn't do it again. As soon as we realized what I'd done, Bishop took over. We cleaned up the scene as best we could, wiped my fingerprints off the gun and hi-tailed it out of there."

"What happened then?"

"We ran back to our own house and locked ourselves in Bishop's room. Knight was panicking, rubbing his hands up and down his thighs, even though there was nothing on them. He kept looking over at me. I went into the adjoining bathroom, washed my hands, checked my reflection to make sure there was no blood on me. Then I went back into the bedroom and asked whether it was time for lunch."

"You wanted *lunch?* Did you understand what had happened? You were only seven."

"I knew what I'd done. I'd killed a man, but I felt it was justified. He'd been hurting someone, and I ... stopped him."

"Did you tell your parents?"

I'd half-expected her to be horrified by my story, maybe demand to go home and get away from me. My sole intention had been to distract her from the blame loop she'd put herself in, but she sounded more fascinated than horrified, so I indulged her question.

"Not immediately, no. Bishop suggested we wait and see if the police came knocking. We hadn't left anything at the man's house, but that didn't mean someone didn't hear the gun go off or saw us entering or leaving. Knight was jumpy for a couple of days, Bishop was focused. I ..." I paused and blew out a breath. "Well, I just carried on with my life. He wasn't relevant to it. I did what I had to do."

"What about the woman?"

I shrugged. "As far as I know, she didn't go to the police, and we never saw her again."

"When did your parents find out?" She shifted on my lap, leaning against me so she could drop her head against my shoulder. "They *did* find out, didn't they?"

I adjusted my hold on her waist, looping my other arm around her and leaning back against the couch cushions. "It was about a month later. My parents came home late, and I noticed blood on my dad's shirt. The spatter reminded me of how it had sprayed out behind the drunk when I shot him. I pointed at it and asked if it was blood. My parents exchanged glances and asked why I thought that. I considered my options and told them about the guy I'd shot. Bishop came running in as I was telling them about pulling the trigger for the first time. He was furious with me, but my parents ..."

I broke off to chuckle. "Turns out killing is the family business. From then on, they brought us into the life my parents led—highly paid assassins ... or hitmen, if you like. They taught us everything they knew. Knight showed a talent for computers, Bishop for planning and development, and me ... well, I inherited my mother's ability to kill without hesitation."

"Are you—?"

"No, I'm not a psychopath *or* a sociopath. I have emotions, I have empathy. I even have morals, believe it or not. I just have a highly tuned ability to separate what I do from who I am. They say that the first kill is the hardest and after that it becomes repetitive, and to a degree, that's true, but for me ... it's not so much that killing is hard, it's not. But while I can form attachments, emotional bonds, I try not to. It interferes with the job. But when I do, I don't use them to further my own interests. So, no, I'm not a psychopath. That's nothing you need to worry about."

"What about your parents?"

"No, they're not psychopaths either. They're a product of another time. They were part of some kind of government thing when they were young and raised to do ... what they do. Eventually, they broke away. I believe they ran away together, changed their names, married, had kids and went into business for themselves. And, as we grew and showed an aptitude for what they did, they trained us."

"Did you have a choice? Could you have said no?"

"Of course. My parents aren't monsters, darlin'. But ... the family business suited me and I made a lot of money from it. Over the years, the contracts changed. The targets became people who

I felt didn't need to be removed, and I found I did ... I *do* have a moral compass of a sort, after all. That's when I decided it was time to step out."

She was still and silent for a long time, and I thought she'd fallen asleep. I was thinking about carrying her up to bed and letting her sleep in comfort when she raised her head.

"I'm glad you let me hire you." She lifted a hand and traced it along my jaw.

I turned my head to meet her eyes. They no longer held the sheen of tears. Instead, there was something else there, a warmth, an intimacy that heated my skin. I smiled. "I'm glad I let you do it, too." My hand rose, brushing a strand of hair away from her face. "Do you want to go upstairs?"

I wasn't asking if she wanted to sleep, and the awareness in her eyes told me she knew it, too. She gave me a small nod. I tightened my hold and stood, taking her with me. Her hands looped around my neck. Her lips found my throat and she pressed soft kisses along my jaw as I climbed the stairs.

Was I making a mistake letting myself grow close to her? Maybe. Was I going to put her to bed and walk out like a gentleman? *Fuck, no.*

I had no idea what it was about this woman, but there had been a subtle attraction there from the start. Something that caught and held my attention. I wanted to spend time with her, to have her scent weave around me. The time spent locked up with her had solidified that to a point where it had been difficult to ignore. I'd set it aside while I worked out how to get us free. Then I'd forced myself to walk away afterward, telling myself the moment we'd shared in the hotel room had been down to the trauma of what had happened. But she came to me, searched me out. And now ... now she was here, in my arms, warm and willing, and I wasn't about to turn her away.

I nudged open the bedroom door with my shoulder, stepped through, kicked it shut behind me, and crossed to the bed. She shrieked when I dropped her onto the mattress without warning, and I smiled, catching her hands to still her scramble across the bed and pinning them in place so I could come down above her. I didn't waste time with whispered words of seduction. I simply claimed her mouth with mine, parted her lips with my tongue, and thrust deep inside.

She didn't fight, mouth opening to accept my invasion, and she pulled one hand free so she could wrap it around my neck and drag me closer. I let her, pushing one leg between hers and bracing myself on one hand while I used the other to find the hem of her shirt and push beneath it. Her back arched, a soft gasp leaving her lips, when my fingers found the curve of her breast, and I separated my mouth from hers to look down at her.

"You're okay with this?"

She nodded, her tongue snaking out to lick over her lips.

I didn't wait for further confirmation, leaning back to unbutton and pull off my shirt. I tossed it to one side and caught hold of her t-shirt.

"Sit up."

She rose up and lifted her arms and tugged her shirt over her head. That joined mine on the floor. She dropped back onto the bed and looked up at me. I swept my eyes over her. She wasn't wearing a bra beneath the pajama top, and her full breasts, tipped with dark pink nipples, were on display. I bent my head slowly, knowing her eyes were on me, and ran my tongue around one stiffened peak.

Her sigh above me was soft, and I smiled against the warmth of her skin before flicking my tongue over the tip of her nipple. It hardened further. I sought out her other breast and palmed it, feeling her nipple press against my palm. I squeezed—a perfectly plump handful—and sucked her nipple into my mouth, caught it between my teeth and laved my tongue over the tip to soothe the sting. She moaned, back bowing, one leg lifting to hook over my hip and she rubbed against my thigh.

I dropped a hand to the waistband of her pajama bottoms, pushed beneath the material and down. No underwear impeded my path and my fingers found the wet warm center of her. I didn't hesitate, pushed a finger inside her, while my thumb found her clit and stroked a small gentle circle around it. Her fingers curled around my forearm.

"Rook." She breathed my name.

I added a second finger, timed the flicking of my tongue with the pumping of my fingers until she was writhing beneath me. Her nails dug into my skin as I thrust deeper into her body.

Dragging my mouth from her breast, I kissed my way down her body, pushed the pajama bottoms down her legs and settled between her thighs.

I'd dreamed about having my mouth on her again, about her responsive moans as I'd feasted on her at the hotel. I pulled my fingers free, spread her open, flattened my tongue and licked all around her clit, sucked on her sweet, wet flesh, while she pleaded for more. I ignored her clit, focusing instead on the soft plump lips to either side, sucking them into my mouth, and lifting my head until they pulled free. I caught one of her hands and drew it down her body.

"Hold yourself open for me," I told her. "Offer your body to me, darlin'."

She didn't question me, her legs widening so she could spread her pussy open with her fingers.

I ran the tip of my tongue over her lightly, a barely there touch that had her body twitching.

"Keep yourself spread open, honey. I want to look at you." I traced around her clit with one finger, dipped it inside her, and then back up to her clit again. "Do you want me to fuck you?"

"Yes." Her response was immediate.

"Say it."

"I want you to fuck me." There was no hesitation.

"Even though you know what I am ... what I've done?"

"Even if you'd gone ahead and killed my brother."

I stilled. I hadn't expected that response. Turning my head,

I pressed my lips against her thigh, kissed my way up and inwards until I could cover her clit with my mouth. I feasted on her, licked ... lapped ... *sucked* until she was writhing beneath me. Her fingers touched my head, slid into my hair, curled into a fist and tugged.

"Stop," she gasped. "Rook, please. I want you to fuck me."

I lifted my head, licking my lips. "I want you to come first."

51

Magdalena

True to his word, he didn't stop until he'd wrung an orgasm from me, one that had my back bowing, and my fingers digging into his scalp as small explosions were set off in every nerve ending. My vision swam, my body a mass of sensation, and I missed him rising from the bed and kicking out of his pants. It was only when I heard the rustle of paper that my eyesight refocused, and I found him standing beside the bed, tearing open a condom. I rolled onto my side.

"I want to do it." I held out my hand. After a second's hesitation, he handed the condom to me. I smiled at the slight frown, pulling his eyebrows together. "What's wrong? Don't you trust me?"

The frown smoothed out. "I trust you well enough."

I swung my legs off the bed and sat up, reaching out to run my fingers over his hip and down his leg. There was a small scar on his thigh. I touched it with one fingertip. "What is this?"

"Gunshot." He turned and pointed at the other side of his leg.

"Exit wound is there."

"How many times have you been shot?" I leaned forward and pressed my lips against the scar. His skin was warm beneath my mouth.

"No clue." His hand dropped to rest in my hair. "Less than fifty, more than ten? I've probably been stabbed more times than I've been shot."

I leaned back to look up at him. "*Stabbed?*"

He shrugged. "I'm not always as sneaky as I need to be when I'm working a job. You can check out all my scars whenever you like." His fingers slid through my hair, and he tugged my head back. "Do you want to do that now or …?" His voice was amused, a half-smile teasing his lips.

I'd never felt so at ease with someone before, never made idle conversation—if you could call discussing the various scars on his body idle conversation—while I was naked and about to have sex. I kissed a path along his thigh, away from the scar and up to his hip.

"I definitely *don't* want to do that right now," I whispered, and wrapped my fingers around his erection.

The groan that rumbled through him caused my body to heat up, and I gave him a long, slow pump before rolling the condom on. The hand in my hair tightened.

"Lean back on your elbows and open your legs."

I dropped back, his hand falling from my hair, and held his eyes with mine as I slowly parted my legs. His gaze dropped, his tongue sweeping over his lips, and then he stepped between my thighs, and leaned over me, bracing himself on his hands on either side of my body.

"Wrap your legs around my waist."

The move lifted my ass off the bed and he raised one hand to slide it between our bodies. He grasped his dick, pressed it against me and then he was pushing inside, inch by slow inch. I could feel him stretching me, *filling* me, and the sensation of him slowly possessing me was incredible. My elbows lost their strength, and I fell back against the mattress, a soft gasp escaping me when he drew back, then slammed his full length into me ... I lost all sense of time as he drove me to another orgasm.

I was on the edge of sleep when Rook came back into the bedroom. The mattress dipped slightly as he slid beneath the covers, and then his warm body pressed up against my back, the weight of one arm across my waist.

"Are you asleep?" His words were a soft whisper against my ear.

"Not yet." But I was close. Speaking was an effort, and his warm chuckle told me he knew.

"I don't know what this is, Dal," he continued in a quiet voice, his lips brushing along my throat and across my shoulder. "I'm not sure we can put a name to it right now, but I want you to know that I *like* you being here ... with me ... like this."

I wriggled backwards until there was no space between us and rested my hand over his, where it lay against my stomach. "I like it, too."

I don't know if he replied because sleep claimed me, and the next time I opened my eyes, it was to the sun beaming through the gap in the curtains. Rook was a warm presence beside me. At some point during the night, I'd turned, wrapping myself around him, and I could hear the steady beat of his heart against my ear.

I eased out of his arms carefully, not wanting to wake him. I had the distinct impression that falling asleep sharing a bed was not something he did regularly, and I wanted the opportunity to look at the man I was quickly developing feelings for, while he couldn't see me.

His eyes were closed, his breathing soft and steady, and I leaned up on one elbow to stare down at him. There was a dark smattering of stubble covering his jaw, with the barest hint of gray here and there, matching the gray at his temples. A faint scar, about an inch long, ran just beneath his right eye, hardly visible unless you were close to him, and there was another to the left side of his top lip. Tattoos covered his arms—skulls, animals, weapons. There was another on the wrist of his right arm, a small clock-like tattoo with markers to show how many people he'd killed and I briefly wondered if he'd add to it after the past two weeks.

I ran a finger over his jaw, down his throat and followed the line of his arm where it lay on the sheets beside him. His hand was flat, palm down, and I linked my fingers with his, comparing the dark tan of his skin with the lighter tone of mine.

"Good morning."

I'd heard friends talk about how sexy a man's morning voice could be, but nothing prepared me for the gravelly tone which broke the silence or the way it sparked my nerve endings to life.

He lifted our linked hands and pressed my fingers to his lips, then moved until he was leaning over me, my hand pinned above my head.

He kissed my cheek, then the tip of my nose, and smiled down at me. "How long have you been awake?"

"Not long."

"Then we need to grab coffee, breakfast, and make a plan for the day." He lowered his head and nipped my earlobe. "Or we'll end up staying in bed all day."

I tangled my free hand into his hair. "I like option B best."

He chuckled. "We have too much to do. Come on, darlin'. Get that pretty ass out of bed." He released my hand and rolled away.

I watched as he rose from the bed and crossed the room, admiring the way the muscles moved beneath the skin of his ass and thighs.

"Stop ogling me." He didn't turn around.

"I'm not."

"Liar." He pulled open the door on the closet and took out a clean shirt and dark pants.

"Don't you ever dress casually?"

He glanced over at me. "Sometimes. When the situation calls for it."

"And whatever you have planned today doesn't call for it?"

"Not in my eyes, no." He stepped into the pants and pulled on the shirt, then faced me. "Come on, *up*. You have ten minutes before I come back and tip you out of that bed."

"Come back? Where are you going?" I pushed up into a seated position, and his eyes dipped to look at my chest before rising to my face.

"I'm going to make coffee." But the direction he moved was *not* toward the door, but back to the bed, and he palmed one breast, stroking his thumb over my nipple. It sprang to attention immediately. His lips twitched upwards, and he bent his head to replace his thumb with his mouth.

I couldn't stop a moan from escaping, feeling the pull as he sucked at my breast right down to my clit. I fell back against the pillows, and he followed me, teeth tugging gently at my nipple, while his tongue flicked back and forth across the tip. And then he let me go, and straightened.

"You really are a delicious distraction that I never saw coming," he muttered, then laughed, shaking his head. "Get up, Dally. I'm not letting you tempt me back into bed."

"But—" I shrieked as the world spun, and I found myself upside down, my face pressed against his back. "Put me down." One hand swatted my ass as he strode out of the room, my stomach bouncing against his shoulder.

"I need coffee, darlin'." He ignored my struggles and carried me down the stairs and into the kitchen.

The world spun again as he placed me on a seat beside the table and cocked an eyebrow at me.

"That was rude." I glared at him.

He smiled. "Trust me, I want nothing more than to feel my dick buried inside you, but there's shit we need to do today, and I need at least one mug of coffee before we get started."

L. ANN

52

Rook

I tossed the t-shirt I'd grabbed on my way out of the bedroom door with her slung over my shoulder onto Dally's lap. "Put that on."

"Why?"

I fiddled with the coffee machine. "Because if you don't, I might forget why we're in the kitchen and just fuck you on the table and call that breakfast."

Her startled gasp went straight to my dick, and I questioned my decision to drag her out of the bedroom. Instead of pulling her off the chair and doing all the dirty nasty things going through my mind, I busied myself making coffee.

"I know someone who owns a gun range in the next town over. I thought we'd go visit and give you a lesson in using a weapon." I kept my voice casual.

"You think I need to learn how to shoot?"

"I think *everyone* needs to know how to use a gun—to ensure they don't blow their own heads off, if for no other reason."

She frowned. "That's a ... an interesting way to look at it, I guess."

I handed her a mug of coffee. "Drink up. Are you hungry? I'm sure I can throw something together, if you are."

She was shaking her head before I finished talking. "I don't really bother with breakfast. Coffee is fine."

I finished making my own and sat opposite her. She seemed no worse for wear after the ordeal she'd gone through. Still a little pale, bruised, and tired, but otherwise calm. I was a little concerned it was a front she was putting on, that she would crash at some point.

"How are you feeling?"

She blinked at me over the rim of the mug and appeared to be considering my question as she sipped her coffee. I waited, not wanting to push her into a response and, eventually, she set her mug down on the table and leaned back on the chair.

"I'm not sure. I feel like I should be freaking out, you know? But part of me is asking what the point would be ... does that make sense?" She didn't wait for my response. "It's like. I'm not there now. I'm *here*. You came for me. If you hadn't arrived when you did, it would have gone a lot worse. But you did, so I'm not sure whether there's anything to be gained from crying over it ... does that make me weird?"

"A little, maybe. But it makes sense. Especially after going through the kidnapping as well. I think after a while, you start to become numb to the bad things and focus on the positives. At least, that's what I do." I reached across the table and took her hand. "I don't want to dwell on what might have been, but there's something I do need you to understand."

I hesitated. I needed to make her aware of everything, but I really didn't want to scare her, so I had to be careful. "I handed over your brother to Sergei—he's responsible for the debt he owes Tomek—but that doesn't mean there won't be any repercussions later. Tomek is his own man. Sergei's control over him only extends so far. I don't *think* Tomek will try to start anything further, but he's hot-headed so there's a slight risk."

"That's why you want me to learn how to use a gun," she whispered.

I nodded. "You're going to want to go back to your life. You don't want to be locked away in my home for the rest of your life, and I doubt you want my brother to organize a new name and life for you somewhere else. It would be a good idea, but I wouldn't force that on you. So, I want you to be protected when I am not there." I squeezed her fingers. "Do you understand?"

She nodded after a second's thought.

"Okay, good. Then go and get dressed, darlin', and we'll head out."

"This doesn't look like a gun range." Dally sat forward in her seat and peered at the building in front of us. "Does that say *Tony's Mechanics* on the sign?"

"Yeah. He owns the garage, but there's a gun range attached to it. It's just not …" I considered my words. "Well, it's not open to the public."

Her head turned toward me. "What you mean is that it isn't a legal business, don't you?"

I chuckled. "Maybe." I opened the car door. "Let's go inside."

Dally was out of the car before I got to the passenger side. She smiled at me. "I know, I know. You wanted to open the door for me and be a gentleman, but honestly ... I don't need you to do that."

"It's how I was raised. Open doors, help a woman out of the car, walk on the outside of the sidewalk." I shrugged. "It's simply good manners."

Dally tucked her arm through mine. "I guess. It's not something I'm used to."

I looked down at her hand where it rested on my arm, and the thought that I wasn't used to this level of intimacy was loud in my head. And yet ... it felt right, comfortable, *normal* even. I covered her fingers with my palm. "Are you sure you're okay?"

She nodded. "I keep thinking that I *should* be freaking out over everything that has happened ... and maybe I will, eventually. But right now ... I'm just going to keep pushing forward and focus on how I want things to be instead of what has happened. I think ..." She paused and licked her lips. "I need to speak to my parents. That's going to be hard. I don't think I'll be able to pretend something hasn't happened, that I don't know where Fr—*he* has gone. But I know you're right. I can't tell them about it. I'm not even sure they'd believe it." She looked up at me, eyes troubled. "For today, can we pretend it didn't happen? That we're just having a fun day out?"

I nodded. "We can do that."

I led her through the door, which led into the small reception area for the garage. A redheaded woman smiled brightly. "Welcome to Tony's. Are you here to pick up a car or drop one off?"

"Neither. Tell Tony that Rook is here."

Her smile faltered before returning brighter than before. "One moment, sir." She disappeared through another door, and I could hear low voices talking, and then she was back, another man behind her.

"Rook!" Tony's hand was outstretched in greeting.

I took it and shook, resisting the desire to wipe my hand once he released it.

"It's been a while. I was surprised to get your call, gotta be honest. But I have you all set up. Come through." He didn't look at or even acknowledge Dally's presence. But that wasn't unusual. He was well-practiced in the art of only seeing what he was paid to see and unless I introduced Dally, he would behave as though she wasn't there.

We followed him through the garage and out the exit set at the far back. A small parking lot held three cars, which we passed without stopping. He pulled out a set of keys and stopped outside another building. "You're the only one here today. I marked it down as a private party." He flashed a smile, unlocked the door, and held it open. "After you."

"You know better than that." I didn't move, and caught Dally's arm as she stepped forward. "You first, Tony."

He huffed. "Do you really think I'm going to set a trap for you? After all these years?"

"I'm still alive because I know people can be bought. You go inside, we'll follow."

He grunted. "Fine." He stepped through the doorway and reached out to the left. My hand drifted to the gun holstered at my back, but he simply flicked a light switch, and the room lit up.

"See. Nothing and no one is waiting for you. Come on in." He waved a hand, indicating we step inside.

I guided Dally inside, looking around carefully. There was nowhere anyone could hide, unless they were tucked down behind the barrier between the range and where you stood. I strode across and leaned over.

"Rook, I swear to you, I haven't been paid off."

When I turned to face him, Tony was standing, hands raised, fingers spread.

I looked at his hands, then up at his face, then shrugged. "Okay."

His throat moved as he swallowed. Dally glanced at him and then at me. "What's happening?"

"Nothing. Everything is fine." I uncurled her fingers from my sleeve and took a step away. "Is everything set up?"

"Sure is." He held out the keys. "If you'll follow me out, you can lock the door. No one will disturb you. The key to the gun cabinet is the red one, the door key is blue. There's a second exit over there." He pointed to the right. "Fire extinguisher is beside it, just in case. Not that I think you're going to start a fire in here, but safety regulations..."

I snorted. "This place doesn't even exist. I doubt you get surprise safety visitations."

"Well... no... but my clientele would kill me if something happened, as *you* well know."

I took the keys and followed him to the door. "Thanks, Tony. If Knight calls, let him know I'll get back to him."

"Knight knows you're here?"

"Him and Bishop." I let a smile spread over my face. "So, you know... if you *were* considering doing something, I'd definitely rethink it."

Tony rolled his eyes. "You're so untrusting. Good job I like you or I'd be insulted. I'll come back in four hours and check in on you." He patted my shoulder. "Contrary to what you might believe, it's good to see you." He nodded his head and threw open the door. "Lock the door behind me." He strode across the parking lot back toward the garage.

I waited until he disappeared from sight before closing and locking the door.

"You don't really think he's going to try and set you up, do you?" Dally said when I turned back to face her.

I shook my head. "No, but it doesn't hurt to remind him what he'll be facing if he ever decides to do that."

"I thought you said he was a friend?"

"He is."

She stared at me. "You have a very strange idea of what friendship is."

I laughed. "Come on, let's get started."

53

Magdalena

My hands and shoulders ached, my ears hurt from the mufflers pressing onto them, and I was fairly sure I was getting eye-strain from staring down the range at the targets which Rook kept pushing farther away.

He'd had me practice with various types of handguns, explaining *in depth* about each one before even allowing me to touch it. Then he tested me on which guns had safety mechanisms, which ones didn't, how each one worked, followed by how to put bullets into them. Not once did he lose his temper or raise his voice, taking me through how to load and then disarm each gun step by step, over and over.

Only when he was happy with how I held each gun did he tell me to try firing them … and then the lessons began again as he talked me through switching off the safety, pointing, and aiming.

Four hours turned into six hours, turned into eight hours. By six pm, I was sure my arm was going to fall off, but we'd found out which gun I was most comfortable holding—not that I could remember what he'd called it. He'd had me practice with that one for most of the afternoon until I could hit the target. I wasn't about to get any awards for my shooting skills, but I was pretty sure if someone was coming toward me, I could at least hit *them* and not any bystanders.

When seven pm rolled around, I placed the gun down onto the counter, and pulled off the ear protectors.

"I need to stop." I said in response to his questioning look. "My arm hurts too much to hold steady."

For a second, I thought he was going to argue, but instead, he nodded. "Do you want to go out for dinner? We could drop back home, get changed, and find a restaurant."

"I'd like that."

But before we left, he insisted on making me go through the steps of making sure all the guns were safe, bullets removed, safeties on, and packed away back in the gun locker. We walked across the parking lot and through the garage. The receptionist had left, probably hours ago, and only the man Rook had called Tony remained. He sat in reception, feet propped up on a table covered in magazines, scrolling through his cell. He hopped to his feet when we walked in.

"All done?"

Rook nodded and handed him the keys. "Thanks. Everything is locked up."

"Great. Coming back tomorrow?"

"No. I think we did enough for now. Did you get the order

for me?"

"I did. Let me go and get it." He strode away, but was back less than a minute later, with a box tucked under his arm. "There's a box of ammo in there as well."

"Track back?"

Tony shook his head. "None. I can make it legal if you want, but right now there's no way of tracing it back to anyone."

"Leave it that way for now. I might change it later." Rook took the box, shook Tony's hand and then he was guiding me back out to the car.

"What's that?" I asked once we were both settled inside, nodding to the box he'd tossed onto the back seat.

"Your first handgun. I'll show you later. Let's eat first."

The restaurant was one I'd eaten at before, located in the center of Glenville. It was a family-owned place, small but popular, and we were led to a table set in one corner of the room.

Rook took the menu from the server and flipped it open. "What would you like?"

I opened my menu and scanned down the list, looking at the words carefully. A tanned hand appeared in front of the page and one long finger tapped the paper. "How bad is your dyslexia?"

My stomach plummeted to my toes, and my eyes jerked up to his. "What?"

"That's what you have, right? It's not simply a case of not being able to read. You're dyslexic." There was nothing in his voice to show what he thought about it.

My mouth dried up. "I ... umm ..."

"Dal ..." His hand rose from the menu and touched my cheek. "Look at me." He waited until my eyes met his. "It's nothing to be ashamed of."

"But how did you know?" I forced the question out.

"Initially, I didn't. Back when you said you couldn't read the ransom demand, I put it down to fear. But then you didn't read the report Knight had compiled about you or your family. You went straight to the photographs. At the diner, you looked at the images and not the words. Tonight, you couldn't hide your dismay when you saw there were no images of the food on the menu. You're not stupid. There's no way you simply haven't learned how to read, so ... " He shrugged. "Dyslexia is the only answer."

I stared at him.

"That's the real reason you don't drive, isn't it? The more I think about it, the more sense it makes. You have difficulty with left and right. When we were looking at the gun safety sheets for each weapon today, you relied on me explaining and not on the words written down." His hand dropped from my cheek and he took my hand. "That's why your mother keeps buying you books to read. She thinks she can fix it by forcing you to read."

"She thought I was lazy ... *stupid*." The words left my lips and I could hear the bitterness in them.

"You're neither of those things."

"I know that now. But it took a long time to figure it out." I shrugged. "It doesn't matter."

I could see he wanted to pursue the subject further, but for some reason he opted not to and instead looked at the menu. "The food here is pretty standard, nothing outlandish. There's steak, fish, or vegetarian."

"Steak is good." I focused on the menu. "It's not that I *can't* read what it says. It sometimes takes me longer to work out the words... that's all." I explained quietly. "When we were... when I had to read the ransom ... When I feel stressed, it's harder to make sense of the words and the more I try, the worse it jumbles together."

"That makes sense. Well, we're in no rush and under no pressure tonight. Take all the time you want."

"No, I'll have steak. I prefer that over the others."

He nodded, and after a couple of minutes, the server reappeared to take our order. Rook ordered two steak dinners and two glasses of cola.

"Is there a story behind the no alcohol?" he asked once the server had walked away.

"Nothing exciting. Alcohol makes it harder to focus, and I don't really like how it tastes."

Silence fell, and I toyed with a napkin. Small talk had never been one of my skills and I cast around trying to find something to talk about. Rook leaned back on his chair, his dark eyes moving constantly around the room. He didn't seem uncomfortable or bothered by my silence.

"Do you find yourself constantly looking for hidden motives behind everything people do?" I broke the silence to ask.

His gaze swung to me, and one eyebrow rose. "Are you asking if I think you have an ulterior motive for being here?"

"No! You just seem to be always watching what other people are doing. Are you looking for weapons?"

His laugh was low and rich. "Not really. Being aware of my surroundings is an ingrained habit. My life choices mean that I've had to always be conscious of what everyone around me is doing, especially when working out a plan to reach a mark."

"A mark ... that's like your—"

"My target, yeah. You learn to assess your surroundings, work out who is a potential threat to your job and who isn't."

"So, if ...." I looked around the room, and jerked my chin toward a young couple gazing at each other over their plates. "If one of those two was your ... *mark* .... How would you do it?"

His eyebrow hiked further, and then he chuckled. "Okay, I'll indulge you." He paused when the server returned with our drinks. "Thanks, honey." Taking a sip, he smiled at me over the rim of the glass. "First, I'd need to decide whether I wanted my target to die publicly or when he was back at home."

I propped my chin on one hand. "Let's say you're supposed to send a public message to someone else in the room."

"Devious, I like it. Alright, let's pretend he works for that older guy." He gave a discrete nod toward a gray-haired gentleman eating alone near the entrance. "The older guy has upset someone with a far reach, *but* he's too important to be taken out, so I'm instructed to take out his son."

"His son being the mark?"

"That's right." He grinned at me and the pure mischievousness of it made me laugh. "I received information that both the father and son are going to be at this restaurant tonight. The son with his girlfriend, the father is waiting to meet with the man who has issued me with the contract."

"I guess you come to the restaurant?"

"First, I follow him around for a couple of days to figure out the kind of things he does. I check out who he spends time with, where he goes, how he spends his days and evenings, where he sleeps, and what he drives. I go deep into his entire life until I know everything about his routine. Okay, let's assume part of the contract is to take him out with an audience. It gives the message that Grey Hair over there is on borrowed time and that the person he's fucking with is serious. I need to make it happen without attracting attention to myself. The easiest way would be to dress like one of the serving staff, but a quick look around will show you that I wouldn't blend in. I'm too old."

"You're not old."

His smile softened. "I'm not *old*, but I'm too old to blend in here. Look around you. The servers are all around your age. Not a thirty-eight-year-old man. It wouldn't work. I'd need to be someone who's here for dinner."

"Okay, that makes more sense. You book a reservation, but not under your name?"

He gave me an approving nod. "Good girl. I use one of my many fake IDs and book a table. I spin a story about how I need one close to the window, because I always feel a little claustrophobic if I can't see outside. There are only two window tables—the one my mark is sitting at and the one behind him. I dress down a little. My suit wouldn't be top of the range, but it also wouldn't be bargain basement. It would be plain, maybe a little rumpled, not something that would stand out or be memorable. I'd wear a white shirt and a plain tie. I'd look like any other businessman who doesn't have a family to go home to, or time to cook."

"Would you get here before or after them?"

"Good question. I'd get here first. That way, I'm sitting down and they have no reason to even notice me. If I walked past their table, one of them would look up. It's a natural instinct. By already sitting down, with my back to them, I'm giving them the message that I'm not important to their night." He paused for another sip of Coke. "I'd probably even be partway through a meal. By the time they've ordered, I'm looking at leaving."

"When do you make a move?" Was I really sitting here discussing how Rook would plan a murder? Yes, I was. I was pretty sure I should be asking what was wrong with me because instead of being scared or creeped out, it fascinated me.

"During their main course. He'll have picked the seat on my side, sitting with his back to me, because he's a gentleman and instinctively he doesn't want his woman that close to another man." He broke off when the server returned with our meals.

"Enjoy!" she chirped as she set down the plates.

Rook didn't speak again until after he'd eaten a mouthful of food. "Once they're deep into conversation and enjoying their meal, I'd lean back on my chair and use a syringe to inject strychnine into his body."

"Why strychnine?"

"It's quick to work. With a high enough dose, it can cause respiratory failure and brain death. By the time the poison had done its job, I would be gone. Just another lonely workaholic businessman heading back to his cold apartment."

L. ANN

54

Rook

She stared at me, her expression rapt as she listened to how I'd plan out a job, and I wondered whether she could handle the life I had lived on a more regular basis. The thought made me stop speaking, and I frowned.

Bringing someone into my life—even now that I'd retired—would be an idiotic move, a *dangerous* move. It was not something I'd *ever* considered and yet, here I was. My mind had already halfway figured out how to make it work. I wasn't sure if that surprised or disturbed me.

I could ask Bishop to relocate us, Knight to build us a new life. I was confident I could talk her into walking away from her family. They sucked anyway. What bothered me was that I *wanted* to do it. I'd *never* missed the things other people viewed as normal—relationships, settling down, two point five kids and a white picket fence. None of it was for me... but sitting here with Dally, I wondered whether it would be possible. Whether I could *have* that.

"You're staring." Her voice was quiet, and I blinked.

Had I been staring?

"Is everything okay? I'm sorry, I shouldn't have asked you to describe all that. Did it bring everything back to you?"

I reached across the table and took her hand. "No. It's not something that bothers me. It was fun to plot it out without actually following through." I wasn't lying, it *was*.

"Have you done that before? Used strychnine, I mean?"

I nodded. "A few times. Not in quite the way I described, though. It was rare that people would pay for a public message like that. It's too easy to get wrong."

"Is there anyone in here that you would view as a danger right now?"

"In here?" I glanced around the room. "No. Unless they're *superb* at hiding micro-expressions."

"Are *you* good at that?"

I smiled. "Very good at it, but in this kind of casual setting, there are still tells if you know what to look for."

"Is everything to your liking?" The server was back, smiling down at us both.

"Yes, thank you. Do you want dessert, darlin'?"

Dally shook her head. "I'm tired. Do you think we could go home?"

"Can we get the check, please?"

The server nodded and disappeared.

"Are you alright?"

"Just tired. You've worn me out with all the practicing today. My arm aches." She gave a quiet laugh. "I'm sure if I compared them, one arm would be more muscular than the other right now."

"You need to learn to shoot with both hands."

"I don't, not really. You're a perfectionist."

I smiled at that. "Maybe you're right."

Dally was dozing when we finally pulled up outside my house. Her eyes fluttered open when I cut off the engine, and she yawned when she unclipped the seatbelt. It was clear she was more tired than she was claiming by the fact she didn't even attempt to open the door, but waited for me to round the car and do it for her. I reached inside and helped her out, and she leaned against my side as we walked into the house.

"Coffee or bed?"

"Bed," she replied around another yawn.

She paused in the hallway to kick off her shoes, and I stopped to watch as she shrugged out of her jacket and hung it up. It was strange how *normal* it felt to have her in the house. There was nothing awkward about her behavior.

"Are you coming up?" Her words pulled my attention away from my thoughts, and I shook my head.

"No, you go on up. I'm going to stay down here for a little while longer."

"Okay." She came back toward me, rested one hand against my chest and leaned up to press a kiss to the corner of my mouth.

"I doubt I'll be awake when you come up."

I chuckled. "I wouldn't bet against that." I brushed my fingers over her cheek. "Go on. I'll be up later." There was no doubt, no question, no *decision* to be made. I wouldn't be sleeping anywhere other than beside her—we both knew it. If I was a lesser man, I'd be scared by how easily we'd fallen into this odd relationship. And that's what it was—a relationship.

I was still thinking about that when I entered my kitchen and took a bottle of beer from the refrigerator.

Two weeks ago, I had no idea who Magdalena McCarthy was. Now? The thought of her not being in my life was something I refused to consider. What did that mean? A side effect from sharing an intense experience or something more? I shied away from the word *love*. We'd known each other for two weeks. Love didn't happen that fast ... did it? Surely not.

I pulled out my cell and called my brother.

"How difficult would it be to move?"

"For who?" Bishop's voice was low, almost a whisper.

I frowned. "Where are you?"

"Hiding from the mafia princess from fucking hell. I swear to god, if I have to sit here and listen to her wail about her fucking nails one more time, I might kill her myself and take the consequences."

"Don't get killed by the mob, Bish. I'd have to come out of retirement to avenge you."

"Good point. I'll try. Thankfully, I'm only here for another twenty-four hours, then she's Dorian's problem. Who do you want to relocate?"

"Me ... and Dally, if she wants to come with me."

"*You?*"

"This whole retirement thing isn't working well. Everyone knows where I am. You know it's only a matter of time before the contracts start rolling in again. I'm serious about getting out of the game, Bish. I'm done. I'm fucking over it. I think the only way I can do that is to make it clear I'm done."

"And you want to take your no-longer-fake girlfriend with you? Have you talked to her about it?"

"Not yet. I don't even know if she'd come, if it's something that I *should* mention."

"Are you in love with her, Rook?"

That wasn't a question I could answer easily. "I don't know. Maybe? I like her ... a lot."

"Pretty sure it's stronger than *like*." Bishop's voice was wry.

"I did say *a lot*. I don't know. Isn't it too soon to say?"

"I don't think there's a hard and fast rule on how quickly you can catch feelings for someone. Only you can say whether it's how you feel. From where I'm hiding, it seems like you do. You've done things for her that you wouldn't do for any other woman."

"Maybe."

"Fuck maybe. You were already fucking her in your head when you agreed to be her fake-date. I saw the look on your face after she left your table. I just didn't see *her*. She had your attention from the second you saw her. How does she feel?"

"No clue. We haven't talked about it."

"Sometimes playing things close to your chest doesn't work. Talk to her. I *can* relocate you. How do you feel about the coast? Maybe a Caribbean island?"

"Somewhere that doesn't have too many people."

"I'll work something out. Let me know if it'll be for one or two people."

55
Magdalena

I sat at the desk to the right of the entrance to the art gallery, with my chin propped on my hand. Sienna, the gallery's owner, walked around showing some of the art to two potential customers. I shifted on my seat, turning my head to look out of the window. An hour to go until closing time. I'd been back at work for two days—against Rook's advice—and while it was nice to be out of the house, it was hard not to startle at every unexpected noise.

For the past week, I'd stayed inside Rook's house with him. I chuckled to myself. Okay, I'd basically moved in. We slept together, *lived* together. I'd gone back to my apartment twice to collect more clothes. I had filled one side of his closet, and all my toiletries were scattered around his bathroom.

He hadn't said anything about it, and neither had I, but we'd settled into a comfortable routine … until I told him I wanted to go back to work and return to a normal life. He'd argued, protested that he couldn't protect me, and I'd asked him whether he really thought I needed protection. He'd been quiet for a few minutes and then reluctantly shook his head. I called the gallery a little while later and arranged to go back.

What I didn't admit to Rook was that I wished I hadn't. I was bored. Before everything had happened, I'd been content to spend part of my day in the gallery. I watched people talk about the artwork on the walls, discussing what it meant, what message the artist had been trying to share. I'd dreamed that one day my own work would be admired in the same way.

Now? Now, every time someone walked in, I examined them—the way they walked, how they observed the room, whether their clothing held any suspicious lumps and bumps. I wondered how many of them had connections to the seedy underworld I'd recently become aware of. I wondered how many of them had tried to hire someone to kill another person.

Nothing about the world was bright anymore. It was dark and scary, unpredictable and disturbing. And yet, I felt more alive than I ever had.

The low beep of the alarm when the door opened dragged my attention back to the room. A tall man, clothed in a dark expensive suit and sunglasses, strolled toward me, hands buried deep into his pants pockets. He stopped when he reached my desk, and one dark eyebrow hiked up behind the lenses shielding his eyes. I tipped my head back and smiled.

"Mr. Chambers."

Rook inclined his head. "Ms. McCarthy." He turned, propping his hip against my desk, and scanned the room.

"You're early. I don't finish for another hour."

"Just calling in on my way past. I'll be back to get you. I need to go and see Bishop first. He's meeting me at the diner. If I'm not here when you lock up, wait for me. Do *not* go anywhere." He pulled off his glasses and nailed me with a hard look. "Understand?"

I rolled my eyes. "I'll stay inside until you arrive."

"Do you have—?"

"Yes!" I cut in, scowling. I was certain he'd been about to ask if I had my gun, and the last thing I needed was Sienna to overhear him. He'd spent a week teaching me to shoot. I'd never be in his league, but I was a lot more confident with it than I had been at the start of the week. "Rook, I promise, I've been listening to everything you said."

His expression didn't change at all, yet I *knew* my flippant tone irritated him. I could *feel* it. I glanced around to see where Sienna and her clients were, then stood and rounded the desk so I could wrap my arms around his waist and lean against him.

"Thank you for being worried about me. I promise I'm taking everything seriously. I'd be stupid not to."

His chest moved as he sighed and one hand rested against my spine. "Fine. I'll stop fussing." I hid a smile at the grumbled words. I couldn't deny the way his protectiveness warmed me. His lips touched the top of my head. "I better go meet Bishop before he comes hunting for me."

I nodded against his chest, but didn't move. His hand slid up my spine, reaching my hair and tugged at it. "Dal?"

"I know." I leaned back and looked up at him. "I'm glad we met."

That damn eyebrow quirked up again, but he smiled and dropped a kiss to the tip of my nose. "Me too." He reached back and unwound my arms. "Don't forget what I said, darlin'. I'll be back soon."

He turned, raising a hand to wave as he walked out. I stood there for a second longer, before returning to my post behind the desk, pulled a pad in front of me and spent the next fifteen minutes sketching him.

"That's good." Sienna leaned over me to say, and I glanced up at her.

"Oh! How long have you been standing there?"

"Only a couple of minutes. I sold two Denver's and a Colton." She referenced two local artists who had paintings in the gallery.

"That's great."

"It is. When are you going to let me sell some of your work?"

My head shake was immediate. "I'm not good enough yet."

"Mags, you *are* good enough. Your work should be on my walls."

"Maybe ... one day."

She huffed. "I might have to have a talk with that fine man who's been picking you up the last couple of nights. I'm sure he could convince you."

"*Rook?*" My cheeks burned. "Please don't. He hasn't seen anything I've done." *Well, other than the sketch of the man who kidnapped us, but that doesn't count.*

"I want to display your work, Magdalena. I know you have enough of it stockpiled for us to do at least one showing. Let me organize it, please?"

"Let me think about it." Maybe I would talk to Rook and see what he thought. I caught the stray thought and laughed. I'd only known him for a month, yet I was *living* with him. We were definitely in a relationship... one we hadn't even talked about starting.

"That's good enough for me. I'll start making plans."

"Sienna! I never said yes."

Her smile was breezy. "You will."

L. ANN

56

Rook

Bishop was at the diner when I arrived, and I slid onto the bench seat opposite him.

"Nice shiner." I flicked a finger toward the yellow and purple bruising around his left eye. His mouth kicked up into a half-smile. "I pissed off the mafia princess, and she took a swing at me."

"What did you do?"

"Told her she screamed like a fishwife at a farmer's market, and acted like a diva and if she wanted to stay alive, she needed to get a personality transplant."

I laughed. "That'll do it."

He shrugged. "She's Dorian's problem now." He waved a hand for the server, who brought over a coffee pot and a mug for me. She topped up Bishop's drink, filled my mug, and left as silently as she'd arrived. "So, are you still thinking about relocation?"

"I haven't mentioned it to Dally yet. She went back to work yesterday."

"How is she doing after the whole ... well, you know?"

"Better than I expected. She has the occasional nightmare, but she's keeping it together pretty well."

"Do you think it's a front?"

I thought about that, then shook my head. "No. I think she's so accustomed to her family being shitty to her that this was just another moment of fuckedupness, and she's filed it away as such. Maybe if it hadn't turned out to be her brother behind it ... that might have garnered a different reaction, but I think she expects her family experiences to be negative."

Bishop leaned back on his seat, eyeing me over his mug. "And you. Never thought I'd see the day you'd settle down with a girl."

I could have denied that, argued that I hadn't settled down, but I didn't. What would be the point? Dally had exploded into my world, and while our beginning might have been drenched in violence and blood, the past week had proved that there was more to the connection we had than an initial need to survive.

She was funny, quirky, sexy as fuck, and I was pretty much obsessed with her. Why bother hiding it?

I raised my mug in a silent toast. "It's hard to explain. She is ..." I shrugged. *Fuck it.* "She's perfect."

Bishop choked on the mouthful of coffee he'd taken. "Perfect?" he repeated once he'd gained control of himself.

"Yeah."

"It's serious then?"

"I think so. We haven't really talked about it. She stayed

at my place after I got her back from Tomek, and we've been back to her apartment a couple of times to collect more of her stuff. I think there's more at my place than hers now. She should probably tell her roommate to find someone new. There's no point in paying rent for somewhere she no longer lives." I wasn't really explaining to Bishop as I was thinking out loud.

My brother laughed. "I guess congratulations are in order, then? When do I get to meet her?"

"You can come with me when I pick her up, if you're that curious."

"Oh, I'm definitely curious about the girl who made you slam your brakes on."

I rolled my eyes. "Is it really that strange?"

The look he angled at me said everything. Yes, it was strange. I had *never* allowed any woman close enough to meet a member of my family. Dally was different, though, in ways I never thought I'd appreciate.

"You have the weirdest expression on your face. I do believe you're in love." Bishop smirked at me.

Was I? I examined the emotions that coursed through me when I thought about Magdalena McCarthy. Anticipation at seeing her, anger when she was hurt, the need to touch her when she was close.

"Yeah, I think you're right." It was worth the admission to see Bishop's jaw drop. He recovered fast.

"Have you told her?"

"Not yet." I smiled. I was already plotting ways to set the scene and tell her how I felt.

"Does she love you?"

"I'd like to think so." *Did she*? I fucking hoped so. I had to believe she did. I didn't want to think of any alternative reasons for why she was staying with me. "Anyway, enough about that. Why are we meeting?"

"No particular reason. I wanted to touch base with you and check in. It's been a busy few weeks for everyone. I'm heading over to see Knight when I leave here. He's been locked away in that apartment of his for too long. It's time he got out and breathed in some fresh air."

"Knight doesn't enjoy going outside, you know that. His beloved computers can't go with him."

We both laughed. Knight hated leaving his apartment where he could watch the world and all its secrets from his computer screens. He argued that there was no reason for him to leave when he had everything he needed right there.

"I might grab Dally and come with you. We could go out for dinner."

Bishop nodded. "Good plan. He might be more open to leaving the apartment if it's to introduce your girl to the family."

We were right on time to pick Dally up. Her boss was walking out of the gallery as I parked, Bishop pulling up behind me in his car. Dally spotted me through the window, gathered up her purse and jacket and came out. I climbed out of the car to greet her, tugging her toward me so I could steal a kiss before turning her toward Bishop.

"Dal, this is my brother. I've told you about him. Bishop, this is Dally."

Bishop thrust out one hand. "I've heard a lot about you."

"Oh?" Dally cast a glance toward me. "Nothing too bad, I hope."

My brother patted the hand he held in his. "Not at all. But I have to admit to being curious about the girl who managed to stop my brother in his tracks."

"Bish." I growled a warning. My brother laughed.

"I'm afraid he didn't get an awful lot of choice in it. Between me railroading him into coming to dinner with me, and then him getting kidnapped alongside me by default, he was kinda stuck with me for a while there." Her voice was light, but I spotted the way her eyes darkened slightly, and her bottom lip trembled.

I dropped an arm across her shoulders and drew her into my side. "And it was a good job I *was* there, otherwise who knows how much trouble you'd have gotten into?" That made her laugh. "Bishop is meeting Knight and going for dinner. I was thinking about joining them, and wondered if you would like to come, too?"

A smile broke out across her face. "I'd *love* that. Can we go home first, though, so I can shower and change?"

I glanced at Bishop, who nodded. "It'll probably take me an hour to convince Knight to leave his precious computers. How about I make a reservation for eight at Montage?" He named a restaurant a few miles out of town.

"Sounds good. Call me if there's a change to the plan." I turned, taking Dally with me, and walked toward my car, opened the passenger door and waited until she was seated, before closing it and striding around to the driver's side. "That put you on the spot. I'm sorry. We can cancel if you want?"

"No! I liked Knight. He was nice to me when he drove me home. I'd like to thank him for that."

"He nearly got you shot."

She rolled her eyes, which told me she knew I was talking about catching her outside my door. "If you were going to shoot me, it would have been while we were still outside. I don't even know why I believed otherwise."

I hid a smile. "Maybe."

57

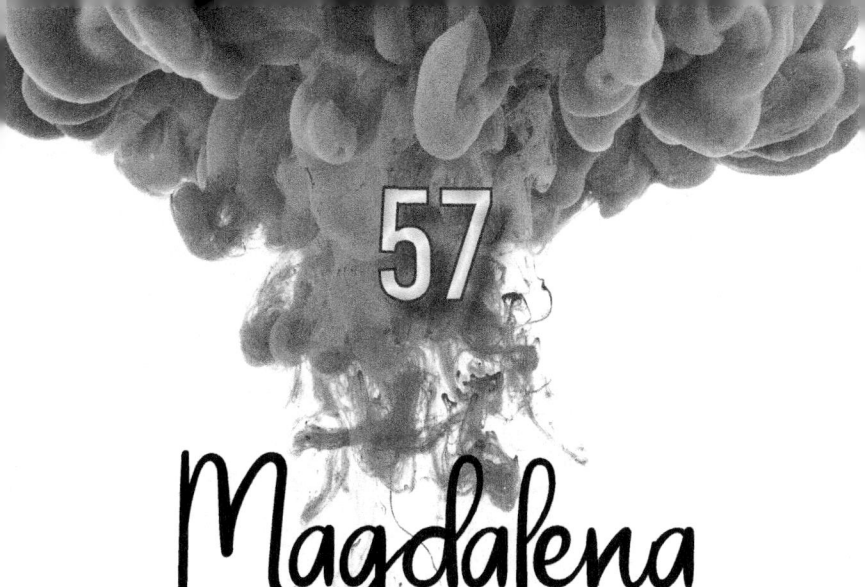

Magdalena

There was a dark red dress laid out across the bed when I came out of the shower. I stroked a finger over the silky material.

"Do you like it?"

Spinning, I found Rook standing in the doorway. "It's beautiful."

"I saw it in town today." One shoulder moved in a half-shrug. "Thought you might like it."

"It's the color of blood." I picked it up and held it against me, my eyes on Rook.

"My favorite color." His voice was dry.

I laughed at that. "You're a terrible person."

He walked toward me, reached out a hand, and tipped my head up. "And yet you haven't run away."

"Maybe I'm a terrible person, too." I was only half-joking. Was I a bad person for finding a man who did the things Rook did so attractive? For falling in love with him? I blinked.

Wait. What? When did I fall in love with him?

His thumb brushed over my lips. "You haven't done your makeup yet."

I shook my head, not sure I could speak, while the realization I *loved* him bounced around my head.

"I'm glad." He took the dress from me and tossed it onto the chair, then lowered his head and captured my lips in a kiss. I fell into it, with no thought of playing hard to get or denying him, when he wrapped his arms around my waist and lifted me off my feet.

Two strides, and he was lowering me onto the bed and coming down above me. "When you ran from me in the hotel room, with nothing but the towel wrapped around you." His lips kissed a burning path down my throat. "And then when you were beneath me, on the carpet, fighting to get free." His nose nudged away the towel covering my breast. "All I wanted to do was rip it off and taste you." His tongue lapped a wet circle around my nipple before he closed his lips over it and sucked.

I let my head drop back against the sheets. "You were fucking scared, exhausted, but there was so much fight still in you." He leaned up on one hand and unknotted the towel with the other. The cool air on my skin made me shiver when he pulled it open. "I knew right then that you were dangerous, that I would burn down the fucking world if you asked me. Fuck, I would do it if you *didn't* ask if it meant you were safe."

He kissed his way down my ribs, my stomach, and licked another circle around my navel. "We'll go for dinner with my brothers." He pushed one thick finger inside me, and my eyes almost rolled back from the pleasure of it. "I'd like you to wear the dress I picked up." A second finger joined the first, and my fingers curled into the bedsheets. "But first …" His breath was warm against my hip. "First, I want to make you come."

I wore the dress he'd bought for me. First, because it was pretty, and I liked it. Second, because, honestly, after giving me three mind blowing orgasms using his tongue and fingers, it was the least I could do to say thank you. His palm was warm against my back as we walked into the restaurant, and I smiled. I loved how attentive he was without it seeming to be a conscious action.

He'd hold the car door open, take my hand and help me in or out. He'd lay his hand on my back, like he was doing, as we walked—not because he thought I couldn't walk alone, but because … Well, I didn't know why, but I know it made me feel special, *important*, and I liked that.

The usher led us to the table where his brothers waited and, seeing the three of them together, their family link was obvious. They were all dark-haired and dark eyed, all tall and, to my inner artist's eye, their facial structure was similar. My fingers itched to pick up a pencil and sketch them.

Rook stood behind my chair, sliding it beneath me as I sat. I tipped my head up to catch his eye and thanked him. He squeezed my shoulder and then took the seat beside me. "Sorry we're late."

My cheeks flamed. We were late because he'd been one hundred percent focused on making me come and we'd lost track of time.

Knight caught my eye and snickered. "No need to ask *why* you're late. It's written all over your face."

"Luckily, it's not written all over mine. I remembered to wash before we left."

I gasped at the obvious innuendo and twisted to face him, my eyes wide. "What ...? Oh my god ... Why would you say that?"

His grin was unrepentant, and his brothers' laughter echoed around the room.

"Are you sure you're hungry enough to want dinner?" Bishop asked, and I groaned.

"That was just the appetizer. I'm feeling pretty hungry for the main course right now."

"Please stop," I whispered.

But that set the tone for the evening, and while part of me wanted to curl up and die from the embarrassment of the jokes his brothers made, another part of me was fascinated by this new side to Rook I was discovering. Playful, teasing, completely at ease with his family, and at times I caught myself watching him as he talked to Bishop and Knight.

When it was time to order, his hand dropped to rest on my thigh, showing that he'd noticed me tense up when I opened the menu. He turned toward me, placed his menu flat on the table and tapped each item with his finger, while he asked what I thought of it. Without drawing attention to my dyslexia, he told me what meal options there were.

I think I fell in love with him a little more because of that.

The atmosphere at the table was a far cry from dining with my own family. There was a lot of laughter, and all three men constantly stole food from each other's plates. Not once did any of them make me feel like I wasn't welcome or didn't belong, drawing me into their conversations with ease and warmth.

We were waiting for dessert to be served when Knight leaned back on his seat and eyed me across the table.

"You know I'm going to claim responsibility for you and Rook getting together, right?"

"How'd you figure that?" Rook asked before I could speak.

"I told her where to find you *and* put it into her head that she should search you out."

"Oh, so you were playing matchmaker and not looking out for her safety?"

Knight smirked. "Couldn't it be both?"

Rook grunted, but didn't reply. I laughed.

"Are they always like that?" I asked Bishop.

He pointed at Rook. "Middle child." His finger moved to Knight. "Youngest child. Self-explanatory, really."

L. ANN

58

Rook

It was a little after eleven when we parted company with my brothers and drove back to my house. There was a chill in the air when we climbed out of the car, and I wrapped an arm around Dally's shoulders as we walked toward the front door.

"I like your brothers."

"Someone had to eventually, I suppose."

She gave a soft laugh. "You're all very close, don't pretend otherwise."

"You're right, we are." I unlocked the door and stepped back so she could go inside. "I've been thinking—" Her cell rang, cutting me off.

She frowned down at the screen. "It's my mother. Why is she calling so late?" Her eyes darted up to mine. "You don't think—"

"Answer the call."

She'd been about to ask if I thought it was about Fraser. It was written all over her face. "Take a breath, darlin', then pick up the call."

She did then lifted the phone to her ear. "Hi. Is everything okay?"

She listened as someone, presumably her mom, spoke to her. Dally's face paled, her eyes widened, and she reached out a hand to grasp my arm. "You want me to come over *now*? Is Charl—Charlotte there?" She sighed. "Okay. I'll be there in about an hour... *No*, I can't get there any faster, mom. I'm in the next town over. An hour is how long it'll take for me to travel there... Okay... okay, yes. I'll see you soon."

She cut the call and looked at me. "She's filed a missing persons report for Fraser. The police have called to say they've found a body and they believe it's him." Her tongue swept over her lips. "She wants me to go to the house. Rook... I don't think I can do this. How can I look her in the face and pretend I don't know what happened to him?"

"Change out of the dress and into something more comfortable. You can do this, Dal. We knew a time would come when you'd have to face your parents. You've done *nothing* wrong. All we have to do is go to the house, act surprised, say you haven't seen him since the dinner, and then leave. That's it."

"And then what? What about when it's time for the funeral? I have to go to that too and pretend I'm *sad* he's dead? I *can't* do it, Rook."

"You don't have to do it. We can be out of town before they arrange the funeral."

"Out of town?"

"Don't worry about that now. Get changed." I turned her

toward the stairs and gave her a gentle push. "It's going to be okay, I promise."

She was silent for most of the journey to her parents, spending the time staring out of the window and gnawing on her lip. When we finally parked outside the house, I reached out and turned her head toward me.

"Darlin', look at me." I waited until she focused on me. "We're going to go inside. Your mom isn't going to give a shit about what you say or do. This isn't about you, it's about her. Just like everything else is about her. What she's looking for is someone to validate it."

"Her son is *dead*, Rook. I think she's within her rights to be upset."

"I never said she wasn't. But that same son organized your kidnapping *and* tried to sell you to pay off his debt. You owe him nothing. She's not interested in how you feel."

"Should I tell—?"

"Absolutely not. If you do that, more questions will be asked and there's a high chance that they would list you as a suspect. I'm not sure I can get away with killing half the police force in town to protect you. I'm good, but that would be a challenge even for me."

"You wouldn't really do that."

I leaned across the console and kissed her. "You can go ahead and find out, if you like."

"Rook." My name was soft on her lips.

"I told you, Dal, I'll burn down the fucking world, if that's what you want me to do." I took her lips again in a kiss that, I hoped, left no doubt that I was telling her the truth, then pulled away. "Ready?"

She bit her lip, then nodded. "I think so."

"Stay there." I threw open the door, exited, and strode around to help her out. We walked toward the house hand in hand, her fingers locked tight on mine.

The door swung open before we reached it and I recognised the maid from the last time I was here. Katy, I thought her name was. The one who Dally hid a friendship with.

"Mrs. McCarthy is waiting for you in the Summer Room." There was no sign of anything but professional courtesy in her voice or on her face. "If you'll both follow me."

Dally's grip on my hand didn't loosen, and we followed Katy through the hallways to the room where I'd first met her mother all those weeks ago. The only differences when we walked into the room was that the sun wasn't shining through the window, and her father was standing beside the bookcase. He frowned when we entered, but said nothing. Her mother glanced at me, and one corner of her lip curled into a sneer.

Oh, this was going to be good.

"Sit down, Magdalena." The older woman's voice was cool. "I want you to explain to me why my son is dead."

"Wh-what?" In the process of lowering herself onto the couch, Dally lost her balance and fell the last few inches onto the firm cushions.

Her mother sniffed. "He contacted me while we were on our retreat to tell us that someone had tried to kidnap you and demand a ransom."

"You ... *knew?*" The color drained from Dally's face.

"Of course I did."

"And you didn't even call me to check if I was okay?"

"You're here, aren't you? Fraser told me it had been a failed attempt, and that you were with ..." Her eyes cut to me. "With him. Your brother was certain *he* was responsible for the demand." Her eyes cut to me.

"Rook? *Rook* wasn't responsible, Fr—"

"You're a piece of work." I spoke over Dally's response. "You were told your youngest daughter had been kidnapped, and you didn't think it was important enough to follow up on? What the actual fuck kind of parents are you?"

Her mother's spine snapped rigid. "Fraser said it was a false alarm, that it was just a trick to try and get money out of us. And clearly ..." She waved a hand at the woman sitting pale-faced and shaken beside me. "She's alive and well ... unlike *my son*."

"That's not her fault."

"Isn't it?" Her cold eyes bored into Dally, who bowed her head.. "I'm sure he went to talk to the people who were trying to extort money out of us and *they* killed him. If she had done as she was told, and married the man I picked out, this wouldn't have happened."

I stared at her. Maybe it was grief at losing her son causing her to lash out. I was certain it wasn't. I closed my hand over

Dally's arm.

"We're leaving."

"Wh-what? No ... we can't." She sounded dazed.

"I *said* we're leaving." I used my grip on her arm to pull her to her feet. She didn't resist. "Take one last look at your daughter because, if I have my way, this is the last fucking time you'll see her."

59

Magdalena

I didn't put up much of a fight when Rook decided we should leave. Hearing my mother talk callously about my kidnapping sent me into some kind of mental shutdown, and it was only the cool night air hitting my face that brought me back to my senses a little.

"I can't leave." I stopped outside the front door. "What if the police need to talk to me?"

"They won't." He kept moving, pulling me along with him.

"You don't know that."

"Your parents aren't about to tell them that they were informed of a kidnapping and ransom demand. Or that they ignored it because it was only their youngest daughter and they don't give a fuck what happens to her."

I flinched. Rook stopped, caught my shoulders, and turned me to face him.

"Darlin', listen to me. You know the truth about them. They

don't care about you, they never have." His tone softened. "Just because that woman in there gave birth to you, it doesn't make her your mother ... not where it counts."

My eyes burned from my fight not to let tears fall. "But they're all I have, Rook."

He shook his head. "Not anymore." Bending his head, he kissed the tip of my nose, my cheeks, and then my mouth. "You have me. You have my brothers. And when you meet them, you'll have my parents, too. *We* are your family now."

His face blurred through the tears. I wasn't sure how to feel—anger at my mother, hurt at the way she'd dismissed me, betrayed at the way my father hadn't even said a word ... then there was the warmth of Rook's words. All the emotions inside warred with each other.

I swallowed. "I don't know what to do."

His palms cupped my cheeks. "Right now, all you have to do is trust me, darlin'. Let me take you home. Let me get you out of here." He pressed another kiss to my lips. "Or tell me to light a match, and we'll watch the world fucking burn."

He stood there, and I had the impression that he *really* was waiting to see what option I'd prefer. I sniffed, and leaned against him, took in a deep breath, inhaling the scent of him, and then pulled away. "Will you wait here?"

"Why?"

"There's something I have to do." I lifted a hand and pressed my palm to his cheek. "Please wait here for me."

I walked back into the house. My parents were still sitting in the Summer Room. They both looked up when I stepped inside.

"Fraser is dead because he owed bad people a lot of money. Instead of taking responsibility for that, he had me kidnapped and a ransom demand sent to you. Only he'd forgotten you were in New York, so he arranged with those bad people to *sell* me to them to pay off his debt. Your son, *my brother*, was willing to put me into a situation that could... No, *would* have eventually killed me. And that's *your* fault."

"How dare—" my mother snapped.

"No! How dare *you*! I am your *daughter*, and yet you've never treated me like one. You treated me like the accident you saw me as. And fool that I was, I tried desperately to get your approval *all the time*. But, do you know what? I'm done, Mother. I'm *done*. You finally have your wish. You only have one daughter, and it isn't *me*."

I didn't stay long enough to hear her response, if she even gave one.

Rook was leaning against the side of his car when I exited the house. He straightened as I moved toward him at a quick walk.

"Take me home."

"You got it."

I found myself bundled into the car before I could say another word.

"What did I do to make her hate me so much?"

"Nothing. Sometimes people are dealt a shitty hand by the

universe, darlin'."

On some level, I knew he was right, but it didn't make it any easier to accept. He dropped one hand from the steering wheel and reached across the center console to take mine.

"I know what you're thinking. You're sitting there telling yourself that you're the bad person for walking out of that situation. Walking away when she needs your support. But you need to understand that she didn't call you because she wanted you to be there for her. She called you because she needed a target, someone to blame."

He broke off to start the engine and reverse down the driveway.

"You've been her whipping boy for years. I could see that after a single interaction with her. And your father is no better. Sure, he's a little warmer, but he doesn't stop her, Dal. He stands there and lets her treat you like shit. You're under this misguided belief that she has the right to do that, but she doesn't. No one does, and I wasn't prepared to let it happen. If you need to hate me for that, so be it."

"*Hate* you?" I twisted in my seat to face him. "I don't hate you."

He squeezed my fingers before letting them go so he could return his hand to the steering wheel. I turned to look out of the window, letting the sound of the engine and the scenery rolling past send me into an almost meditative state. A sound intruded, a repetitive thud, and I turned my head to see his fingers drumming against the steering wheel as he drove.

I caught him glancing my way. He frowned, muttered something

I didn't catch, and veered across the road and pulled over.

"Why are we stopping?"

"I want to talk to you." He cut off the engine and turned in his seat to face me. "I'm thinking about leaving town. I spoke to Bishop about it a couple of days ago. I want him to find somewhere I can relocate to, where I'm harder to reach. Too many people know where I am now, and if I stay here, I'm going to end up getting dragged back into a job I don't want."

"Oh." *He was leaving?* There was a dead weight in the pit of my stomach. "When?"

"That depends entirely on you."

"Me?"

"I want you to come with me."

The dead weight turned into butterflies.

"Look, Dal, I'm not going to lie. You have completely disrupted my life. I moved here to get away, to slow down, and then you exploded onto the scene and turned everything upside down."

"That doesn't sound like a good thing." I scowled.

He laughed. "Three weeks ago, I'd have agreed with you."

"Then why ask me to come with you?"

"Because I don't think I can live without what you've brought to my life, darlin'."

"Chaos, more death, and fighting?"

He shook his head and stroked a finger down my cheek. "*You.* I can't live without you. If you want to stay here, I'll find a way to make it work. But I think moving away would be good for both of us." He unclipped his seatbelt. "You're an incredible woman, one that I want to spend the rest of my life waking up with."

There were tears in my eyes again. For different reasons this time. I swallowed past the lump in my throat. "But we barely know each other." My protest was half-hearted.

"We know *enough* about each other. Relationships have been started on less. I know that I've never felt for anyone what I feel for you."

"What ... what do you feel?" I could barely hear myself talk over the rapid beat of my heart.

"I'm in love with you. But I think you know that already."

"But—"

"Tell me you don't feel the same way and I'll drop you at your apartment and leave you alone. But I don't think I'm imagining this, am I?"

I shook my head. The butterflies in my stomach were performing somersaults. *He loved me?*

"No, I'm not imagining it, or no, you don't feel the same way?"

"You're not ..."I licked my lips. "You're not imagining it."

He nodded. "Think about what I said." He fired the engine back up and pulled back out onto the road.

And that's what I did for the rest of the journey home. I weighed up the pros and cons of throwing everything I'd built my life into over the past twenty-four years aside to move away with a man I'd known for barely a month.

Granted, it had been an intense month where we'd gotten

to know each other in ways most couples never would. But was it enough? Could we build a stable relationship from how it had started?

I stole glances at him from beneath my lashes as we drove through the dark. The man beside me had killed people, *many* people. He had lived a life that I'd only read about in fiction books. My eyes dropped to his hands where they held the steering wheel. He had killed in front of me, *for* me.

How did that make me feel? I analyzed the question. Could I live with someone I knew had murdered people? Because that's what it was, really. He had murdered people for money, and I only had his word that they had been bad people to begin with.

"I can feel you looking at me." He didn't look in my direction, eyes steady on the road ahead. "Do you want me to find somewhere to park?"

"No." I chewed on my lip, then took a deep breath. "Do you ever think about the people you've killed?"

"Think about them, no." He didn't even hesitate in replying. "Can I tell you the name of every single one, what they looked like and what their last words were? Yes, I can. Do I regret killing them?" He glanced over at me.

"I'd have been terrible at my job if I couldn't deal with the aftermath of taking someone's life. Maybe … one day … on my deathbed, I'll regret it, but right now? No. It was what I was paid to do, and I performed my job to the best of my abilities." His mouth twitched into a half-smile. "For the sake of complete honesty, I was *very* good at it."

60

Rook

"Where are you thinking about moving to?" She didn't acknowledge my last comment.

"Near the coast somewhere. Maybe even a Caribbean island with a minimal amount of people. Hell, I could *buy* an island and become a recluse."

"Would your brothers allow that to happen?"

I laughed. "Probably not. Or they'd buy neighboring islands."

"Is that even possible?"

"If you know the right people and have enough money, anything is possible. What about you? Where would you move to?"

"It's not something I've ever considered. Choosing to move to the next town over from my parents was hard enough."

"Did they try to stop you?"

Her laugh sounded bitter. "Of course not. I think my mother would have preferred me to move out of state."

"What's the deal with your dad? You seemed to get along with him at your birthday dinner."

"I did ... I *do*, but he follows my mother's lead and won't rock the boat too much."

We'd reached the house, and I cut off the engine and turned to face her.

"Look, Dal, I'm going to lay it all out, okay? I'm not asking you to declare your undying love for me. With everything that happened, we've moved fast and maybe you think we're just hooking up, but I don't. I'm not a young kid. I know how I feel. Contrary to what my brothers might say, I *have* had relationships, but they were never serious and didn't last. There was always something missing. Something that stopped me from making any genuine commitment. Whether it was because of my line of work, or the timing, or even a difference in outlook, *something* always made it easy for me to walk away."

I paused and waited to see if she had anything to say. She stayed quiet. "I can't walk away from you. Even the idea of it sends my mind into a spin, planning ways that I can stay here with you and not get dragged back into my old life."

"Is that possible? I mean, can someone force you to go back to doing ... what you did?"

"Not *force*, no. But after the last few weeks, my activity will have been noticed. Contracts will be sent my way and the people who send them can be difficult to refuse."

"How will moving away change that?"

"It sends the message that I am not available without insulting anyone."

Her brow furrowed. "Your life is so complicated."

"It's not. It's actually very simple. It's different from what you're used to, that's all." I threw open the door and climbed out. "You don't have to decide right now, Dal. There's time to think about it."

She'd unbuckled her seatbelt and opened the passenger door by the time I rounded the car. I held out a hand and steadied her as she climbed out.

"I don't need to think about it."

I waited for her to expand on it, but she didn't. Instead, she tossed me a smile and headed for the house.

I tightened my grip on her hand and tugged her back to face me. "Going to share?"

"You mean you *don't* already know?" Her smile turned mischievous. "I quite like the idea of keeping you in suspense for a while."

I mock-growled and backed her toward the car. I *hoped* her teasing meant she wanted to come with me, but I needed to hear her say it. "Tell me what your decision is."

Her back hit the side of the car and I planted my hands on either side of her and leaned forward. She tipped her head back, her tongue touching her top lip as she looked at me.

"Or what?"

"You're very brave all of a sudden."

"I've survived a lot lately." Her voice was steady. "It's shown me that I can handle things most people can't. Things I would never have thought I could handle."

"That's very true. You've shown a remarkable amount of bravery in the face of some tough situations." I dipped my head. "But those people you faced weren't me," I whispered in her ear. "Can you *handle* me, darlin'?"

Her laugh was soft, and she lifted her arms to loop around my neck. "Do you know what? I think I can handle you just fine," she said, and closed the gap between us to kiss me.

EPILOGUE

Magdalena

EIGHTEEN MONTHS LATER

I took a step back and admired my handiwork. The long sheer curtains hung from the windows, blowing gently in the slight breeze, taking away the smell of the paint. This was the final room in the house that had needed attention, and finally, six months after moving in, it was done.

I'd found an inordinate amount of joy in throwing myself into the whole design and decoration process. I poured over samples of material, paint, flooring, and drove everyone crazy around me as I argued with myself. But it had been worth it. The sprawling villa that had seemed cold and uninviting when I first saw it was now warm, appealing and, more importantly, *home*.

"Dally? You up here?"

I turned, just as the man who had changed my life completely over the past eighteen months came through the door. He slowed to look around as he moved toward me.

"You finished it."

"Do you like it?"

"It looks stunning." His expression darkened a little when he saw the stepladder. "Tell me you didn't climb that."

I rolled my eyes. "It's not high. I couldn't reach the runner for the curtain."

"You should have called me."

"I didn't *want* to call you. Anyway, you weren't here, and I wanted the room finished before you got home."

"And I don't want you falling and hurting yourself. Compromise with me a little."

"I won't climb any more ladders."

"Promise me."

I huffed. "Fine. I *promise* I won't climb any more ladders."

"Good, because walking down the aisle with a cast on your leg is not going to be a good start to our married life, is it?" He caught my hand and tugged me closer. I let him, looping my arms around his neck and leaning up to kiss him.

For the last eighteen months, I'd woken up beside him every morning, and fallen asleep in his arms every night. Three months after I'd cut my parents out of my life, he'd surprised me with the announcement that he'd actually bought an island. A *small* one, granted. Close enough to the mainland that we could get there in a couple of hours, but far enough away that people couldn't drop by for an unannounced visit. He'd brought me here, showed me around the villa, and then stopped in this very room. There had been a table in the center, and wait staff had appeared through the large French doors with food and non-alcoholic wine.

That's when he proposed and, soon after, let me loose on a complete redesign of the villa.

When our lips parted, I smiled up at him. "I love you. You know that, don't you?"

"If I didn't, I'd be questioning why we're getting married tomorrow." His lips quirked. "I'm looking forward to showing you how much I love you for the rest of our lives." He pressed another kiss to my lips. "Come and sit down." He drew me over to the chair beside the window.

I frowned at him. "Why?" He didn't reply, staring pointedly at the chair. I sank onto it. "Rook..."

"My parents' flight was on time. I've already shown them to their room."

I sat up a little straighter. I'd known when he left for the mainland he was going to collect them and bring them to the island, but knowing they were *actually* here sped up my heart.

What if they didn't like me? What if they decided I wasn't good enough for their son?

Warm palms cupped my cheeks. "Get out of your head, darlin'. My parents are nothing like yours. They're going to love you."

I blinked and found Rook crouched in front of me. "I know, but—"

"But nothing. That's not why I wanted you to sit down, though."

"Then why?" Tension snapped my spine taut. "Has someone tried to contact you?" It was my only fear over the last year and a half. That someone might decide to send him a contract.

"No, nothing like that. They know I'm not available. No ..." He licked his lips, and the action made me scowl.

"Rook, what is going on?"

"Your sister is here."

I shot to my feet. "*What?*"

"Sit down." He barked the instruction.

I caught myself as I lowered myself back on to the seat, and glowered at him. "Don't do that."

"No, I'm going to use whatever means necessary to make you do as you're told." He took my hands in his. "Listen to me, please." His voice softened. "There's no easy way to say this."

The nervous beat of my heart sped up further. "Rook, just tell me whatever it is." My voice came out as a whisper.

"Your mom died." His eyes were intent on my face. "She had a heart attack two months ago. She was gone before the EMTs arrived."

My vision wavered, grew dim, and I sucked in a breath.

"Charlotte tried to find you to tell you when it happened, but, of course, she had no way to contact you. Knight saw the obituary on one of his random checks on your family. He reached out to Charlotte for details and told her he could let you know."

"So, why is she here?"

"Because she wants to see you."

"I don't want to see her." I attempted to pull my hands free from his, and his grip tightened. "Take her back to the mainland."

"Dal, do you remember when you told me you and your sister were close when you were young? And it was only after she got married that things changed between you?"

"Yes, but things *did* change."

"Do you know why?"

I finally freed my hands and pushed myself to my feet. "It doesn't matter why."

Rook straightened and followed me as I walked toward the windows. "It does matter. It matters a lot. Charlotte overheard your mother and Radall Delacour talking about money and thought your mother was trying to talk him into marrying you."

I stopped and slowly turned around.

"Charlotte argued that you were only eighteen, far too young to be married. Your mother denied that's what she was trying to do."

"She wanted me out of her house, so I was no longer her responsibility."

"She wanted a share in Randall Delacour's business, because—"

"She was *selling* me." I cut him off. "Like mother, like son, I guess. Maybe that's where Fraser had the idea."

"In a way, but Charlotte had the wrong idea. All she saw was your mother trying to get money from a man thirty years your senior. She promised to give Delacour an heir, if he gave your mother what she wanted."

"So, why is she here now?"

"She divorced Delacour almost a year ago. She found out he and your mother were having an affair."

"An affair?" I blinked. I hadn't expected to hear that.

"The money your mother wanted wasn't because she was trying to marry you off to him. It was to blackmail him."

"Blackmail him?"

"Come and sit back down, darlin'."

"Rook, just tell me why she's here!"

"Delacour is your biological father."

My vision went dark, and I fainted.

Rook

I caught her before she hit the floor, lifted her into my arms, and carried her across to the bed. Laying her down carefully, I sat on the mattress beside her. No more than a minute later, her eyelashes fluttered, and she opened her eyes. I leaned forward and brushed her hair from her face.

"What happened?"

"You fainted."

"You said Charlie's husband is my father." Her tone was accusatory.

"I did. Your mother was going to tell the world unless he paid for her silence. What your sister overheard was him telling your mother that he wanted *male* heirs. She took that to mean he wanted to marry you to give him those heirs, when he meant he didn't want to be linked to a daughter."

"How did Charlie find out?"

"Just after we left town, she found out she was pregnant. The scan said it was a girl. When Charlotte told your mother, she responded with a comment about how it would be another girl he wouldn't want. Charlie pressed her until she told your sister who your real father was. She confronted Delacour, who admitted it was the truth. Charlotte walked out the same day."

"You still haven't told me why she came here … why *you*

allowed her here?"

"Because I miss you." Her sister's voice replied before I could. "After I married Randall, I distanced myself from you because I thought it would be better for you."

I stood, and Dally got her first glance at the sister she hadn't seen in over twelve months. She was carrying a baby on one hip, and was dressed in casual joggers and a t-shirt. Her hair was loose instead of the formal pinned back hairstyle she'd worn all that time ago, and her features seemed softer.

"Rook told me everything you went through, Mags. I'm so sorry you had to deal with all of that. I wish I'd known. I really do." Charlotte took my place on the mattress beside Dally.

I moved toward the door. "I'm going to give you two some time alone. Dally, if you need me..."

She gave me a wobbly smile, and I assumed it was okay for me to leave. I stood for a second longer, watching the two women talk quietly. When Charlotte leaned over to wrap her arms around Dally. The action told me everything I needed to know.

The two sisters would work things out. And tomorrow I'd put my ring on Magdalena's finger, with at least one member of her family there to witness it.

I smiled, slipped out of the room and pulled the door closed behind me.

AUTHOR NOTE

Thank you for coming on a new adventure with me. I hope you enjoyed Rook and Dally's story. The author's note is usually the place to share something deep and meaningful, but you're not going to find that here!

Thank you to all the usual suspects for listening to me whine, giving me a firm talking to when I reach the stage of "everything about this book sucks", and not letting me quit.

Keep watching for Bishop and Knight's stories—yes, they will be getting theirs.

If there's anything you've read that you want to talk about—once again, we've opened a spoiler room specifically for this book. You can find it on Facebook, using the link below. Make sure you answer the questions, otherwise you'll sit there … in limbo … forever.

Rook Spoiler Group

https://www.facebook.com/groups/rookspoilerroom/

If you're not already a member, you can join me in my

Facebook Group

https://facebook.com/groups/lannsliterati

I also have a **newsletter** where you get a free story for signing up!

https://lannauthor.com/keep-in-touch

BOOKS BY L. ANN

FORGOTTEN LEGACY SERIES

Tattooed Memories - Book 1

Strawberry Delight - Short Story

Strawberry Lipstick - Short Story

Shattered Expectations - Book 2

Guarded Addiction - Book 3

Exquisite Scars - Book 4

Broken Halo - Book 5

MIDNIGHT PACK SERIES

Midnight Touch - Book 1

Midnight Temptation - Book 2

Midnight Torment - Book 3

Midnight Hunt Book 3.5

Midnight Fury - Book 4

Midnight Pack Full Series Boxset

(ebook only - includes the short story "Midnight Link")

Printed in Great Britain
by Amazon